On Silver Tides

ON SILVER TIDES

SYLVIA BISHOP

ANDERSEN PRESS

First published in Great Britain in 2024 by
Andersen Press Limited
20 Vauxhall Bridge Road, London SW1V 2SA, UK
Vijverlaan 48, 3062 HL Rotterdam, Nederland
www.andersenpress.co.uk

2 4 6 8 10 9 7 5 3 1

British Library Cataloguing in Publication Data available.

ISBN 978 1 83913 358 9

Printed and bound in Great Britain by Clays Ltd, Elcograf S.p.A.

For everyone who needed an escape from the 2020 lockdowns; and anyone who needs an escape right now.

1

Kelda's little sister seemed like a perfectly normal baby until her seventh day, when it was time to throw her in the river. Then they found out she couldn't breathe underwater.

It took a moment for everyone to realise. When Kelda's mam emerged with the baby in her arms the family were all waiting at the side of the boat, and they threw petals and cheered, and Uncle Abe struck up something complicated and twirly on his fiddle. But then she handed the baby up to Kelda's father, and the little body was very still and tinged a strange grey-blue, and everyone stopped cheering.

The fiddle carried on, unfurling reels like streamers, because when Uncle Abe was playing he stopped really paying attention to anything else. Somewhere from an islet to their left, a reed warbler answered him.

Normally, Kelda's family were quick to respond to danger. They knew how to fix a boat's engine, and bail out and mend a leak; they could handle nymphs and grindylow without breaking a sweat; they knew the cures for every kind of river worm and parasite. But none of them knew anything about drowning. Kelda's mam just shook and wailed. Kelda's father leaned low over the little body, peering through his spectacles, and asking Mam questions in a low, urgent voice. Kelda's younger brother Firth nudged Uncle Abe. But none of this made the baby any less limp.

Kelda had seen a drowning man once. She had been left on the boat to practise knots while the others went silverside, as a punishment for cheek, so she was the only one who saw the man get scooped out of the canal. He wasn't limp like the baby; his limbs twitched horribly. One of the women had knelt down in a puddle of skirts, torn off his ridiculous cravat and collar, put her mouth over his, and breathed into him until he revived. She had reminded Kelda of her family – the way she knew just what to do, and set about doing it without any nonsense.

The others missed all this, only arriving in time to see them pull away in a motorcar, which caused great excitement. But Kelda had dreamed for weeks about the poor landman who spent too long silverside.

Mam let out an especially keening, broken wail, and Kelda suddenly understood that no one else was going to do anything. So she ducked her head under her father's and put her mouth over her sister's, as the woman had done to the drowning man. The baby was so tiny, she covered her whole mouth and nose. She breathed out.

She only gave a very slight breath. She had been marvelling at the sheer littleness of her sister all week, and instinct told her that those small lungs could not hold too much air at once. One tiny breath – two – three.

The baby was still.

She tried again – one, two, three.

The baby coughed, and opened her eyes.

That wasn't the end of the danger. They stayed up with her in the galley all night, keeping her close to the warmth of the stove, burning candle after candle as they watched her cough and splutter and squirm and, just as terrifyingly, sleep. But it *was* the moment that saved her life. And it was the moment in which Kelda, until then her own wilful, wild person, was understood by everyone to have become her sister's guardian.

They didn't do the naming that night, of course. No one was really in the mood for it the next night either, but Mam had already made the bitter chowder, and it would go bad if they put it off any longer. The trouble was, the family were old-fashioned, and usually went in for water names – but it seemed cruel to give the little girl a name meaning 'strength of the river' or 'sea goddess' or something. Like they were mocking her.

Mam was the most pious of them, and she wanted to give her a water name regardless. They were still arguing about it while she lit the lanterns strung up along the deck.

'She's *got* to have a water name,' Mam said. 'She's part of the family.'

'It's not right,' said Dad. He hadn't said much else since the baby had spluttered back to life – at least, not in front of the children. He and Mam had held a muttered argument which they thought Kelda and Firth hadn't heard, but the walls of the boat were thin. Besides, Kelda was old enough to know what Dad suspected. In the end, it was Mam's piety that convinced Kelda, and it was probably what mollified Dad too.

Keeping anyone of landman blood on board was absolutely forbidden, and the River would sicken and spoil. If the baby wasn't silverman through and through, Mam would never have her on the boat.

'Well, what do you suggest, Murphy?' snapped Mam. Her voice had the thick edge it got when she was trying not to cry. 'Do you want to brand the poor thing as a freak?'

'There must be something watery that isn't untrue,' said Uncle Abe, ever the peacemaker. He spread his large hands out, palms up, his favourite gesture. 'She'll still live on water, after all. Something about "near the water", or ...' – he floundered here – '"On – on a boat".'

The unnamed baby whimpered in Kelda's arms. Kelda was inclined to agree. Her sister didn't deserve a half-hearted name, which just said what she *nearly* was. She wasn't a half-thing. Her name should feel complete.

There was no help to be had from Firth, who was leaning over the edge of the boat to watch the lantern-light dance on the black water. Mam and Dad, meanwhile, were strung up tight as fiddle-strings, and neither could bend from their position without snapping. So Uncle Abe turned his spread-out hands and spread-out smile to Kelda. 'Well,' he asked, 'what does the hero of the hour think?'

For a moment there was silence on deck, as Kelda considered this. The only sound from the river was the reed warbler, disturbed on its islet. Kelda loved river islands. They were neither bank nor water: they were a world unto themselves, with reeds and willow trees and nesting birds and secrets of their own.

She reached for the chowder, and took the first spoonful, even though that was supposed to be Mam's job. Nobody protested. She had earned the right.

It was bitter and salty, and she had to work to keep the disgust from her face as she swallowed. Then, with her sister in the crook of her right arm, she emptied a second spoonful into the river, and announced:

'Isla.'

An extract from 'Zoology' in:
The Waterways: Essays on a Hidden World
....

Amphibians can breathe both on land and in water. While a few have gills, most absorb oxygen directly through their skin from the water. It is difficult for a landman to understand what this feels like. Imagine if your skin could feel how peppermint smells: that's quite close.

It is commonly thought that there are three orders of the class *Amphibia*. The same zoological wisdom tells us there is one living species of the genus *Homo* – *Homo sapiens*, the common or garden human. But there should be another species of *Homo*, or another order of *Amphibia* – or both.

You could call them *Homo aqua*, if you want to think of them as people. Or *Anura sapiens*, if you prefer to think of them as an unusually wise sort of frog. Or you could just use their own word for themselves: silvermen.

2

For the first five years of her life, nobody suggested sending Isla away. When she was still a baby, Firth did once say he wished she *had* drowned, but Kelda had set on him like a wild animal. It had earned her a week's confinement on the boat, but it had shut Firth up.

As far as Kelda was concerned, it wasn't Isla who was the problem. All she did was be born. The problem was everyone else. Sometimes they were still as they should be: Mam humming old songs to herself, Dad's face set in his crinkle-eyed half-smile; family expeditions up tributaries for crayfish or caddis fly eggs or whatever the local up-water delicacy happened to be; evenings spent together round the poplar stove. Those were the good days.

But Dad's suspicion had lodged like a thorn, and he would retreat regularly into baleful silence, and long moody walks. Every now and then, after an especially bad argument, he would disappear for days at a time. And whenever Dad was moody, Mam – who used to give as good as she got – didn't say a word about it, but went through the motions of her day with grim determination, like someone observing a penance.

She was more pious than ever. She kept up an endless parade of River tributes, as though she was atoning for whatever sins she had privately decided were the cause of Isla's strange birth, and she would allow no deviations from strict Lore observance on the boat. A lot of Abe and Dad's more radical ideas were buried under a stiff silence.

As for Firth, finding everyone else had grown sullen or sorry or devoted-to-Isla, he withdrew into books and some private corner of his mind. Only Uncle Abe remained the same.

None of this was Isla's fault. She was easy to please, mostly wanting to potter about Abe's roof garden and eat aster drops and know the names of birds. She had the same flat grey eyes as everyone else, and the same slight sheen to her skin. She learned to swim well, and she diligently memorised her sailing knots and guardian knots, and all the key stanzas of the Lore. When they passed other silverman boats, no one looked twice at her. She was no trouble.

That's what Kelda thought, anyway.

The two of them were out collecting bayroot when Meredith Jupp came along to think otherwise, so they missed the beginning. It was the February of Kelda's sixteenth year, Isla's seventh – her silver year, when she was old enough to be a proper part of their boat. She had been given her first piece of silver that name-day: a pendant in the shape of a knotted eel, just like Kelda's, and Firth's, and all the Pades before them.

That evening the banks were treacherously muddy, and there was a film of mist over the river. The smoke of a landman town rose in the distance, a smudge of darker grey against grey cloud. In black trees, nothing stirred.

Kelda had already spotted the Jupps' boat upriver, the windows warm with lamplight. Which meant that Aeron Jupp would be sure to come by later – he always did. Kelda had drifted from most of her friends once Isla was born, and when their boats crossed it was Firth now who would spend the day with Aeron; but unlike the rest of their crowd, Aeron had doggedly kept visiting Kelda too, sitting with her on the deck for earnest chats once Isla was in bed.

Kelda normally looked forward to this, but tonight, she was nervous. They had heard word a few months back that little Fossy Jupp had got mer-sick and died, and their boats hadn't crossed paths since. Kelda always found it hard to know what to say when the River took someone. Fossy had been younger than Isla.

She told herself that this was why she felt flustered at the thought of seeing Aeron. It was half-true.

'Ooh,' said Isla, 'the Jupps' boat, Kelda, look!'

'Sure is. That bayroot looks *good*.'

Isla looked at her slyly. 'Uncle Abe says you and Aeron—'

'Uncle Abe had you believing there are sharks in rivers for a whole day once, remember? Come on – see the patch I mean, over there?'

Isla was not interested in the bayroot, but she was *very* interested in defending her theory about sharks. The diversion was successful. But as they picked their way along the bank, Kelda found herself glancing back at the bright little boat, checking for a figure in the mist.

Stupid. Silverside would clear her mind.

They were just far enough inland for the water to be fresh,

but she squatted down on the bank to test first, for any hint of the brackish water where river met sea. She had to lean a long way down – it had been a dry winter, and the rivers were low.

No salty sting of pain: the water was fresh. 'Ready?' she said to Isla.

Isla wrinkled her nose, which was how she always felt about water in winter, and which more-or-less meant yes. So Kelda leaned forwards. Then she dropped from the bank, and slipped straight down through the current.

Her skin woke up; her grey eyes blinked, narrowed their pupils, adjusted; and the world became shades of silver, and silent. Basket in hands, she floated just underneath the shimmering bayroot, and began to gather it in.

Thirty seconds later she was shooting back up into the air again, because Isla hadn't followed.

'*Isla*,' she said. It's hard to look stern when you are just a head bobbing about above water, but Kelda had had plenty of practice. 'What are you doing?'

'There's a duck!' Isla explained, pointing. She was not wrong. There was indeed a duck. There often are ducks, when you live on rivers. Kelda couldn't quite match her excitement.

'It's duck*weed* we're after, little miss. Come on.'

'I think it wants to be friends.'

Kelda didn't comment on this either way. Maybe it did, maybe it didn't. It was hard to tell, on account of it being a duck.

'We can make friends later,' was all she said. 'Silverside. *Now*. Mam needs this by dinnertime.'

So Isla reluctantly followed, but as soon as she had to go

up for air, she stayed up. Kelda could see her feet paddling, and next to her, the little blobby shadow of the duck with its flappy feet working furiously. Sighing was not an option, since Kelda wasn't breathing through her mouth right now, so she rolled her eyes instead. But she left Isla to it. There wasn't much bayroot anyway, as the current was only just slow enough; it had been a surprise to spot any here at all. They didn't really need both of them to gather it.

She stayed silverside hunting for more wispy roots long after she had enough. She liked the feeling of the river rippling past her, on its way to somewhere else. Her parents were having a moody day, and the current was the opposite of all the stiff, buried sadness on the boat. But when Isla's legs disappeared, doubtless back on to the bank, she let herself grow light, and drift back topside.

Sure enough, her sister was squatting in the mud. There was algae knotted in her curly hair, and she was cradling the duck. It was hard to be certain, but Kelda thought it might be slightly stupider than the average duck.

'I'm going to keep him,' Isla announced.

Stubbornness was a family trait. 'No,' said Kelda.

'Yes! I promised him.'

'You'll have to unpromise,' said Kelda. 'Mam will never allow it. Look at all this!' – she brandished the basket enticingly. 'Dinner's going to be good.' And actually, the weed *did* look especially good – it was glossy, and a rich, deep green. But Isla was not so easily distracted.

'You can't unpromise a promise,' she protested. 'It wouldn't be a promise if you could just unpromise it.'

Since Mam was going to ban the duck anyway, and a bitter dusk was falling, Kelda decided not to waste any time debating the nature of promises and their applicability, or not, to ducks. Let Mam do the parenting this time. Kelda wanted to get by the stove, and warm her fingers seasoning the stew. 'Mam won't allow it,' she said, setting off for the boat. 'And I don't want you to be disappointed. But do what you like.'

'I'll explain to Mam,' said Isla, trotting behind, 'about the promise.' And the duck gakkered quietly to itself, pleased with this idea.

The galley was warm, and thick with the smell of sage and thyme and lemon balm from the pans that were already simmering on the stove, and the hot mint tea in a pot on the table.

The duck stretched out its neck, with an enthusiastic *quawwk?* But Kelda was thoroughly distracted by the woman sitting at the table, drinking the tea: Meredith Jupp.

She must have come while they were silverside. Kelda was instantly on edge. Talking to Meredith felt like diving headfirst into saltwater, boiling your blood. She was permanently smug, even if you were only talking about the weather – as though she somehow possessed better, more *correct* weather than you did.

Worryingly, she seemed smugger than usual today. And Mam, normally so pale beneath her dark hair, was looking flushed – almost, Kelda thought, *angry*.

'Mam!' Isla announced, ignoring Meredith. 'I've got a duck!'

Quakkerquakker, qwrrrrk, agreed the duck. But Mam

12

ignored the duck, every bit as firmly as Isla ignored Meredith. It was a family trick.

'Girls,' she said, 'go to your room for a minute please.'

Isla did not protest: this was the best possible reception the duck could have received. It was Meredith who demurred. 'Surely she should stay, Lyn,' she murmured, glancing at Isla – who was too busy with the duck to notice. 'Then we can straighten this out right away.'

Mam drew herself up very straight. 'Meredith,' she said, quietly, 'I will *not* ask my child to be subject to—'

'Come now, Lyn,' said Meredith, 'You're getting emotional. Take a breath.' And she smiled, a chummy smile that instantly raised Kelda's temperature and made her fists curl. Suddenly the galley's warmth was too much. She put down the basket.

'Mam,' she said, 'what's going on?'

'Nothing, Kelda. Take Isla to your room.'

The duck chose this moment to flee his loving captor's arms and waddle under the table, quickly followed by a cooing Isla, so Kelda could not have obeyed this instruction even if she had wanted to. Meredith moved her knees out from Isla's path, rather ostentatiously.

'I've just come about some little rumours, sweetheart,' she said to Kelda. 'I'm sure it's nothing. My Aeron and your Firth were talking, and Firth made some rather strange claims, and I just wanted to *check*.' She swung her knees back as Isla and duck re-emerged, and added plaintively, 'As a *friend*. I didn't think it would cause so much upset.'

Mam fixed on a not-upset smile, but her eyes were furious. 'Well, you've checked. I'm afraid I need to get back to the

13

stove. Will your boat be moving on tomorrow? Let me give you some aster cake – I remember your Aeron's sweet tooth . . .'

You had to hand it to Mam: she was good under pressure. Kelda could never have been that polite. All she could think of was finding Firth and repeating the pummelling episode. True, Aeron was a friend – and yes, Abe liked to joke that he was courting Kelda, and there might be some truth in it. But *no one* could be trusted with Isla's secret. And here was proof – Aeron had already blabbered everything to Meredith.

'Thank you, Lyn, but I really wouldn't be comfortable taking food from this boat until I can be sure that . . . well . . . you understand, I'm sure. Perhaps Isla could just go silverside with me for a few minutes?'

At the sound of her own name, Isla finally clocked the conversation happening above her. 'But I've just been!' she protested. 'It's yucky tonight.'

The tension in the room tightened. No normal silverman would describe the water as *yucky*, even if they happened to be six years old.

'Lyn Pade,' said Meredith, 'I am sorry to insist, but if I don't see Isla silverside tonight, I will have to take this to . . .'

'Really,' cut in Mam, 'there is no need' – but just then Dad opened the door from the deck. Sometimes his walks worked off his mood, and this seemed to be one of those times; he smiled at them all from the doorway now. The smile faltered when it alighted on the duck, and positively wilted at the sight of Meredith.

'Murphy,' said Meredith, without preamble, 'my Aeron says your daughter is a landman. Is that true?'

14

Isla's eyes widened, and she looked at Dad. Dad paused in the doorway for a moment, all trace of the smile gone, a grim figure against the mist.

Then he shut the door. He crossed the galley, and sat down. He poured himself a tea from the waiting pot, and took a sip.

'No,' he said.

'I see,' said Meredith. 'Perhaps you might have some suggestion as to what your son could have mentioned, that would have misled my Aeron?'

'I have no idea, Meredith,' said Dad. And he gave her one of his thickest silences, and took another sip of tea.

'You realise, of course, the trouble you would bring on all of us if you were covering anything up. The health of the River . . .'

'Of course. *If* I was.' Dad fixed Meredith with an unwavering look over the top of his spectacles, the kind that always told Kelda she was about to be confined to the boat for at least a week. 'I think if the River's going to suffer over anything, it would probably be your husband's night-fishing. Don't you?'

He said this calmly, but it was an explosive thing to claim. Diving for fish at night was forbidden. It was supposed to make the moon angry, but it was pretty obvious to Kelda that it was just a way to stop anybody using the cover of darkness to break the other fishing rule – don't take more fish than you can eat fresh. It stopped overfishing; the moon had nothing to do with it. But silvermen were riddled with superstition.

'I wonder,' Dad went on, 'if you've got through all the

pickled fish yet. That must really be coming in handy, while we're all struggling with the low water.'

All the smugness had drained out of Meredith in one great rush. She said nothing, only staring at Dad. Kelda was astonished. Pickling fish! It would be humiliating. And a serious contravention of the Lore. But it was plain from Meredith's face that it was true.

Dad drained the rest of his tea in one gulp, then stood up. 'I am not the only one who knows,' he said. 'I promise you there are enough of us to pass our testimony at Equinox. Now,' – and he crossed the galley as he spoke, and opened the door – 'get off my boat.'

There was a long silence, apart from the gentle sound of Uncle Abe's feet on the roof overhead as he pottered about his garden, and some gakkering from the duck. Twice, Meredith seemed to be about to speak, but changed her mind.

Then she stood, and went to the door. When she reached Dad, she looked up at him with haughty dignity. 'You should be ashamed,' she said.

Dad didn't waver. 'I will never be ashamed of Isla. Goodnight, Meredith.'

He shut the door behind her, but it didn't block out the sound of her footsteps crossing the deck, and no one spoke until they heard the soft *splosh* of her slipping off over the side. Kelda realised her palms were aching from her dug-in fingernails. She tried to uncoil.

'Why did she want me to dive?' said Isla, clutching the duck. 'Does she know I dive different? I kept it secret. Did I do something wrong?'

'No,' said Kelda. 'Mam, where's Firth?'

Mam and Dad ignored both their daughters. Dad sat, took off his glasses, and rested his forehead in his hands. 'We can't hide it forever, Lyn,' he said. It felt like he was just picking up where they had left off, in an old, tired conversation.

Mam's face tightened, the saintly-patient face she wore on bad days. 'She hasn't seen,' she said, with terrible quiet reasonableness. 'She can't testify.'

'You are being deliberately obtuse—'

'Don't take that tone, Murphy, I'm not a child. Can we talk about something else, please?'

'No, we salting can't.'

Mum's patient face grew extra-patient, and she pressed her hands together, and looked away from him.

'Lyn.' Dad massaged his head where his frown crinkled it. 'Listen. Secrecy is not an option, not for a whole lifetime. And if the River gets any worse . . . Better to be safe, send—'

'No.'

'It's for her own safety.'

'Is it?' said Mam, and now she really *was* angry. '*Is it*, Murphy?'

Isla looked from Mam to Dad, trying to make sense of it all, uncertain tears brimming. Kelda bent down to kiss her. No one would be sending Isla *anywhere*.

'Where's Firth?' she repeated. It was all she could think about. She didn't even look round when Uncle Abe came in with a cheery hello, and started making appreciative noises at the good smells coming from the stove. She just said it a third time, louder: 'Where's Firth?'

'Kelda,' said Mam, 'please don't *aggravate* things—'

But before Kelda had any chance to really start aggravating things in earnest, there was a howl from behind them, so chilling that it commanded everyone's attention at once – even Kelda's – even the duck's.

Uncle Abe had dropped Kelda's basket on the floor, spilling the bayroot – or rather, Kelda realised, it was spilling *itself*, uncoiling and inching across the wood, already at least five times the size it had been. And there, in the basket, in the clutches of a coil of weed, was the top half of Uncle Abe's finger.

Everyone sprang up at once, grabbing anything silver they could lay their hands on. The weed had grown hideously while they were all distracted: they would have a job to hold it back, even with all of them.

'Firth!' hollered Mam. 'Get the nets and get in here! Kelda's picked Wicked Jenny!'

AN EXTRACT FROM 'BOTANY' IN:
THE WATERWAYS: ESSAYS ON A HIDDEN WORLD

....

Lemnoideae is a subfamily of freshwater plant, which also goes by the popular names of water lentil, water lens, bayroot and duckweed. It is abundant and nutritious, making it an excellent addition to the diet of a water-dwelling species. However, care must be taken, as it is difficult to distinguish from the vicious plant known variously as Jenny Greenteeth, Ginny Greenteeth, or Wicked Jenny.

A crop of duckweed found in flowing water, or looking unusually lush and verdant, should arouse particular suspicion. Wicked Jenny is usually confined to brackish water, the half-salted murky world where river and sea collide, and only found inland during hot summers; but it may spread upriver at any time, if the River's health is poor.

Landmen's tales of Wicked Jenny have grown confused. The name is still used for duckweed, but the stories that survive mostly paint Jenny as an old river hag. This is perhaps because landmen tend to think of plants as mindless things, neither good nor evil – which is true enough, on land.

It is not true on the waterways.

3

Dusk had only just settled into night, and the nocturnal Jenny was still dozy. The coil that had snapped Abe's finger now curled up around it happily, darkening in colour as it absorbed the blood. But the other tendrils were busy. They lengthened steadily, and unfurled themselves up the stove and round the shelves of jars and along the steamed-up porthole, exploring.

The Pades wasted no time. Kelda handed the medicine tin to Uncle Abe with one hand, and seized the silver pot full of trout stew with the other. Abe left for the roof, the only helpful thing he could do while he stank of fresh blood, and called again for Firth.

Mam and Dad had taken two slim silver scythes from the door and positioned themselves wordlessly, taking strategic angles either side of the Jenny. Kelda loved to see them working together – it was as though they could read each other's minds. Even Isla had wisely seized the empty silver teapot, although less helpfully she was putting most of her energy into cramming a defensive spoon into the duck's bill. The duck was not cooperating.

A moment later Firth had joined them from the roof with the net, face pale. He was the only one of them who wasn't calm in a fight. He was *good*; it wasn't that he panicked. But while everyone else was just dealing with the problem in front of them, he always looked as though he was fighting a great spiritual war against all the faceless forces of evil in some personal underworld. He clambered on the table with the net, nodding his readiness to Mam. Then he stared down at the Jenny, dark head bowed, lost in his own private moment of fiery solemnity.

The Jenny had established that the stove and jars and porthole were all part of a corner, and that the corner didn't have any ways out, and didn't have any food. Long tendrils began to loop down to the floor and try the other direction. More and more of them moved out into the centre of the galley.

'Steady,' said Mam. 'Not yet.'

Touching the Jenny would tell it which way to turn. They wouldn't have long to act once it knew where they were. Best to wait until all its tendrils were close together, easier to fight.

'Kelda,' said Mam, 'stew by that far stool.'

Dad and Isla took one step back from the stool in question. Firth adjusted the angle of the net. Kelda fished out the juiciest pieces of trout, and dropped them – a few here, a few there – spread out enough to keep the whole Jenny busy, but close enough to keep it contained.

One tendril found the first piece. It weaved, questing for more. The scent was strong. Three more tendrils joined the first.

'Wait,' said Mam.

Half a dozen tendrils joined the fish feast. But three more were still too far away, trying out the edges of the porthole.

'More,' said Mam. Kelda dropped more fish, but that was the last of it; and still the last tendrils of the Jenny didn't come.

'That's all,' she said.

'Well,' said Mam, 'we'll have to take it anyway then.' They only had a few seconds before the fish would be gone, and the Jenny would move on. With a few flicks of the head, Mam and Dad determined who was going to take the tendrils by the fish, and who was on defence against the rogue remainders; then Mam said, *'Now.'*

She and Dad sliced through two tendrils each. Instantly the stubs and the remaining tendrils all reared. Those by the fish were in easy reach of Dad's hook, and with each slash he took chunks off at least two at once, felling them like wheat, marginally faster than they could regrow. It would have been an easy contest with Mam there too.

But she was busy. From the far corner the other three tendrils came sailing through the air, a liability. One came straight at Mam's left and she sliced it easily. Kelda stunned a second en route to Dad with the stew pan, yelling 'Here, Mam!' as it shook itself dizzily – and Mam took it with a clean sweep.

The third came arcing highest of all, whacking itself against the low ceiling with a thud. Unperturbed by the wood, it came bucking forwards again, straight at Firth. He was still looking down, keeping vigil with the net.

'Firth!' yelled Kelda, too late, as the tendril flew straight to the crown of his head.

'GO!' cried Isla, throwing up the duck, which squawked in confusion and flapped up to a shelf, sending jars crashing – and its silver spoon fell from its bill and swiped the Jenny en route, causing a second's recoil. In the time it bought, Mam sliced. Firth blinked upwards, shaken but untouched. Isla cheered.

Below, Dad had decimated the rest of the Jenny. Twitching coils lay everywhere, oozing white sap across the boards.

'Net!' he called – and although Firth was shaking, his aim was always good, and the next moment the hacked remains of the Jenny lay stupefied under fine silver netting, woven with tight guardian knots. The plant twitched and writhed a moment, but the knots held. Then it lay still.

Mam nodded, put down the hook, took a tray from the oven, and slid it under the lifeless bundle. Dad got kindling from the stack by the wall. Kelda wondered if she was going to get a telling-off for picking it, or if they could skip straight to congratulating each other.

But all Dad said was, 'It shouldn't be so far inland. Not this time of year'; and all Mam said was, 'Not now, Murphy.' She didn't sound angry now – just tired. They left without another word to burn the Jenny on the bank, and the galley was still.

Kelda realised she was still clutching the pot. She put it back on the stove.

'Did you see the duck?' said Isla. 'Kelda, did you see him? Firth, the duck saved you! The Jenny was gonna get your head!' She looked up at the duck with enormous satisfaction. 'Mam will *have* to let him stay.'

Firth was too busy having a reverential moment of grace to quibble. He sank to his knees on the table, and ran a hand through his hair – a habit acquired from Dad, but Firth had inherited Mam's thick, pliable hair, so he always resembled a windswept hedgehog. He said nothing about the duck. Isla was having unbelievable luck. First Mam had ignored it, now *Firth* was ignoring it: this was the equivalent of a welcome party.

Kelda decided to join in the general ignoring – of the duck, of Meredith, of everything. If the rest of them could, she could too. 'Well done,' she said. 'Let's clear up.'

So Isla picked up pieces of trout and broken Jenny, while Kelda found a cloth and mopped at the sap, and Firth marvelled at the glory of their salvation from his table top. Some of Kelda's pummelling mood had been spent on the Jenny, and anyway, she couldn't demand answers from him in front of Isla. She left him to it.

Uncle Abe came back in as they worked, his finger stump bound. A poultice of woundwort and knitbone kept his blood safely inside him, but he was pale and shaking. He sat, holding the arm up above his head, and Kelda put on a pot for sweet tea.

'What shall we have for dinner?' she said. She found she needed to be busy: she almost wished she was still fighting the Jenny. 'We should do something simple. I could fry up the leftover chara cakes?'

'Yummy. Is your finger gonna grow back?' asked Isla, staring in fascination at Abe's bandaged stump.

24

'Nope. Your uncle's a three-fingered fiend now.' He did a ghostly smile at her in a bid to show that this was all right, and added, 'Nice duck you've got there.'

'I'm gonna call him Robin Hood,' she said, 'because of his green feathers.'

Robins had brown and red feathers, and Kelda didn't know where hoods came into it. But Isla didn't always make sense, so she just said, 'That's a lovely name,' and took down the tin of cakes. 'Can anyone see the oil?'

From his table top, Firth scowled. 'Isla, that's a landman myth, isn't it? Robin Hood?'

'He steals from the bad,' said Isla, 'and gives to the good. Uncle Abe was telling me.' Uncle Abe smiled at her weakly.

'River and moon,' muttered Firth. He didn't push the point, but on the other hand, he didn't help find the oil either. After a minute of heavily waiting for anybody else to take anything *seriously*, he slammed into his cabin – in the bow of the boat, next to the galley – and left Kelda to get on with frivolous things like handing Uncle Abe his sugar-laden tea, and making them all dinner.

She found the oil, and put the cakes on to fry. They sizzled and spat as they browned.

'Robin Hood didn't like Meredith,' said Isla.

Kelda turned the cakes. 'Robin Hood is spot on there. He shouldn't listen to a word she says.'

Isla was crouching very still, contemplating the duck. 'She said I was a landman. Because of my diving?'

Kelda and Uncle Abe exchanged glances. From Abe's expression, it was clear he had heard it all through the open roof hatch – and presumably, then, Firth had too. But before Kelda could decide how best to assuage the fears of Robin Hood, Mam and Dad came back in. So that was the end of *that*. Even Isla knew better than to try and ask them her questions, especially in this mood.

So instead, they all got on with beside-the-point discussions about where they had gone to light a fire and the otters that had come to watch and how much sage to add to the chara cakes. Their reserve of useless conversation was exhausted by the time the cakes were served, and they ate in near-silence, Firth wolfing his in record time before returning to his cabin. Nobody mentioned Meredith, or the Jenny, or everything that such misplaced Jenny implied about the state of the River.

After dinner was Isla's bedtime, and today it was Uncle Abe's bedtime too. Abe slept in a hammock in the galley ('And what do I need a poky bed-cabin for,' he had said, when Kelda had once queried the justice of this, 'when I've got my roof garden?'). He took a draught of something strong from the cabinet that only he and Dad ever used, and he went to sleep as soon as his head touched his pillow.

Isla slept in the middle cabin with Kelda, on the top berth; Mam and Dad had the stern. Isla had been persuaded to climb into her berth with the bribe of keeping Robin Hood for the night but, unlike Uncle Abe, she was wide awake. So she and Kelda curled up in her blankets and talked. Kelda told her that Meredith was an idiot, and she knew nothing, and was just throwing her weight around because she was that sort of silly person, and that nothing bad was going to come of it. She was

26

good at sounding confident. Slowly, her sister relaxed against her warm body.

But even once Isla was mollified, she was still not sleepy. So Kelda sat up, lit a lamp, and told shadow-stories.

She had learned all the hand shapes from Mam. The shadows of grindylow and lavellans and fuathan danced across the wall, and white-water spirits too – kelpies and selkies and wyrms, for the stranger stories. Firth would have approved: they were good River stories. Kelda didn't know any others.

'How big are wyrms?' said Isla.

'Big enough to eat you UP,' said Kelda, flattening her hand into the snake-like body.

'But HOW big?'

'You'll have to ask Uncle Abe.'

'Why don't we have any in England?'

Kelda was not a nature scholar, and Isla was meant to be getting sleepier. 'I don't know. Not enough white water?'

'What do spirits eat?'

'Little giiiirls.'

'Liar liar. Are spirits born like fish are?' Isla had recently become acquainted with the facts of life, and was embarrassingly fascinated by them.

'I don't know. Now—'

'Do you think if you had silver you could—'

'I don't *know*, Isla. Spirits are very mysterious, all right?' She stroked her sister's arm, and dropped her voice dramatically. 'Shhh, now . . . it's time . . . for the story . . .' she bunched up her hand, with pointed fingers for a rodent's snout, 'of the little girl who stopped a *lavellan's heart*!'

'The little girl called *Isla*,' said Isla.

'Sure.' And Kelda told the story in the silkiest, sleepiest voice she knew. She wished Mam would tell the stories sometimes; she was much better at it. She hardly ever did these days.

It took a while tonight, but the stories worked their slow magic. By the time the little girl called Isla had stopped the heart of the giant water-rat and saved a whole village of shadow people from its venomous bite, the real Isla was finally asleep.

Kelda extinguished the lamp, and the shadow-world vanished.

Kelda crept back into the galley to find Dad preparing mugs of tea in the dark, trying not to disturb Uncle Abe. The door to the deck was ajar.

'Your mam's lighting the fire,' whispered Dad. 'Call your brother.'

So they *were* going to talk about it, after all. Good. Kelda crossed the galley, and tapped the door with her knuckles.

'Firth.' She raised her voice just enough to carry through the wood. 'Tea on deck.'

There was a pause. She was about to tap again. Then Firth said, 'Coming.'

A minute later they were all gathered round the poplar stove with blankets, hands wrapped around mugs of tea – apart from Firth, who had wrapped his hands around his knees instead, drawing them up to his chin and staring into the flames. Beyond their small circle, the river and the sky were endless dark, and the only sound was the ceaseless murmur of the water as it hurried onwards. In the firelight, their grey eyes looked silver, and the silver pendants at their necks winked gently.

'So,' said Dad. His voice was measured, and full of care: he only ever snapped at them over trivial things, the everyday bickering that didn't really matter. 'I think it's time we all talked.'

In winter, brackish creatures like Jenny should not be inland, far from saltwater. It's a sign that the River is sick.

Salt and summer and sickness all starve rivers, robbing them of oxygen. Some creatures can't survive this. Others *like* the choking water – the halibut and mullet, the fly larvae, the yellow eel. And the ones that landmen only know as myths: Wicked Jenny and Tiddy Mun, grindylow and lavellan. If you are unlucky, fuathan. These are the brackish creatures. They are stupefied by silver, and held by guardian knots.

Travel away from the lowlands and the sea, up into the hills, and the rivers breathe. Where these rivers tumble over rapids and waterfalls, there is white water. And where there's white water, there are shape-shifters: kelpies and water bulls, tangies and selkies. If you are unlucky, a wyrm. These are the white-water spirits, and they can't be held; only appeased.

The inhabitants of marshes and fens and the deep groundwater are outside the River's dominion, and don't concern silvermen: knuckers and water leapers and will-o'-the-wisp. They would be held by reed-knots, if landmen knew how, but most have forgotten.

4

Kelda pulled her blanket closer, and looked from Mam to Dad, trying to guess which way this talking was likely to tend. Neither of them was angry now, and it was a little unsettling. She felt something had slipped out of her control this evening, and it wasn't something that she quite understood yet.

Mam had brought silver thread and was beginning on a new net. She did not look up.

'First,' said Dad, 'you have some explaining to do, Firth. And then I think we should talk about everything that happened tonight. And Isla's future.'

There was a moment of silence, apart from the fire and the river.

'So. Firth.' Dad's voice was kind. 'You've never been a gossip. What happened?'

The silver-eye effect of the fire gave Firth a slightly manic look, but when he spoke, his voice was tight and small. He didn't meet anybody's gaze. 'Aeron's been studying since Fossy died,' he said. 'She got sick round when the River first started going bad. He wants to understand – he's been reading loads of old lore, medical lore – he wants to be a healer. I thought he might be able to help.'

'What, help his pious family throw Isla into the River to heal it?' said Kelda. Aeron hadn't come by that night to see her. Good: he should be ashamed.

Firth didn't look at her, but there was the slightest shake of his head. 'I've been thinking maybe there's a reason she's like she is. Maybe she could be cured . . .' He trailed off miserably.

'Did you really think a teenage boy could teach us anything we don't know, Firth?' said Dad.

'He's going to look through his books,' said Firth defensively. 'And he's a friend. I couldn't exactly just ask Willig, could I?' Willig was the healer the family usually sought out, on the rare occasions one was needed. He brought exceptional tonics and ointments, but he also brought the gossip of half the waterways. He was the last person you would trust with a secret. 'And we have to do *something*,' Firth said, warming to his theme. 'We all just sit around pretending it's not a problem. I can't stand it. I wake up worrying about her every day. *Every day.*'

It was hard to be sure because of the firelit-silver-glint thing, but Kelda thought there was a film of tears in Firth's eyes. This was a surprise. She was caught off-guard, her retorts faltering.

'What if someone finds out?' Firth went on. 'And if by some moonsafe no one does, what happens when she's older? When she's supposed to have her own boat, and fish and harvest for herself which she *can't*, and marry?'

Kelda knew the answer to that. She had already designed

the boat she would build for herself and Isla: she had the sketches in her cabin-chest. And she had imagined all the little touches too, although they changed with her mood. At the moment it was going to be cherry red, with a roof garden for Isla, and white paintwork on the trimmings. They wouldn't marry. Uncle Abe made his jokes about Aeron, but Kelda had always known she wasn't going to make a love-match, with *anyone*. Isla was more important.

But Firth didn't want answers, or hypothetical cherry-red boats. He wanted to impress upon the family the numerous and terrifying nature of the questions which beset him every morning, and which he felt they were failing to take seriously. 'Does anyone really think she'll get away with it forever? Are we just supposed to all live sick with worry till then? And what if she *is* causing the trouble on the River? I know she's not a landman, Mam,' he said hastily, when Mam's gaze snapped up. 'But the Lore isn't clear. We might be doing wrong keeping her here, even so, when she's . . . like she is. I don't know. We don't know. And it's her silver year now, and *something*'s stirring up the River – Jenny inland in winter is the least of it. People are getting the mer-sickness all over, and there's grindylow infestations, and Aeron heard an actual lavellan's woken up inland, and—'

'We know all that, Firth,' said Dad. 'That's what I want to discuss. It's a dangerous time for Isla, when everyone's scared – and very bad timing for it to happen in her silver year, you're right. But *you* know she isn't making the River sick, don't you? That's just superstition.'

Firth looked at Dad, and his look was pleading. It seemed

like he was trying to say yes. But all he managed was, '*How* do we know?'

Dad ran his fingers through his hair, at a loss. He was no Lore scholar. Firth had probably thumbed his copy of the River Lore more times in his fourteen years than Dad had in his forty. Dad had made his children learn to tie the knots, and recite the stanzas on brackish creatures; apart from that he never bothered much with it. 'That's just something people believe, Firth,' he said. 'It's not . . . right thinking. But your other worries, we share. We do. I'm sorry we haven't talked about it. We'll talk about it now.' He put another log on the fire, which leaped up, hissing. 'But promise me you won't go talking about this to anybody else, please? However many books they've read. This is a family affair.'

Firth nodded. He looked like he might have more to say, but he just huddled his head on to his knees again, and went back to staring at the fire. Kelda looked at Mam, opening her mouth to appeal for proper discipline – Mam could normally be relied on, when Dad was soft.

But Mam was crying. Kelda hadn't seen Mam cry since the night they almost lost Isla. The tears were silent, but they kept coming, copious and hopeless, as she tied knot after knot in the net and watched her own hands at work, and said nothing.

Suddenly Kelda understood, properly, that something new was happening. She looked away from Mam quickly, out across the formless dark.

'Now,' said Dad, 'Isla. As you both probably know, your mam and I have had disagreements about this. We decided, when we were burning the Jenny, it should be something we all

34

talk about together.' He looked at Mam as though to hand over to her, then he saw what Kelda had seen, and kept talking. 'So. *I* think Isla should be sent away to a landman home. Uncle Abe has made some enquiries with his landman friends, and there's a family who know about our kind who'd be happy to have her. It's—'

'You've already planned it all?' said Kelda. This was worse than she had expected. 'Without talking to us?'

'It's just an option, Keldie,' said Dad. 'We haven't accepted their offer yet. I didn't want to stir everybody up airing my concerns until I had an alternative. And now I do – so we're talking. We wouldn't decide anything without consulting you, I promise.'

Kelda just glared at him.

'Hear me out,' said Dad. He held her gaze. 'Anyone of landman blood living as part of a silverman boat is an abomination in the Lore. No one's ever heard of a silverman like Isla, and we can't expect anyone to believe us. I know we've all been living on the hope that no one will make it their business to investigate, and I think maybe that's worked to a point – I'm sure some people have their suspicions, and are keeping themselves to themselves. But there are hard times ahead. Firth's right, the River's sick – it's worse than it should be, even with the rainfall this low. And this is February. It's going to be a hard summer.'

Summer was the sickly season. The rivers thinned. The winterbournes disappeared entirely, and the rivers that remained were poorer water, tight on the skin, glutted with algae. And at the same time the waters grew crowded: the other river creatures spawned, and most of the spawn died. The Lore said it was the time when the gates of life were open at both ends.

'I strongly feel,' said Dad, 'that Isla should take this chance to leave in spring, before the search for blame really begins in earnest. The landmen are happy to take her on our way back from Equinox. I'd like to leave her on the way there really, but we'll have converged with half the other boats by then, so it'll be too late to pretend anything's happened to her.' Kelda opened her mouth at that, and Dad raised his voice slightly. 'Better to pretend she's died than let it come true. Kelda, you haven't seen a hard year. They won't just send her away – it's too late for that now she's come into her silver. If she's held responsible, she'll be drowned.'

Kelda knew the Lore, but it was just an abstract idea. She couldn't really grasp it, or feel afraid of it. Isla leaving, on the other hand, was something she had imagined, dreaded, set herself against. She might have found it easier to listen if Dad had cried too; but he was too calm, too sure.

'We'll keep her safe,' she said. 'How would anybody know? As long as Firth keeps his mouth shut—'

'Kelda, don't make this about blame, *please*. It's hard enough as it is.'

'But if he hadn't told—'

'We would still be having this conversation. There have been – remarks – from other boats before tonight. It's never been safe. Never.'

She turned to her mother. 'Mam. You don't want this?'

There was a long pause.

'Of course I don't,' said Mam at last. Her voice was miraculously steady, as though the tears belonged to somebody else. 'I've been against it all along. But Meredith gave me a scare tonight. Something became . . . real. Maybe it's the right thing, even if we don't want it.'

'But it would break her heart,' said Kelda.

'I know,' said Mam, so quietly it was almost just part of the river.

'It's a good plan, Dad,' said Firth. 'I vote yes.' And before Kelda could turn on him, Dad quickly leaned forward, and took up the reins again.

'Right. So it's clearly me and Firth in favour. But I'm not tearing this family apart against its will. Mam and Kelda?'

'No,' said Kelda, 'Never.'

'Mam?'

This time the silence went on and didn't stop. First it was the silence of Mam not answering, and then it was the silence of nobody knowing what to say about Mam not answering, and then it was the silence of everybody thinking their own thoughts. It was a full minute before anyone spoke again.

'Well, I've said my piece,' said Dad. 'I need to sleep. Think it over, and we'll talk again soon. Don't be late, you two' – this to Firth and Kelda – 'last one to bed, see to the stove.'

He stood, and put a hand on Mam's shoulder, but she didn't look up. Firth stood too, springing up like an animal released from a trap. But while Dad walked away, Firth hovered. He seemed to be waiting for permission to speak. Kelda looked studiously at the fire.

In the end, he spoke without permission. 'You're not the

only one who loves her, Kelda,' he said. 'If you love her, you should think about this. Otherwise it's just selfish. It's just because *you'd* miss her.' And then he *did* leave, very fast, with the speed of someone who knows perfectly well when a pummelling might be coming their way.

Only when they had both gone did Kelda cry. She stayed with Mam, and they talked and worked the net together until the fire died down.

She woke early, and lay listening to Isla's breathing in the darkness, punctuated by the occasional sleep-gakker from Robin Hood. Kelda wondered if ducks had dreams. They were probably nice easy dreams about worms and weeds. Kelda's dreams had been more tiring than being awake.

The morning light began to turn her porthole silver. She slipped out of bed and pulled on her fly-silks. Then she padded across the boards, into the galley and past Uncle Abe in his hammock, out onto the frosted deck, over the side and into the water.

It was a sharp river here, the kind that ran over granite and let in very little of the soft water from the ground below; and at this time of morning it was cold. Kelda's skin burst into life. It was good. She wanted her skin to feel busier than her mind.

She stayed down there for a long time, sinking right to the bottom, letting the tiny eddies and whorls around the riverbed boulders tickle at her skin, feeling the current push against her out-turned palms before hurrying on with its journey. She stayed until the surface up above was almost white with light. Then she put her hands in the moss and pushed, launching herself to the surface in a rush before she could change her mind.

Uncle Abe was awake. He was on the roof of the boat, sitting on a stool, playing something lopsided and lilting on his fiddle. Kelda didn't realise *why* it was lopsided until she had climbed the ladder to the garden, and saw that he had taken off the third string, the one he would have played with his snapped finger.

He stopped, seeing where her gaze fell.

'It's a musical experiment,' he said. 'I'm trying some of the old reels with those notes missing, first. I can work out how to play them with three fingers – but it's interesting without them, isn't it? Something haunting about it.'

Kelda nodded. 'It's pretty. Kind of sad.' She was picking her way to the other stool, opposite his, which was a tricky business because of all the sprawling stems and delicate buds to be negotiated. The smell of soil and mulchy growth was overwhelming. She made it to the stool at last, with only minor injury to plant-life.

Uncle Abe put down the fiddle, picked Kelda a mint leaf to chew, and said, 'So. What hook are you wriggling on this morning, Keldie?'

'Is it a nice house?'

'Ah. You've talked.' He picked some mint for himself. 'Yes. It's a nice house. Very nice. In this big old forest. Lovely people – brother and sister, old friends of mine. You've heard me talk about the Parsons – Judith and Peter?'

Kelda nodded. Uncle Abe's landman friends were rarely mentioned these days, since Mam had become so much more pious and uptight; but in that other-world before Isla she had heard the names – Dad would join Abe on his trips back then, and once or twice even Mam too.

'You think she'll be happy?'

'Yes.'

'How could she be happy without us?'

Uncle Abe's hands spread. 'She's young. She'll adapt. Better do it now, while that's still true. Although she might throw a fit about the duck, I suppose.' Kelda didn't laugh, but Uncle Abe was unperturbed. 'I've been teaching her landman things,' he went on, 'and she loves it. She loves their stories best, the ones in forests and fields and mountains. And she loves to hear about the way they live, their houses, their towns, how they play together.'

Kelda just chewed, and they both sat, looking out across the misted river to the trees on the bank beyond.

'She doesn't like swimming, Keldie,' said Abe. 'Let her run.'

Dad was the only one awake inside. He was not good with mornings. He was currently trying to work out why his egg wasn't frying on an unlit stove.

Kelda lit it for him.

'Aha,' he said. 'Yes. Good. Now, tea.'

'She should go,' said Kelda.

'Good. What?'

'She should go to the landmen. But I hate it.'

Dad blinked at her. This was clearly a lot before breakfast. 'Right. Well, Keldie, I agree with you.'

Kelda didn't look at him as she went back into her cabin, and said, 'I'm still going to kill Firth.'

Dad smiled at that. Overhead, Uncle Abe's reels lolloped on, the same but different, and the egg fried like normal and the sun warmed to the day like normal and the river kept right on flowing, on and on, unstoppably out to its end.

Apart from their respiratory systems, perhaps the greatest difference between silvermen and landmen is their social structure. Landmen have a habit of clumping together in large groups, and very often of staying stuck to one place; hence the silverman saying, 'sticky as a landman', for an unusually clingy or needy person.

Each silverman boat is essentially independent, constantly on the move to maintain its own supplies, and charting its own course. Fishing, foraging and gardening are key. Besides survival, many silvermen occupy their time with scholarship – most commonly as natural scholars, Lore scholars, history scholars and water scholars – or crafts, usually in wood or reeds or metalwork. Boats only gather en masse at the two Equinoxes: at the Avonmouth in the south in autumn, and east in spring, at the Humber.

In the past this required most boats to fill up barrels of fresh water and brave a sea voyage, but when the landmen laced the rivers up together in the middle with a criss-cross of waterways, few continued to risk the sea. The boats became narrower, to fit within the canals, and sea sails were abandoned.

The Equinoxes are mostly a time for certain restricted trading, and a more or less continuous round of eating and drinking. They are also an opportunity for any complaints against the peace and health of the River to be tried.

Once the Equinox has passed, the boats disperse once more.

5

As always, the Spring Equinox brought boats to the Humber. Up from the Nene through the Soar and the Trent; up from the Weaver and the Dee through the Macclesfield Canal; longer journeys from the chalk streams of the Wey and the Lea; short sails south from the Ure and the Ouse, the Derwent and the Hull. To the south and the west, the waterways were emptied of silvermen.

Spring brought others too, not only to the Humber but all over, even to the unnavigable northern waters: elvers and salmon fry stirring in the streams, sand martins and wagtails returning on the air, carpets of algae on the rocks and marsh marigold on the banks. The air grew warmer, but the water was still cool and deep, with only the thinnest winterbournes running dry. It was a rich time for the rivers.

The silvermen watched these signs of the summer to come, and the landmen who lived on the banks of the Humber watched the boats that arrived on their shores every year. Odd traveller types, they never caused any trouble *exactly*, but no one liked to get too close. The more superstitious believed queer rumours about them. The less superstitious believed you couldn't trust anyone who couldn't settle down in good bricks and mortar like everybody else, and besides this their songs were strange, and their parties looked suspiciously like a wild amount of *fun*.

They were, too.

The day on the Humber itself was the day of salt. The Humber is an estuary at the mouths of the River Trent and the River Ouse, and the water is heavy with salt, and with the silt that turns it brown. Unable to dive, every boat brings a barrel of fresh water and when they go from boat to boat visiting each other, they refresh their skin in those barrels. As well as the visits, there is the trading on shore, and the rowdy gatherings of musicians and singers, and the earnest gatherings of the more scholarly minded in day-long chitterings.

Then, at dusk, all the boats move down the Humber, past the point where the two rivers meet, and on down the Trent, until they pass the tidal head – which shifts its location depending on the winds and the rains and the moon and a hundred other things which only the most dedicated water scholars understand – and cross over into fresh water once more. And the parties on the Humber are nothing compared to the moonlit party after the freshwater crossing.

Kelda usually loved Equinox. This year it felt unreal, a sickening ride that was happening around her relentlessly, whether she wanted it to or not. She couldn't say that she was sad, or anything so calm and simple as that: she was just strung up tight in every muscle, and constantly felt sick, and wanted it to stop.

Which it would, soon enough, and then she would regret

wishing the time away. She concentrated on knotting a chain of asters to be wound around the water barrel, while Firth scrubbed the deck, and Mam worked at the stove. Dad was diving for seasonings, with strict instructions from Mam – her cooking at Equinox was a point of family pride. There had been a careful, desperate peace between the two of them since the night of the Jenny.

Isla was decorating the garden with Abe. She had taken the news well, considering. They hadn't exactly explained that she could be flung overboard, but they had said that it was time for her to go because of her diving, and that they would visit often, and that Uncle Abe's friends had horses that lived in stables full of hay, and trees for climbing, and a house with an upstairs. And that it was a secret, just for their family. She had nodded solemnly, as if she had somehow always known that the boat was not hers forever; and she had climbed into bed with Kelda that night, and solemnly cried herself to sleep. The solemnity had been worse, somehow, than tantrums. But slowly it wore off, and she asked Uncle Abe more and more questions. He drew her a map with the cottage on it, and told her stories about the people there and the horses they kept, and the woods; until she tentatively seemed almost . . . excited.

Kelda didn't know *what* to feel about that. On the roof now, Abe and Isla were singing – a song of one of the weirder old histories, where the rivers turned to blood. It ended in someone being sacrificed to the River. Kelda wished they had chosen a different song.

'*Turn back and weep, all you who keep,*' boomed Abe.

'Your vigil at the sandy head,' piped Isla.

'Spring tides hold sway, the Crescent Bay will turn to waters thick and red! All Caledonia, red!'

This last line was sung with hefty gusto and slightly dubious harmonies. Kelda concentrated extra-hard on her work.

She needed to work fast. The Pade boat had arrived at the Humber at the last moment, the night before the day of salt, so they had all got up at the crack of dawn to prepare the boat. Now others were stirring, their boats already gleaming and festooned, their barrels elaborately decorated.

Her speed was severely compromised by Robin Hood's attempts to eat the flowers – he had been allowed to stay as a concession to Isla's happiness, which was quite right in principle, but often very annoying in practice. By the time she had finished, the earliest risers were pushing off in alder boats to begin their visits.

'Well done, you two,' said Mam, ducking out from the galley and looking at their work on the deck. 'Good. That will do nicely.'

'Can we go?' said Firth. He looked forward to the chitterings all year. Kelda was keen to go too, to take Isla and get away from the gossip and speculation about the River that would come with the visits this year.

'Yes, love. Are you taking the alder?'

Uncle Abe called down from the roof. 'I'll row you upstream, Firth. I've got some trading to do.'

'Dee Marshmen is trading *weather loaches*!' said Isla, her excited face popping out over the roof, silver pendant dangling.

'And Uncle Abe says if anyone knows anything about white-water spirits it will be Dee, but that nobody knows much, but I can ask her and see.'

Kelda did not particularly trust the wisdom of Dee Marshman, and was old enough to remember Uncle Abe's last weather loach: a drooping fish in a glass tube who was supposed to swim frantically when the atmosphere changed and a storm was coming. In Kelda's lifetime he had been elderly, and never managed more than a worried bubble. But she smiled enthusiastically, and called back, 'Great! Come and get your skirt, then.'

The girls ducked inside and tied on their wrap-around skirts, which they wore to avoid scandal in landmen towns. Their usual one-piece suit of moon-coloured fly-silks, ending in practical trousers, would apparently cause outrage – it was something about showing women's legs that was the problem. Happily, landmen were too stupid to spot the difference between silk from silkworms and the tough, waterproof silk from caddis flies – so although the disguise looked foreign, it didn't look *too* alien.

Kelda loved the skirts. Hers was moss green, and she had made herself a headscarf to match, which she tied now over her long brown plait. Isla's skirt was deep red. They spent a minute parading about the room doing their best landman impressions.

'What tosh!' cried Kelda. 'You are a CAD!'

'Perfectly top-hole!' agreed Isla, who loved this game, but didn't know exactly what all the landman slang meant. But they weren't really trying to make sense, so it didn't matter.

Kelda collapsed dramatically on her bunk. 'The RAIN! I shall die of it!'

Isla switched roles at once, and began enthusiastically playing the part of the rain.

'Are you girls ever coming?' called Abe, from the galley. 'Boat's ready!'

So Kelda stopped dying of the rain, and they hurried to cram themselves in behind Firth and Uncle Abe in the alder boat, Robin Hood in Isla's lap.

The boat was shaped like a canoe, but moved much faster, cutting easy slices through the water. It was always strange to Kelda, to look out at the inviting ripples on all sides, and know that there was nowhere to dive. She dipped a finger in the water just to feel the shock, a little burst of blistering heat just below the skin. One minute in there, maybe two, would mean death.

Isla leaned over to try it. She left her fingers in, all of them, smiling to herself. Innocently demonic.

'Hands in the boat, Isla.'

'But you—'

Kelda used her no-nonsense voice. '*Hands in.*'

They landed a short way upstream, on a sheltered stretch of mud and shingle. It was a singularly grey slice of earth, but it was dotted with colourful rugs, where people had laid out artwork and bound books and carpentry and clockwork, and small plants and seeds for roof gardens, and some of the more unusual feats of basketry and weaving, and sealskin and silver. Around each rug people squatted in the mud, bartering lazily.

To the right of the rugs a chittering was already underway. A speaker stood on the wooden stump in the middle, and the listeners squatted round them, chewing mint, heads cocked. When the oil lamp at their side burned down, it would be the next speaker's turn. The topic was the speaker's choice.

Firth hurried over at once, to where his usual crowd were already crouched, attentive. With a jolt of her stomach, Kelda spotted Aeron Jupp. He looked her way, and she looked away quickly.

'Right,' she said, 'where are these weather loaches, then?'

Dee Marshman was near the back, with her usual silverware, some landman curiosities, and half a dozen loaches in their glass tubes: morose, mottled fishes with tentacled faces. They looked remarkably like Dee. But her hangdog face brightened at the sight of Uncle Abe – they were both nature scholars, and old friends – and she waved them all over.

'Thought you'd be along for one of these, Aberforth!'

'You're a temptress, Dee.'

'Brought me something special from your garden? These are rare.'

'Oh, I daresay I can interest you . . .'

Isla was thoroughly disappointed in the loaches. While Abe fell to bartering over the fish and, to his great excitement, a battered pocket-watch, she tugged at Kelda's hand. 'Can we look at the rugs?'

'Of course,' said Kelda. 'I've not brought anything to trade, mind you . . .'

So they wandered the rugs, the duck's feet slapping along the mud behind them. Kelda usually liked to look at the beautiful woodwork and copper in particular, privately picking out what she and Isla would have on their boat. She caught her mind still doing it now, automatically trying out that clock for her imagined galley, or this weathervane for the roof. She held Isla's hand extra-tightly.

Isla had never spared a thought for decorating a boat, and wasn't overly interested in anything beautiful if it didn't grow or move. She was briefly entertained by the rug full of books, and had to be reminded, several times, that they were very valuable. (Silvermen had heard of the printing press, but held no truck with it: they maintained that knowledge lightly gained was lightly held and quickly lost. Scholars borrowed and copied out complete texts, lovingly binding them in skins of all kinds.)

Isla quickly eliminated the weighty histories and Lore, and picked up a slim book in vole skin, decorated with hemlock flowers in gold. *Lavellans: On the Origins of the Water-rat.*

'Can I have this?'

'No.'

'Please?'

'No.'

'*Please?* I *really* want it. Firth said there's an awake one now, in big dark caves inland . . .'

'Well, when you're grown up and a nature scholar you can copy one out and have it.'

Once Isla had established to her satisfaction that no amount of wheedling was going to result in her getting a present of any kind, she began to lose interest in the rugs, and stare at the chittering instead. She tugged Kelda's hand. 'Can we listen?'

This was fine by Kelda. She was aching from all the

not-thinking-about-her-cherry-red-boat. It was less good that Isla chose them a spot right opposite Firth and Aeron – Kelda almost tugged her on. But then someone shot them a dirty look, as though to say that a chittering was not really for six-year-olds and ducks; after which Kelda squatted down *very* firmly exactly where she was, because she wasn't going to be bossed around by dirty looks.

'. . . with the poisons from these mills increasing by the year,' the speaker was saying, 'and no sign of the landman greed abating. Consider the once-great River Mersey . . .'

Qrrrrrk, said Robin Hood, who had just found a worm, and did not wish to consider the once-great River Mersey.

Kelda didn't blame him. This was an exceptionally boring speaker, and the poisons of the landmen were always a boring topic, since they were more or less constant and everybody agreed and nobody could do anything about it. No one stood to raise a question or argument for the entire length of her very dull speech. It was a relief when her oil burned down, and the next speaker stood: a short, portly man, with more than the usual sheen to his skin, and an excitable puff of red hair. At his feet he set a bulging sealskin satchel.

It was Willig, the healer.

'Thank you, friend,' he said, indicating the last speaker; then he put his fingertips together, the way he always did when he had something to impart – which was more or less always. 'My friends, I wish to discuss the matter of the mer-sickness. I have been working to improve my cure, and I believe I have made an important breakthrough. Our dear friend Cordelia has agreed to join me' – and he stretched out an arm.

51

At the cue a young woman stood, and came to stand by the oil lamp. The whole of the left half of her face and neck was covered with the unmistakable grey, leathery skin of the mer-sickness.

'As you will all be aware, we have seen a bad season this year. The sad state of the River means the sickness is rife among eels, and I must urge you all to be highly vigilant against eel-bites, especially as summer approaches. I believe my esteemed friend' – he nodded to another healer in the crowd – 'is hoping to speak later on her research into the causes, and her theory that the bite is especially potent when the eels are newly arrived to fresh water from the sea. I wish now only to present the results of my new cure.' He produced a bottle of inky liquid from his satchel and held it up, taking his time, enjoying himself. 'Cordelia,' he said, 'was administered this cure a full two hours after contracting the illness. As you can see, it has not spread beyond her face.'

A murmur went up at this. The window to treat mer-sickness was normally measurable only in minutes from the first patches appearing. The sooner it was treated, the less it might spread when it really took root in a few hours' time. A face like Cordelia's was manageable. But when it took the whole head until it became more fish than silverman – or began at the feet and worked up, fusing the legs into one leathered tail – or began on the belly, until the whole torso was a flibbering black rope that couldn't hold itself up straight – then the unfortunate victim was no longer silverman enough to survive on land. There was an obligation to throw them overboard once they were more than half-consumed, but most threw themselves into the water before that, when the agony of two incomplete bodies became too much to bear. They would usually be found belly-up shortly after. And even this slim hope for survival was an improvement on the old ways, before the cure, when Lore required that you slit the throat of anyone infected immediately.

If Cordelia had waited two hours for treatment, she was a miracle. She stood proudly by the lamp, a large silver moon hung around her neck, her long hair tied back to better show the leathered skin.

Willig began explaining the subtle changes to his processing of the eel blood used in his cure, but Kelda wasn't listening. She couldn't tear her eyes away from Cordelia. It was so rare to see a survivor. The skin looked tough, but cracked. It looked like it must smart when she moved.

She was so engrossed that she didn't notice Aeron Jupp stand and walk around the circle, and she jumped when he tapped her shoulder.

She whipped around, and seeing who it was, her eyes narrowed.

He jerked his head: *Come with me.*

She raised her eyebrows: *Why would I?*

He squatted down next to her, and whispered, not looking at her: 'I'd like to talk to you. It's important. Firth can watch Isla.'

She didn't want to hear him even say Isla's name. And she didn't feel like a chat. But if Aeron Jupp thought he had something important to say, she ought to hear it. Better to know. Before he said it to other people, whatever it was.

She stood, putting a hand out to ruffle Isla's hair as she whispered where she was going. Isla didn't even look round. She was entranced by Cordelia, gazing up at her, hugging Robin Hood tightly.

'All right,' Kelda muttered to Aeron. 'What is it?'

He gave her a small smile. It didn't seem malicious; just pleased, glad that she had agreed. As if she had a choice, and he didn't hold power over her whole world, and was just a young man hoping for a chat about the weather.

'Not here,' he said. 'Follow me.'

They walked along the bank until the chittering was well behind them, not speaking. Kelda was disconcerted to find that Aeron, who had always been tall, had shot up since last Equinox and was now about as tall as Dad. It was unsettling.

She glanced back automatically for Isla, but from this distance, she was hidden in amongst the chittering. Kelda was so distracted that she didn't register where Aeron was steering them until they had reached the little copse of oaks. He stepped among the trunks, into the shadows, out of view. Kelda followed, but not before glancing about to see if anyone was watching them go. The last thing she needed was *gossip* about this.

'Thanks, Keldie,' said Aeron. 'I was hoping I'd get a chance to speak to you.'

Kelda just glared, but mostly at her feet. He had a way of locking his eyes on her with alarming intensity, which made it difficult to look straight at him.

'I wanted to say sorry about my mam,' he went on. 'That's not how I would go about things. And I didn't tell her, for the record. She overheard us.'

Still Kelda did not reply. Her skin itched. She knew she couldn't really be dried yet, but she wanted fresh water, and silvery quiet.

'And I wanted to tell you,' he pushed on, unperturbed, 'there's been a case like Isla before. I'm investigating it – I'll know more today, I hope.'

'There's – what?' This was totally off-script, a scenario Kelda had not even considered. She looked up at Aeron. 'When? What was wrong? What happened?'

He shrugged. 'Seventy years ago or so. But that's all I know. There's a record in one of Willig's old books he lent me – he collects other healer's records when they pass on, they're pretty hard to interpret most of the time, but they're interesting, and he has this amazing collection of old Lore too – anyway. It just notes the case, as part of this whole page about a really bad year for the River, and it says *sickness cured.*'

'River and moon,' said Kelda.

'It was a big relief to find it; I thought . . .' He trailed off, not voicing that slightly different world – the one Kelda had inhabited only moments before – the one where Isla was unexplained, and righteous Aeron had to be her enemy. What was there to say about that? So instead he said, 'Your brother did the right thing, you know, telling me.'

Kelda snorted, but Aeron didn't seem to notice.

'And I'm glad I know,' he went on. 'I see why you vanished from our lives, now. We thought you were just sick of us.' And he smiled, and Kelda was suddenly ten again, because it was the smile he had used when they had both understood something that their little siblings hadn't grasped – conspiratorial, knowing.

It had the same uneven kink to one corner, and slid his long nose off-centre.

Then she remembered, with a jolt, that Aeron's little sister was dead. She'd been found belly-up not long after going overboard.

'I'm sorry about Fossy,' she said. It sounded small, stupid.

He shrugged, the smile gone, and it took him a second to find his voice again. His face was unbearably soft in that moment, and Kelda felt a sudden urge to comfort him, but she didn't know how – so she just stood, feeling foolish.

'Thanks,' he said at last, 'me too. It's . . .' He gave in at this, and said instead, 'Willig's work is amazing, isn't it?'

'You already knew about it?'

'Uh-huh. I'm apprenticed, I'll join him full-time soon. He's been giving me books to copy whenever we pass. Mam doesn't know.'

Aeron had always been scholarly, but it was histories he had loved before. Healers lived strange lives, turning their boats at any hour to wherever they were needed, rarely keeping a family or a regular course. 'She'll go full loony,' said Kelda. 'When're you planning to tell her?'

'She'll cope,' said Aeron, not answering the question. 'I've got to do *something*. Willig lost a son to mer-sickness, he knows how it feels. I want to know why the River gets sick like this, how we stop it. It's awful this year – it's not just the eels – everything's sick, and the brackish creatures are way inland. And a lavellan! They haven't woken for decades. We're lucky it hasn't come hunting here, with all of us in one place.' Aeron's voice was raised, too loud in the little copse. 'People aren't taking the Lore seriously. All the old texts Willig has are incredible – there's so much we've forgotten. I want to make it right.'

Kelda could just about remember Willig's little boy – a couple of years older than her at the time, maybe Isla's age, when he had died. Did every healer have a story like Willig's, like Aeron's? She hadn't been able to imagine what she would do to fill the hours without Isla. She would probably have hit on something in the end, but all she had been able to picture were the blank spaces. Maybe her mind had never quite been able to picture it because she had always known, somehow, it wouldn't happen.

'That sounds good, Aeron. Really good. Can I – can I do something? You said you were investigating, about that other case?'

'Best I do it alone. I've had to twist Willig's arm to get him to introduce me to the family. If I make it a circus show . . .'

'I could listen secretly! From outside? If I hid—'

'Risky. If they spotted you, they'd *never* talk.'

Kelda still badly wanted to listen. But Aeron was right that people were fiercely private about sickness. And if she interfered, and then they refused to tell him what they remembered . . .

'You'll tell me all about it? Straight away?'

The smile was back. 'Yep. I promise.' He put an unexpected, slightly awkward, hand on her shoulder. 'It's going to be all right, Kelda.'

'Well . . . thank you.'

'No problem.' He didn't move the hand. 'When I thought

Isla was making the River sick,' he went on, 'it was awful. I'd finally got an explanation, for Fossy, for all of it, and it was the last thing I wanted it to be. But Firth was so hopeful that there could be another explanation, I promised I'd look.'

Kelda swore to herself that she would try and be nicer to Firth. Maybe she could even persuade Uncle Abe to trade something to get him a book. He'd like that.

'Thank you,' she said again, slightly uselessly; and Aeron dropped the hand at last, but seemed to be waiting for something. There was a little silence.

'I'm speaking at the chittering, next lamp but one,' he said. Of course he was – when it came to chitterings, Aeron was precocious. He took a step closer, and his intense gaze was, impossibly, even more intense. 'We've got a bit of time still, I think.'

Kelda regained her studious interest in her feet. 'I should get back,' she heard herself say. 'I'll need to get Isla home for lunch soon.'

'Ah, of course,' he said – but he made no move to leave. Instead, he said: 'We miss you, Kelda. The rest of us.'

Kelda had a feeling that there was a right thing to say to this, or to do, and that with every passing second, her danger of making an idiot of herself grew. So, without quite deciding to, she found herself turning and hurrying back to the edge of the oaks, back out into the sunlight. Aeron followed, loping to catch up with her. They walked a few paces without speaking.

'By the way,' said Aeron, 'why was that duck following you around?'

'Don't ask.'

'Isla's?'

'Of course.'

What wasn't Isla's? Kelda's hands were always hers to grip; her eyes were always watching for her; her voice was a sing-song sister voice learned especially for Isla, until she had almost forgotten there were other ways of speaking. And naturally, everything colourful and curious that found its way into her world was brought there by Isla. Up to and including the duck. As the chittering came clearly in sight again, Kelda was entirely Isla's sister once more. Aeron, striding at her side, was already half-forgotten.

6

Kelda had never known such a beautiful crossing as they had that evening. The heaped clouds had turned dusty shades of blue against an apricot sky, and as the drums sounded out the spring tattoo, a great murmuration of starlings flocked overhead, black against the sunset. Then the drums concluded, with three pounding beats, and the boats began to move.

Mam was at the tiller for the Pades this year, and the rest of the family sat on the roof, watching. Uncle Abe had his fiddle out, and played answering reels to the calls of musicians on other boats. He was getting very good at skipping round the missing finger. The music ebbed and flowed from all around them, with some people singing, and others just stamping time on their decks.

It was a long crossing, longer than usual. It normally took a couple of hours, give or take, but the tidal head is not a fixed point, and has to be rediscovered each year. A group of water scholars led the way in an alder boat, and when they were sure they had crossed into true fresh water, they lit a torch on a long pole fixed to the bow. This year they were well inland when the flame at last appeared, a burst of light against the now-black sky.

A cheer went up across the boats, starting at the front but flooding quickly back across the ranks. Isla and Abe and Kelda danced, and even Dad smiled, listening intently as though he could absorb the happiness. At the tiller, Mam was stamping time and cheering.

'Why's it so far inland?' said Firth. He had been silent for the last half hour, waiting for the flame.

'Dunno,' said Kelda. 'Low water?' She poured him a cup of water from the jug they had ready, and said, 'Lucky Equinox, Firth Pade.' She meant to give him the cup, but found herself giving him a hug first. His whole body was tense, and not just because of the hug, although that did make him flinch. She was going to have to try and help him learn to relax. He made himself so unhappy.

'I spoke to Aeron,' she whispered. 'Thank you.'

Then she gave him the cup, and the jug; and he went off to pour a cup for Dad, who poured one for Isla, who poured one for Kelda.

'Mam or Abe first!' laughed Kelda, pushing away the cup. 'You can't close the circle yet!'

Isla had her stubborn face on. 'I *will* do them first, but I want to do you one *before* the first one.'

Abe rolled his eyes at Kelda. 'Blatant favouritism,' he said, and he took the jug. 'Take it, Keldie, I'll do mine and Mam's. Lucky Equinox, Lyn Pade!' he called down, handing a cup to Mam at the tiller.

They were nearly at the torch: when they passed it, they

all drank. The water was cool. As soon as she had finished hers, Kelda leaped down to the deck and took her first dive of the season, one great looping arch down into the river and up again, before coming back to sit on the edge of the deck.

It was a while after that before Mam could find an unoccupied space to moor. But there was no rush. While Abe and Dad had drinks on the roof, Kelda, Firth and Isla sat on the deck, legs dangling over the bow, eating all the aster drops they could want.

'I *love* Equinox,' said Isla.

Kelda nodded. 'Me too.'

'I like autumn best. I wish we did the bonfire at spring. And the chestnuts.'

'Well, next September,' said Kelda, 'we'll have to save some chestnuts, and see if we can keep them good till spring.' Then Firth shot her a sharp look, and she remembered that she wasn't meant to be promising Isla next years.

It was too late. Isla was delighted by this idea. 'Maybe we'd have to pickle them' – she had recently learned about pickling, and wanted to pickle everything the Lore allowed – then, 'Can I come for Equinox? Abe says landmen don't do Equinox. They do *Christmas*. You can come to the house for Christmas, and I can come to the boat for Equinox.'

Kelda looked at Firth. She had avoided giving Isla any false promises, and if all was going as planned, she most definitely could *not* come home for Equinox. But that was *if* all was going as planned. She couldn't work out how to answer.

'We'll see,' said Firth, rescuing her. And then, against his every natural instinct, he distracted Isla by adding, 'What's Christmas?'

Isla launched into a lecture on saviour babes born unto man and dead trees covered in candles and ribbons, and Kelda gave Firth a grateful look over their sister's head. He listened to the wonders of Christmas with good grace, all the while scanning the river, as though to reaffirm where he belonged. Where *they* belonged.

Then Kelda slipped down to help Mam moor: a lighterman's hitch for the mooring rope, and a half-hitch shield knot in the silver rope – plus an extra guardian knot to be on the safe side, since they were near the sea. She loved their boat. She felt she had never loved it quite as intensely as she did tonight.

Once all the boats had been moored, the party spilled on to land and river. It was late now, and landmen were generally in bed; the celebrations were incautious. The Pades joined the dancing on the banks. Mam danced with Isla, song after song after song, although really there was more hugging and kissing and tickling than dancing.

Kelda left them to it. They should have their goodbye, just in case. She wanted to find Aeron.

He wasn't with his mam and dad, but that was no surprise. She threaded through the dancers, looking for Aeron and Firth's crowd. But when she spotted Aeron at last he was alone, climbing out of the river.

He saw her at the same moment. She hurried over. But someone else reached him first – by the lamps of the nearest boat, Kelda made out Cordelia. She looked very beautiful in the lamplight, leathered skin and all. She put a hand out to

Aeron, then followed his gaze, and spotted Kelda. Her eyes narrowed slightly. She turned back to him, hand on his arm now, tugging.

The look he gave Kelda was apologetic – almost *too* apologetic, as if he expected her to mind about him and Cordelia. But he still turned away, and disappeared into the dark.

Kelda stood feeling slightly stupid. It was selfish of Aeron, running around with Cordelia, when he knew how badly she wanted news. But it was Equinox, and at her age, that was when you looked for love-matches. She stared at the piece of darkness where they had been.

'Never mind, duckie,' said Dee Marshman, suddenly materialising at her side. 'He'll be back. Saw you two moseying off from that chittering earlier. "Courtship in the dark is but a shadow show," quoth she, "Courtship in the light means marriage sure."'

This was so wildly irrelevant that Kelda didn't know what to say. But that didn't matter much: Dee was drunk. She leaned in close, conspiratorial. 'Take me and your uncle. Many a night at Equinox, when we were young. Didn't amount to nothing.'

This was an entirely unwanted addition to Kelda's already muddled feelings.

'Still fancy him, mind,' she added. 'That missing finger's sort of sexy. Swashbuckling.'

'Dee,' said Kelda, 'I have to go.' And not even bothering to come up with an excuse, she took the nearest exit route, down into the river. She just had time to hear Dee shouting that she should wrest Aeron back from that cow Cordelia or live in regret, loud enough for half the party to hear, before the welcome blanket of silverside deadened all sounds.

Not that it was peaceful down here tonight, of course. She felt as much as saw the acrobatics of countless others, racing and diving and loop-the-looping in the black current. She set herself against the flow of the water, back to where the family were dancing. She wouldn't chase around after Aeron – she couldn't exactly prise Cordelia off him and demand a private chat. She would hear his news soon enough. And he was free to do whatever he wanted, obviously.

But although she stayed up all night, she didn't see him again. Her hope for good news about the cure was faltering now, and she didn't want to feel that, so she threw herself into dancing and stamping and singing until dawn. Isla had been put to bed much earlier, Firth had disappeared off to his own friends shortly after, and Mam and Dad had given in and gone to bed an hour or two ago. Only Abe and Kelda were out dancing until the very last.

'Bed, Keldie,' said Abe, when the birds began to sing. 'Bed. Never let the sun catch you addled.'

Kelda *wasn't* addled. But by sudden silent agreement, all the last stragglers were turning back to their boats. The night was spent.

Kelda crept as quietly as she could into her cabin, but she needn't have worried. Isla was already awake. 'Hello,' came the small whisper.

'Hello, little one. Why aren't you asleep?'

'I was for *ages*. I'm hungry.'

'There'll be egg hash soon. Try and sleep.' Although

actually, Kelda was hungry too, and not sure she could sleep herself.

'Kelda?'

'Mm?'

'I don't want to go.'

You won't, she wanted to say. She *wished* she could have talked to Aeron. Instead, she said, 'Let's talk about it when everyone's up. Shall we watch the dawn come in?' *Watch the dawn come in* – that had been Isla's phrase for it, when she used to wake early, and drag Kelda up on deck at first light. They hadn't watched-the-dawn-come-in for a couple of years at least.

But Isla was mollified by the idea. They took a blanket to share: it seemed much colder suddenly, now that the party was over. The boat was moored by a small tangle of trees, and they sat under a roof of green, and watched as the weak light strengthened. Then Isla grew restless, of course, and dropped on to the bank to collect daisies for a new kind of chain she had *just thought of* which would be *amazing*. Kelda watched the position of the sun, and wondered how long she was obliged to wait for everyone before she could just go ahead and fry up breakfast.

It happened in a flash: a barrel, still strung with asters, rolled out from the trees and knocked Isla into the river. It fell in after her with a heavy *splash* – it must have been full.

Isla took a gulping 'Oh!' of river water down her gullet, and came up spluttering and coughing. Kelda was straight in after her, rushing under her shadow and up from beneath her, pulling her to the bank. Isla could look after herself in the river, but not when she had just inhaled a lungful of it. No silverman enjoyed having water in their lungs, but anybody else would be able to keep taking oxygen in through their skin. Isla flailed and choked.

Kelda got her out on to the bank and slapped her back, and the slapping turned to hugging as the coughing and retching turned to sobbing, and they stayed like that until they were both still.

'You're all right?'

'I'm all right.'

Only then did Kelda have time to think. The barrel was gone, sunk straight to the bottom of the river. But where had it come from? One minute Isla had just been picking daisies, then . . .

She released her sister, and walked into the knot of trees. 'Hello?'

There was nobody there now, of course. But full barrels didn't just career into people of their own accord.

'Keldie?' called Isla.

'Right here, little one.' Kelda was scanning all around, but the patch of scrubby woodland stretched well beyond the bank. All she could see was trees.

Isla's voice came again, hopefully. 'Keldie? D'you know what *I* think?'

'Mm?' There had to have been someone. Perhaps it had just been an accident? But had they seen . . . ?

'What *I* think is,' said Isla, with great gravitas, 'you should probably make the egg hash now.'

*

Aeron wasn't on the Jupps' boat when Kelda went to look for him, so she waited for him on theirs, all day, up on the roof so he couldn't miss her. She fell asleep up there eventually, a fitful sleep full of dreams of Aeron which were not entirely about Isla, and which she swiftly stashed away in a never-to-be-spoken-of corner of her mind on waking. But he didn't come; or else he came and didn't wake her. Instead she was woken by Firth, creaking across the deck below and ducking inside.

Yawning, she sat and watched the crowds below: diving, or chatting on the banks, or here and there rowing in alder boats, which were just for fun now that they were in fresh water. But there was no sign of Aeron.

She didn't go inside until it was dark, and time for dinner. Firth had gone out again; the rest of them ate leftovers in the galley. Then Kelda put Isla to bed. It took Isla a while to sleep, so Kelda lay curled around her until she drifted off.

As she always did when they lay like this, Isla twisted her head to Kelda's chest, waited a few moments, then said, with great satisfaction, 'I can hear your heart.'

'That's good,' said Kelda, as she always did. 'Still alive then.'

When Isla was at last asleep, Kelda lay there a while longer anyway. Then she wandered back into the galley, not quite sure what to do with herself. But before the uncertainty could linger on or drag her into worry, there was an urgent tap at the door, and the shiny face and red hair of Willig filled their porthole.

Mam groaned – she had no patience for the healer, and Dad always joked that she would rather amputate a limb herself than suffer one of Willig's speeches – but she opened the door with a polite smile. 'Hello, Willig. Come on in.'

Willig looked behind himself, then stepped inside. For a moment he didn't speak, which was so out of character it made Kelda wonder if he was violently ill, or possibly dead. He pressed his little fingers together, but harder than usual, turning the tips white.

'Willig?' said Mam. 'What is it?'

'I came to warn you,' he said. 'I'm so sorry, Lyn. There are three testifiers gathered, and they're planning to raise a quorum. It's about little Isla.'

In the past, silvermen were governed by a Weard, an old word for *guard*: a council of twelve men and women, who would oversee matters of justice. However, the institution was abolished after a rotten Weard betrayed its people, and silvermen now govern themselves. Transgressions against the Lore are tried as follows:

Three testifiers must speak of their own free will. They must be first-hand witnesses of the transgression. They must come from three separate boats.

Thirty-nine others must be gathered, no more than two from each boat, to witness the trial. Of these, nine will be selected to be judges by the drawing of reeds.

Seven of the nine judges must be in agreement for a transgression to be denounced.

7

Mam, Dad, Kelda and Uncle Abe all stood frozen round Willig in the galley. The healer's face was shinier than ever, and he kept glancing nervously at the portholes and the door.

'Are you sure?' said Abe.

'How have they got testifiers?' said Mam. 'We've always been careful. Some people know, but no one's *seen*.'

'I gather,' said Willig, wetting his lips, 'that Aeron Jupp and Cordelia Elver concealed themselves and orchestrated a fall into the river, so that they could witness. They already knew, apparently.'

'But Aeron's going to help,' said Kelda stupidly, as though by saying it she could make it true. 'There was another case like Isla . . .'

'Yes.' Willig looked at his feet. 'I regret, now, facilitating that particular line of enquiry. It seems that the infant in question was thrown overboard by their family, on their healer's advice.'

'But' – Kelda could not let this hope go, did not want to move on to this present and infinitely worse reality – 'the records said they were cured . . .'

Willig shook his head. 'Unfortunately not. It transpires that *sickness cured* was a reference to the River. It was having a hard year, which improved shortly after the unfortunate infant's demise. And this particular healer *was* always rather pompous about his role in these matters.' He sighed heavily. 'So, young Aeron has taken the parallels with our current situation rather to heart. Regrettable, but understandable. I was zealous for answers myself, at first, when I lost my own boy . . .'

Having imparted his news, Willig was voluble again; it seemed to soothe him. Now was not the time, however, for one of Willig's speeches. Kelda opened her mouth to interrupt him, but Dad got there first.

'Who's the third, Willig?'

'Ah – the third what, Murphy?' said Willig, not meeting his gaze.

'The third testifier.' Dad crossed his arms. 'Aeron, Cordelia – and who?'

Willig's fingertips pressed together as though he was trying to snap them off, and he attempted to speak once or twice with limited success. Kelda's insides clenched. She was suddenly very sure that she knew exactly who it was.

'He's very upset about it, *very*,' said Willig, 'desperately unhappy, but his friends have quite convinced him it's his duty – poor lad, he honestly believes there are innocent lives at stake; but really, that part of the Lore is frankly—'

'*Who*, Willig?'

'It's – well, it's young Firth, I'm afraid.'

Even though Kelda had been sure, it still hurt.

A silence followed, which was unbearable to Willig, so he began filling it almost at once: 'Quite beside himself. I wonder, Abe, if he took a trip to Camberley—'

Mam scowled. 'What for? That nonsense . . .'

'It's not *nonsense*, Lyn,' said Abe hotly. 'Maybe if we'd taken him years ago, we wouldn't be in this situation.'

And before Kelda could ask what anyone was talking about, Dad cut in, 'Well, we *are* in this situation. There's no time to lose. I'll get supplies – Abe, get on the roof and keep watch – Kelda, the alder boat. Lyn, wake Isla.'

'The alder?' said Mam. 'Shouldn't we dive?' Although alder boats were fast, a silverman swimming at full speed could keep pace – nowhere up to the speed of the river's fish, but several times faster than landmen.

Isla was just as fast over short distances, but as she depended on her gasps of air to power her, she tired quickly. 'We won't get far enough with Isla,' said Kelda. 'Anyway, the river's full of divers tonight – just as bad as topside.'

'We could go inland?' suggested Abe.

'Much too slow,' said Dad. 'We'd need to come back to the river soon enough, and any search party on the water could easily outpace us. Take the boat, right now, before everyone knows what's happening. Mam with Kelda and Isla. Me and Abe will follow silverside. Lyn, you remember which way to set out for the Cave?'

'The what?' said Kelda.

'The Mercy Cave. It's a hide-out. We'll explain. Get the boat.'

'What about Firth?' said Mam.

73

Abe put a hand on her arm. 'He made this bed, Lyn. There's nothing we can do. We have to get Isla away.'

So while Willig, after a furtive glance left and right, slipped over the bow, Kelda dived starboard and unhooked the alder boat from its cubby hole in the side of the hull. It bobbed on the current, tethered to their home by a rope. Moments later, Mam and Isla appeared, each clutching a blanket from the girls' beds. Isla scrambled into the boat, and Mam threw down the second blanket.

'Cover Isla,' – as though that would help. 'I'll help Dad.'

Isla was wide-eyed as Kelda tucked her under a blanket, but not crying. Kelda squeezed her hand.

Beside them, the other blanket honked. But before Kelda could question the wisdom of bringing Robin Hood, she heard voices from the boat above, and forgot about the duck entirely. She strained to hear.

'. . . come to see that you stay,' said a man's voice, 'while the quorum is assembled.' It was Maxwell Jupp's voice – Aeron's father. Kelda suddenly remembered her dreams of Aeron just hours earlier. She felt hot with shame and rage.

'River and moon, can't you put away the knives?' That was Dad. The bundle that was Isla gave a sudden sob.

'Just a precaution,' said a woman – Kelda didn't know who. 'We're sorry, Murphy, but it's our duty to see you stay on your boat.'

'With weapons?' said Mam. 'What makes you think we'd try to go anywhere?'

'Come on, be reasonable.' The woman's voice was

unctuously soothing. 'Aeron's just left to gather a quorum; once word spreads, you could've easily been warned.'

'Where's the girl?' demanded Maxwell.

Kelda had heard enough. She untied the rope that bound the little alder boat, took up the oars, and rowed as she had never rowed in all her life.

They travelled upstream through the darkness, against the current, with its countless thrusting fingers of flow trying to push her back up the Trent and out into the sea. She was grateful, now, that they had taken so long to find a mooring spot – they were one of the furthest boats upstream, and there were not many more to pass. Those they *did* pass looked unbearably cosy, with their brightly lit portholes set in panels of red and green and navy blue, and their strings of Equinox asters. But there was no time to envy them. She rowed.

As they passed the last of the glowing boats, the darkness thickened. The waxing moon was obscured by cloud, and there were only a few weak stars.

She heard the figure squatting on the bank before she saw him. He was heaving sobs from somewhere very deep within him, like an anchor being hauled on shore, breath after aching breath. It was somewhere between crying and retching. Kelda had not heard Firth cry since they were very small, and never like that.

She turned her face away, willing him not to lift his head from his hands, and rowed. They passed, and the sobbing faded as Kelda's strokes carried them onwards. She became aware of a quieter answering sob from Isla's blanket, like an echo.

Despite herself, Kelda looked back. For a moment, she

thought Firth was looking right at them. But the darkness had almost swallowed him, and it might have been a flicker in her imagination.

On they rowed, well past the boats now: through a cluster of poplar trees, then out across an open field, with the earliest stubs of some landman crop squatting in the darkness. Kelda's muscles began to protest. She was a strong rower, but this speed was exhausting.

Robin Hood came out from his blankets, and pecked at her ankles encouragingly. She rowed. All the time she listened for the sounds of pursuit. Maxwell and his crew must have established by now that Isla was missing.

In fact, with the advance guard snooping around, there might be a search party much sooner than the family had anticipated. Maybe she and Isla *should* get off the river, and go inland. Kelda would need to sneak back for fresh water in the morning, but that was tomorrow's problem. The bank ahead twinkled with landman lights. Would somebody put them up for the night? What was landman etiquette on house guests? Could you just knock and ask?

But before she could make up her mind, the river changed.

One moment it was pushing against them; the next it seemed to rise and swell under them, and carried them forward, faster than Kelda could ever have rowed. In the sudden rush she lost one of the oars, and hastily pulled the other on board before it too slipped away. The landman lights rushed towards them as the little alder boat surged upstream.

Isla's face appeared from her blanket. 'Keldie,' she said, 'What – ?'

76

The boat spun a full circle, as if it was giddy with excitement. Beneath them, the great surge of water seemed to breathe in and then redouble, expelling them further upstream. Trees and houses and one of the pointy church things flashed by, and then they were past the village and speeding through the darkness again.

'No idea,' said Kelda, finding Isla's hand and squeezing it. 'But it's – it's going the right way. Hold tight.'

For the Pade sisters, there was no terror as the little boat lurched and swung on the sudden madness of the river. Being tipped overboard wouldn't bother Kelda, and she could easily rescue Isla, who had never learned proper fear of water. No terror, then, but stupefied wonder, as the great surge kept subsiding only to refill its lungs and push them forward again, faster than ever.

They held each other tightly. They spun speechless through the dark, past shadow-trees and stretches of glowing town and the hollow black expanse of fields. The water pressed on. It was hard not to feel as though the River was rescuing them.

Kelda didn't know how much time passed, or how far they travelled. She had a feeling they had left the Trent, maybe swung into the Idle – or further, even – she had lost track, and her head was spinning in eddies that seemed to somehow run counter to the river. She had never been so lost on her own waterways before.

Then at last – how many hours later? – there was one last heaving subsidence, and no answering swell. The river began to calm.

The alder boat bobbed on upstream, still carried by the

discombobulated water. It spun a final semi-circle of amazement as it drifted under a curtain of willow tree, and slowed.

'*Wow*,' said Isla.

'Wow's about right,' agreed Kelda. She was dizzy. 'Well, I have no idea where we are now. But we're far away. That's good.' She kissed Isla's head, and didn't add that it didn't matter much *where* they were, since she had no idea where in all the wide world they would go now.

Isla's face was wet with recent tears, but for now, completely overtaken by wonder. 'What *was* it?'

'Some kind of – tide?' Kelda offered. 'I'm not sure.'

'It was amazing.'

'Sure was.' The boat was drifting softly now, and came out into what seemed to be a wide lake. Tentatively, Kelda took up her remaining oar, and steered them closer to the land for a better look. The lake was in some sort of forest clearing; the only sounds here were rustles from the trees and undergrowth. They seemed to Kelda like small, safe rustles.

There was a last, sudden gasp of momentum from the echoes of the tide, and it bumped the little boat right up on to the mud. Which felt like a hint.

'I guess we stop here,' Kelda said. Her body didn't know if it was still panicking, or still spinning on the river, or just sitting now in the safety of this quiet clearing.

Isla hugged her more tightly. 'Thank you for coming with me.'

'Don't be soft. What was I going to do? Push you upriver and wish you luck?'

'Now they'll want to get you too, won't they?'

Kelda wasn't actually sure how this worked, and her stomach lurched with the sudden realisation that the whole family was probably eligible for exile. Possibly excepting Firth the Righteous. But she bottled up this thought, and repeated, 'Don't be soft. Nobody's going to be getting anybody. We're miles and miles away now.' She gestured to the surrounding trees. 'What do you reckon? A camp under the willows? Does his lordship Mr Hood approve?'

And then Isla cried; not the half-sobbing from the blanket, but a proper cry, because a camp under the willow trees is only fun when it's for play, and when you know there is a warm, welcoming boat somewhere underwriting your adventures. In the end, Kelda used the last strength in her tired arms to carry Isla ashore, swaddled in the blankets, duck on board. She found them a spot slightly inland, out of sight of the lake. Then she settled Isla between two tree roots – as though that made any difference, two stumps of indifferent wood – and went to drag in the boat.

When she came back, they lay curled together under the blankets: Kelda round Isla, Isla inside like a heart. The ground was hard, but this didn't bother Kelda nearly as much as how still and unbending it was. There was no lulling movement, no constant murmur. It just sat there. Up above, the dark sky unfolded relentlessly away from them.

Isla turned her face round, to lie against Kelda's chest. 'I can hear your heart.'

Somewhere overhead, an owl hooted. Then there was stillness.

'That's good,' said Kelda. 'Still alive, then.'

8

It was late when Kelda woke, but the light was still gentle, sifted by leaves overhead. She sat up. Isla was asleep – so was Robin Hood – so, it seemed, was the morning itself, apart from the soft ripple of the leaves.

She knew where they were, now; she had brought Isla to these lakes, when she was still teaching her to swim, for the privacy and the still water. Which meant that the strange current had taken them upstream along the Trent, all the way along the Idle, and partway up the Maun. It was a miracle.

It was hard to feel it was a bad miracle. The lake shone with trees and sky, waiting for her, and Kelda hadn't felt the thick balm of still water in a long time. She would dive for breakfast first, then wake Isla.

She went to the lake's edge, and shifted her weight forwards. Reflections gave way to lake-bed as she looked down through the water.

'Don't!'

She jerked her head up. There was a man on the other side of the lake.

'Brackish,' he hollered.

Kelda recoiled automatically at the word, although her brain still hadn't quite caught up. The man was saying something she couldn't hear now, and pointing. She looked where he pointed: the water there was peppered with dead frogs, belly up. They lay like slime-bubbles across its surface.

'River and *moon*,' she breathed, feeling a little sick. The morning's spell was broken. This was not a miracle-glade. This was a trap full of mysterious strangers and inexplicable inland brackish water. And the mysterious stranger was making his way around the lake, heading towards her. She resisted the urge to glance around to where Isla lay, hidden among the trees.

As he came closer, she could see that he was perhaps not quite a man, after all – he was around her own age, she would guess, perhaps a little older. He had the slightly loping movements of someone who has only recently acquired their longer limbs and broader shoulders, and doesn't quite know what to do with them. And, she realised, he wore landman clothes: heavy trousers held up by braces, over a cotton shirt. He was barefoot, like a silverman, but some soft leather boots hung by their shoelaces from the satchel he carried. She relaxed very slightly.

'You all right?' he asked. 'Have you got some fresh water on you?'

'No – I – I didn't know.'

'I've got some. You'll need it, the saltwater carries on a way upstream. I've just come from King's Mill . . .'

Kelda blinked at him stupidly. There was no sheen to his

skin, and he was wearing all that heavy cotton; but he hadn't shown any surprise at her clothes, and he had grey-silver eyes, an unlikely combination with his red hair for a landman. And he seemed to know all about what she was. Unless he was just offering her a drink? She could see now that he also carried a bow and a quiver of arrows – but that was equally unusual for silverman *or* landman, so it didn't help.

He had taken a square of cotton out of his pocket, and now he set down the satchel, and crouched down to open it. There was a tin flask inside, and he emptied water on to the cotton, stood, and offered it to her. Not a drink, then. She took it, and ran it across her arms and face.

'Thank you.'

'You're welcome.'

'Keldie?' Kelda spun around, and there was Isla, pale and yawning. The stranger looked at her. Kelda tensed.

'Morning, little one.'

'What's for breakfast?'

This was a good question. Kelda's own stomach was aching.

The boy looked from her, to Isla, and back. Then without a word, he opened the satchel again, produced a wax bundle, unwrapped it, and took out four round somethings that looked almost-but-not-quite like chara cakes. He held them out to Kelda.

'Oh,' said Kelda, 'that's kind.' She hesitated.

'Go on,' he said, pressing them into her hand. 'You can't get anything yourself in *that*' – and he jerked his head at the water.

Isla had been blinking at him steadily all this time. At last curiosity overcame her, and she asked, 'Who are *you*?'

He raised his eyebrows. It felt like the same thing as smiling, somehow – as though his face was upside down. 'A passing kindly stranger,' he said, 'and provider of breakfast.'

'I'll make a fire,' said Kelda. And, because it seemed the least she could do, she added, 'Will you join us?'

'No. I'm going to vanish back into the woods like a spirit.' He wiggled his fingers spookily at Isla, then bent to pick up his satchel – which, it transpired, was being investigated by a duck.

'Oh, *sorry*,' said Kelda, 'he's with us – Robin Hood, get away from that . . .' She lunged for the duck, who gakkered indignantly, and scooped him up. 'Bad duck,' she said, uncertainly. She wasn't sure if telling off a duck was normal, but she felt she had to say *something*. She handed him to Isla.

'He's called Robin Hood?' said the stranger, his eyebrows shooting even further up in his amusement. 'Well! I hope Robin Hood is enjoying Sherwood Forest.'

'We're in *Sherwood Forest*?' said Isla, wide-eyed.

He nodded, and said to Kelda, 'Don't you know where you are?'

'Of course. We're on the Maun,' said Kelda, a little defensively. She prided herself on knowledge of the waterways. She had no interest in forests.

'Ah, right, obstinate silverman geography. Well, this bit of the Maun is in Sherwood Forest. Which is in something mysterious called Nottinghamshire. Which is in something *very* mysterious called England.'

She allowed a half-smile. 'England I've heard of.'

But Isla was taking this all very seriously. 'Nottinghamshire! The place we're going is in Nottinghamshire!'

'It is?' said Kelda. She had only thought as far as breakfast. Where they were going was a whole other question.

Isla nodded enthusiastically, bopping Robin Hood on the head with her chin. 'Yes! In a village called Basset which is like a small version of a town. Uncle Abe told me.'

Isla's landman family. This was, actually, a surprisingly good plan. Kelda looked at Isla in amazement.

The stranger nodded at the far bank. 'Basset's back that way. Where the Idle meets the Trent, in your terms.' Then to Kelda – 'Do you want some more water for your sister?'

'What? Oh . . .' Kelda felt a stab of panic at the slip she had almost made, even if he *was* just a landman. 'Yes, of course, she'll be needing it. Yes. Thank you.' And she took the square of cotton once he had rewatered it, and wiped Isla down. Thankfully Isla was too occupied with the news that they were in her beloved Sherwood Forest to put up much protest.

'Thanks,' he said, as she handed it back. 'And now I must do the vanishing act I promised before I met your charming duck.' And with that he raised his eyebrows once in farewell, turned, and walked away.

He was soon lost among the trees. Isla watched him go with a small frown.

'He was dressed like a landman,' she said.

'Yes.'

'But he knew all about us.'

'Yes.'

Isla considered this a moment in silence. Then she decided, 'He was nice.'

'Well,' said Kelda, 'he gave us breakfast, so *that's* nice.' But she wasn't so sure about the stranger. She had instinctively liked him, but now he was gone, she was uneasy. She wished she had thought to ask him for water for Isla straight away. He had sounded curious, almost suspicious, when he had reminded her. And, she realised with growing horror, all the other silvermen were at the Humber, and two young girls down here alone would be easily identifiable as the two who had run away. Who *was* he? How did he know silverman business? And how much silverman business, exactly, did he know?

There was nothing she could do: he had seen them, and he was gone. At least, she told herself, they had a plan now. And breakfast. 'Let's build a fire,' she said to Isla. 'Help me search.'

Five minutes later they had a small but serviceable fire burning, and the smell of wood smoke mingled with the fresh smell of the morning, a hopeful sort of smell. The strange cakes added their own scent, heady with herbs that Kelda couldn't place. But whatever was in them, they were delicious.

The two of them ate mostly in silence. Isla looked oddly like Mam, pinched and withdrawn, and Kelda couldn't think of anything to say to her. What was there to say? All she could do for her was make her breakfast, and take her somewhere safe.

'It was very clever of you,' she said, 'to think of the landman house. Well done. We can get there by dusk, if the boy was right. Do you remember the address?'

'The house is Camberley Cottage.'

'That will do. Well – are you ready?'

Isla nodded.

'Is Captain R. Hood prepared to sail once more?'

She nodded again, unsmiling. Which was fair enough. Kelda dropped the false jollity, and set about putting out the fire.

As she was putting blankets back into the boat, she noticed a trail of hemlock at the water's edge, and paused. *Hemlock springs where a lavellan treads*, River Lore, stanza fifteen. Of course, hemlock also just grows, sometimes, without the need to invoke the malign influence of a giant water-rat. But now Firth was in her head, telling her about the lavellan waking, and telling her that the salted inland lake was a clear abomination, and she didn't want him in there telling her anything at all.

She looked at the belly-up frogs, and shivered. 'Time to go, Isla!'

They left the rippling glade behind, Kelda rowing slowly with the remaining oar. Looking straight down into the water, she could see the bellies of fish overlaying the muddy bed. What had *happened* here? Had their current last night been a sea tide?

Her tired arms were grateful to be working with the current this time, although it was gentle here – even gentler than she might have expected for the little river. The Maun had been swollen by the strange tide; despite the dry winter it had overrun its banks now, and the trees that normally lined them now rose out of the flood, their roots underwater. The river wound among their trunks like a secret, slipping past oak and ash and under willows. It was hard to remember it was salted; it looked so perfect.

'Ooh, Isla, look,' she said, 'kingfisher.'

Isla loved kingfishers. But she was asleep. She hadn't been asleep a moment ago. It looked heavy on her, the kind of sleep you plummet into when being awake is suddenly unbearable. Looking at her then, Kelda could cheerfully have killed Firth and Aeron and Cordelia and anyone else who dared to even *look* at her sister – killed them with her bare hands, if they had been there.

But there was no one there. Probably. It was hard to tell, with the closely wooded banks. The kingfisher darted away among the leaves, and disappeared.

The next time Kelda saw any wildlife, it was a pair of dead voles, carried along by the water that had drowned them.

Maun met Meden and became the Idle, which wound through more trees, weaving and arcing through the meaningless land that was apparently Nottinghamshire. There were more dead animals, rabbits and mice and once a fox cub, strangely serene on the current. The shadows of the trees began to bother Kelda more and more, as did the peculiar stranger. Was she being very stupid, heading to this Basset place when he knew they were going there? She had no reason to think he meant them any harm, she reminded herself; and once Isla was hidden inside the landman cottage, she would be safe from prying eyes, even if someone *did* come looking. They had nowhere else to go, and they were vulnerable out in the open on the banks.

But still.

It didn't help that in all her childhood stories, landmen who knew about silvermen were bad news. In the days of the River Weard, relations had been better – there had even been a Land Weard, too. But now landmen only ever appeared in stories to snatch children or break hearts.

She reminded herself that she was rowing straight into the arms of some landmen, so this was a wildly illogical prejudice.

It was something in the way he raised his eyebrows that bothered her, maybe.

The afternoon was softening into early evening by the time the trees began to give way to washland, and Kelda could see banks once more, at the far side of the suddenly-swamped flood plains. They were empty. She relaxed a little.

'Nearly there, little one,' she murmured. Isla was still asleep, but Robin Hood looked at her, head cocked, doing his best impression of intelligent interest. So Kelda addressed herself to the duck. 'I hope this Basset place isn't too big. Sometimes the landmen put so many houses together. I don't know how we'll find the right one. I guess we'll just knock on doors and ask.'

Robin Hood bowed his head solemnly in assent.

'D'you think they'll have you and me to stay as well?'

Robin Hood did not have an opinion on this.

'I'm sure I could get used to living on land. Don't look at me like that. I *could*.'

And at that, Robin Hood obediently put his head under one wing, so that he wasn't looking at her like anything. Then Kelda had no one to talk to but the sky.

She landed the boat by dusk. They were coming up for the

crook of the Idle and the Trent, and there were houses, but not many; it was one of those older smatterings of landman houses that didn't come with any of the other buildings, like churches or shops or the houses for their noisy trains. Not even streetlamps, here. The water had rushed the bank, but the houses were built far enough back that they had stayed dry – clearly, the landmen had learned their lesson in wetter winters.

She woke Isla, and they clambered ashore. She wasn't sure what to do about the telltale alder boat. For now, she dragged it on to the bank and into some bushes: if they were staying, she would have to hide it properly somehow, in case anyone was out looking for them.

'All right, then,' she said, taking Isla's hand. 'Let's go.'

Helpfully, the landmen had all labelled their houses, which was a sensible system – although the names were less sensible. They passed gates with signs saying *Hope Home* and *Rosy Cottage* and *Honeysuckle Farm*, and Kelda wondered to herself why they all wanted to live in things that sounded like syrup. But then, after a while of winding path without anything at all, they reached a wrought iron gate marked *Camberley Cottage*.

Isla looked at Kelda.

'Looks nice, hey?' Kelda said, squeezing Isla's hand.

'Mm-hmm.'

It *did* look nice, in a ramshackle way. It was a grey stone pile with a black slate roof, and it had a peculiarly jumbled shape, as though rooms had just been stuck on one at a time as they were thought of without any heed for the overall sense of the thing. The grassy garden smelled sweet in the evening air, and a light glowed in the window.

Kelda pushed open the gate.

The garden was dominated by an oak tree, under which there was a peculiar stone cylinder with a little roof. Kelda couldn't place it at first, but then understood – it was a landman well. Which meant it led to groundwater. Which meant the water would be fresh. She wondered if it was rude to help yourself, and took a few steps nearer to examine it.

Closer, she could see a net over the top of the stone. It was hard to be sure in the dim light, but it looked like it was made with reeds. The side of the well, she saw with a shock, was inlaid with a stone knot – which looked almost-but-not-quite like the guardian knots she knew. For a moment she stood stock-still, staring.

'Isla,' she said, 'did Uncle Abe tell you how he knows these landmen?'

'Yes,' said Isla. 'But,' she added importantly, 'he said it was a secret.'

'Right.'

'Because he said it would make people mad if they knew.'

'I see.'

'Because what they're doing isn't Lore.'

'Right.'

'But it's a secret and I can't tell you.'

'Yep,' said Kelda, 'that's good of you. Well done.' She was suddenly remembering Mam's face when Willig had said *Camberley*, back on their boat. *That nonsense*, she had called it, but Kelda had a feeling she would have used a worse word, if she hadn't spent a decade and a half of motherhood training herself out of all the bad ones.

Kelda was not exactly pious herself, but even she felt her heart pound as they approached the house, with its bindweed growing up around the door and its doormat of rushes woven into slightly-wrong guardian knots. She knew these from childhood stories, and the stories were not reassuring.

But they had nowhere else to go. So she knocked.

The last River Weard did not betray its people alone. In those days, the River Weard still worked closely with the Land Weard – a small group of landmen who knew about silvermen, and protected the groundwater, using reed-knots and herbs as instructed by the Land Lore. There is more water underground than in the rivers, and they kept this dominion safe.

At the time of the betrayal, landmen were keen on burning people they believed to have devilish powers. Thanks to the two rotten Weards, many silvermen were burned.

The uprising that followed killed the Land Weards. After that, silvermen no longer confided their world to any landman. 'Land Weard' became another word for bogeyman, monster, devil: a byword for fear. The nightmares of children featured their guarded well, their door ringed with bindweed, their charmed reed-weaving.

There was a Sea Weard once, too; but they were killed centuries earlier, for reasons that have long been obscured by a tangle of legends.

9

The woman who answered the door didn't *look* sinister. She had a round, pink face with a mop of curling coppery hair piled up on her head, and cheeks that seemed permanently bunched upwards, ready for a smile.

'Oh,' she cried, beaming at them both, 'thank goodness. Thank *goodness*. Oh!'

Which was an odd way to say hello.

'Come in, come in,' she said, stepping inside, and shooing with her hands. 'I can't believe it – oh thank *goodness*!'

They were ushered down a long corridor with doors on all sides. The woman opened one of the doors, and they all filed inside.

'Peter,' she said, 'it's them! Girls, this is my brother Peter. And I'm Judith, of course. Oh! I'll put on a brew.' And she bustled out, leaving them in a softly glowing room full of mysterious furnishings and paintings of bits of land and china statues of people and dogs. It didn't look any more sinister than Judith.

Kelda had heard that landmen used a new kind of gas light, and was quite disappointed to find oil lamps. There was some sort of open stove set into the wall, too, where a fire blazed, and the room was much warmer than she was used to. Robin Hood gakkered contentedly, but Kelda wasn't so sure.

The man called Peter rose up from a huge, high-backed chair-thing. He was very tall, with Judith's coppery hair and her all-over smile; and he compounded the likeness by grasping first Kelda's hands, then Isla's, and saying 'Thank *goodness*.'

Isla, apparently taking this for a landman greeting at this point, said, 'Thank goodness' solemnly back.

Peter spent a while longer grasping Isla's hand and beaming, overcome. Then he sat, and gestured to Kelda and Isla to do the same. 'We've been looking for you all day. Your uncle's here, but he's out still . . . Judith made him promise he would stop back here when it got dark, at least for dinner, so I daresay he should be here soon . . . Now, I'm rambling. Forgive me, I'm quite taken aback. What a splendid duck, Isla – is he yours?'

While Isla and Peter exchanged enthusiasm about the duck, Kelda tried to marshal her thoughts. She had been thoroughly disconcerted by the way the chair sort of smooshed under her, and was struggling to keep up. 'Uncle Abe's here?' she said, when she could get a word in.

'Willig helped him to escape last night – your parents too. I suppose you know Willig?' Kelda nodded. 'Your mam and dad are looking for you up the Ouse and making their way to the Cave, in case you've found your way there; Abe came down to check the Trent, and rally us to the cause. We sent telegrams first thing, there are friendly landmen watching out for you now up and down the waterways – ah, thank you, Judith.'

Judith had reappeared with a tray full of mugs, and handed

them round. Kelda was reeling. None of this was what she had expected. It was a huge relief to hear that the others had escaped. But Peter's story was baffling: how many of these 'friendly landmen' were there?

She didn't get a chance to ask. By the time Judith had handed out the tea and offered everyone sugar and said 'Thank goodness' some more, there was a knock on the door, and Peter went to open it.

Then Kelda could hear him, in the corridor: really, truly Uncle Abe.

They heard his voice rising in surprise, then footsteps, and there he was – like a dream, but more solid. Kelda stood up and hugged him hard. Isla, out of nowhere, burst into tears. Abe put out an arm and pulled her into the hug, and they all stayed like that for a long time.

Kelda pulled away first. 'Uncle Abe,' she said, 'what happened? Everyone's safe?'

'Yes, yes, all safe,' said Abe. He looked as though he had more to say, but then looked down at Isla, still clinging and sobbing into his shirt. 'Ah,' he said. 'I think the *first* thing is to take this young lady to her bed.'

Isla said something incomprehensible, which may or may not have been in favour of bed. Uncle Abe put a hand on her head. 'Come along, little one. It's *upstairs* – like the roof garden, but inside, remember?'

Isla made more noises, which sounded slightly more acquiescent, and allowed herself to be scooped up by Uncle Abe. 'I'll be right back, Keldie,' he said. 'Well done, my girl. Very well done.'

Then he took Isla away. Kelda could hear him murmuring, until the walls of the house swallowed his voice, which she wasn't used to and didn't like. It was as though they had vanished. But she was grateful that Uncle Abe was going to take care of Isla for a moment. She had no idea how to talk to her, properly, about everything that was happening.

There was a moment's silence in the hot little room. Kelda sat back down.

'So,' she said at last, 'Are you – ah,' – it seemed almost rude to say it – 'I mean, from the front garden, it looked like you might be the Land . . .' She trailed off. It *was* rude, to make an accusation like that.

'Land Weards! Yes,' said Peter proudly. Seeing Kelda's face, he laughed, a booming chuckle. 'You look like I've said we're demons! I gather our reputation is still not good.'

'Oh dear me, not good at all,' beamed Judith. 'But the office never died out, you know, and there's been nothing untoward since that horrid business with the witch trials.'

'Tremendously bad business,' Peter agreed. 'But someone must guard the groundwater. We work with a few of your kind who still know us – your uncle, naturally, and your father once upon a time . . .' This was a revelation, but Peter didn't notice Kelda's face, and rolled straight on. Kelda had the strong impression that, behind the kindly smile, he was very, very tired. 'We need all the help we can get, frankly. We've been worked off our feet with everything that needs doing this season – one of the worst I've seen. The holy wells are barely holding.'

'Oh, it's madness,' said Judith. 'I never saw a winter like

this in all my life. I shouldn't wonder if there's even fuathan in summer. And now, with the catastrophe last night . . . we'll have to revisit all the guards in the area to keep it from the groundwater, but I've no idea if that will even *help*, we don't know what happened . . . we've had a telegram from a friend saying something similar happened on the Nene, but whether it's anywhere else . . .'

'Let's not panic about all that now,' said Peter, 'when the girls have only just got here. Kelda – you must need fresh water. There's a well in the front garden. Finest water in Britain!'

Kelda said a polite 'Thank you'. It felt as though somebody very meek and very, very tired had taken over her body. She couldn't muster the gumption to ask any questions; she could barely even *think* them. The meek-and-tired somebody stood her body up, and took it back out of the room.

It was good to be away from the heat. She stood still a moment, breathing in the strange mustiness of the house, then went outside.

It was dark now. By moonlight Kelda examined the well, then peeled back the reed-net and experimentally turned the handle, which successfully lowered a silver bucket. When she heard it *sploosh*, she brought the heavy bucket back up again, and untied it. She set it down, and knelt beside it to wash.

For a moment, she hesitated. The Land Weard's well.

But they were friends of Abe. They were the most harmless-seeming people she had ever met. And her skin was throbbing a steady tattoo now; it was like being wrapped in a headache all over. So she began to wash.

Peter had not been lying about the water. It was superb – soft, clear, gently nudging Kelda's skin into life like stars waking up a sky. She took a second bucket eagerly, all hesitation gone, and washed until her body was drenched. Then she restored the net and bucket to their places on the well, and for a minute stayed out there, squatting on the ground, feeling her skin hum happily to itself and heal.

With her skin sated, her thoughts felt more pounding than ever. She went back inside.

In the room with the chairs, Abe had returned, and a heavy pie had been served up, which smelled a little like the cakes from the stranger in the forest. Remembering him now, Kelda felt relieved. If there was a network of well-meaning landmen with silverman knowledge, then he had not been so strange after all.

'Isla's asleep,' said Abe. 'I haven't told her who testified – she doesn't know the niceties of the Lore, so I think we can leave that out . . .'

'Good.' Kelda tucked into the pie: it was delicious. She felt the meek-and-tiredness slipping away. 'So – what's the plan? Someone needs to meet Mam and Dad at this Cave, right? Then are we all going to stay here?' She checked herself, and added, 'Ah – if that's all right, I mean . . .'

'Oh, we'd have you gladly, of *course*,' said Judith. 'But we all feel you'd be safest with our sister Maggie. She's at Moray Firth – in a lighthouse of all things! – at the end of the Caledonian Canal, the old Sea Weard seat. In Scotland.'

Scotland! Most Scottish rivers are not navigable, so it was wild country to silvermen. In some of the more sensationalist histories, there were legends about sheltering there in times of crisis, but Kelda didn't know anyone who had actually been.

Abe leaned forward. 'There are people out looking for Isla, Keldie. Hunting parties. Not everyone, you might be interested to hear – even after the business with the tide, there are plenty who'd rather see her escape. But still. She can't have any kind of freedom in England. I told her the new plan just now. She liked it – she made me sing her "All Caledonia Red" for a lullaby, and wants to find the Crescent Bay. Macabre child.'

'Appropriate,' said Peter. 'The river hasn't quite turned to blood, but it comes to much the same thing.'

Isla's voice singing from the roof filled Kelda's head: *Turn back, and weep all you who keep your vigil* . . . She didn't want to think about vicious old histories, or about the strange tide. But the others were settling into the theme.

'That tide,' said Judith, 'was very unfortunate timing.' Her round face was sombre, which looked wrong on her – everything that should be lifted in a smile hung slack, making her look undercooked.

'But it saved us,' Kelda pointed out.

'Yes,' said Peter, 'and that's a blessing. But look at it from their point of view. Isla escaped: the tide came. Perfect proof that the River is angry, if you believe that sort of tosh.'

'It was nasty,' Abe said. 'Moorings came loose, boats smashed into banks, into each other . . . Dead fish everywhere . . . And some of our people were in the river when the saltwater came.'

Kelda thought of the frogs, and felt slightly sick. 'Who?' she said.

'I don't know,' said Abe. 'We were racing to get out of there before we were seen.'

'What *was* it?'

Abe looked at Peter and Judith, who looked at each other. 'We're not certain,' said Judith. 'I don't believe it was caused by anything on the rivers. Maggie sent word last week that there's something strange out at sea – that might explain a great deal.'

'What sort of something? Like . . . a wyrm?' hazarded Kelda. 'They can be in saltwater if they want, can't they?'

Peter shook his head. 'Wyrms are nasty, but they don't turn tides. Maggie's investigating – she studies Sea Lore, or what's left of it. But that's a tricky business . . .'

'I just pray last night was the end of the trouble,' said Judith. 'Your poor people.'

They all nodded gravely at this, because it felt like they should; then Abe took up the thread again. 'So, some of them are out for blood. We'll wait it out here for a few days until they stop hunting, then go to meet your mam and dad, and head to Scotland – well clear of our people. We can live on the canal there. Start over.'

Kelda nodded. She realised she had been clinging to the idea that with Isla gone, people would forget about her – that once she wasn't living on the River, there would be no cause to hurt her. She had been stupid. That was not what their precious Lore demanded.

But: Scotland. That wouldn't be so bad. They would be separated from all the others by miles and miles of unnavigable tumbling streams. They could see the famous lochs. Maybe they'd see the shape-shifting spirits that lived there; she would leave the murky, brackish creatures of the lowlands behind. And she and Isla and Mam and Dad and Firth and Uncle Abe could live there forever and grow old together and nobody would bother them.

Then she checked herself, and mentally crossed Firth off the list. She took a steadying breath.

'Thank you,' she said.

They didn't stay up much longer. Everyone was exhausted. Peter and Judith went to fetch the alder boat, and bury it under hay in the stables where they kept their horses. And the house hid Isla. So for now, they could sleep.

Isla and Kelda slept in separate rooms. Kelda's bed smooshed under her even more than the chair. She didn't know if all landmen loved fabric this much, or if it was just Judith and Peter. She had been given a cotton dress thing to wear, and she had layers of fabric on top of her, and under her, and there was bunched-up fabric inside a bag of fabric under her head, and soft fabric on the floor like moss, and heavy fabric drawn across the square porthole. It was oppressive.

She slept heavily for several hours, but woke in the night, and couldn't judge the time without the sky. For a while she just lay there, too hot and too still; then she shook off the covers, squatted on the bed, and pulled back the porthole fabrics.

Outside, there was the faintest whisper of grey. Dawn was not far off. She moved herself on to a ledge next to the porthole, a wide alcove in the stone, painted white; and she curled up there to watch the dawn come in by herself.

She was so lulled by the gathering light that it took her a moment to react when figures appeared at the gate. She pressed her nose to the porthole, looking down. They seemed to be consulting a piece of paper. They wore hooded wool cloaks against the cold dawn – in the silverman style.

Then one head lifted, and Aeron Jupp was looking straight at her.

She didn't know if he could see her through the glass, but it felt as though he must have – his eyes had seemed to lock on hers. She rolled off the ledge and on to the bed, out of sight, and prayed to the moon that she had imagined it.

Then her brain began to work properly, and she realised that it didn't matter whether he had seen her or not. They were here, which meant that somehow, they knew.

It was time to go.

10

A minute later Kelda had roused the others. Peter and Judith were already awake, and came hurrying up the stairs when she called; Abe woke quickly, as though he had half-expected to be needed. Isla was firmly asleep.

'Is it time to go to Scotland?' she murmured.

'Yes. Now. Right now.'

'I have to get the yellow rabbit.'

'*Isla.*' Kelda shook her more firmly. 'Wake up properly. Wake *up.*'

Then the knocking on the door began. It came in intermittent bursts at first, but by the time they were grouped in the upstairs in-between room, it had grown to a steady rhythmic hammering. They stood shivering in their nightgowns, except Isla, who had somehow acquired a sort of pink quilted coat thing that was much too big for her.

'How strong is the door?' said Kelda. 'It might be safest just to stay here?'

The pounding continued.

'No,' said Abe. 'It's not unbreakable. We should get out.'

'We need the horses,' Peter whispered. 'Perhaps if – if I cause a diversion, then . . .'

'I don't suppose they'll have left the back door unguarded?' said Judith.

Kelda stared at her. 'There's a *second door*?'

'They've never looked around a house, Judith,' said Abe, with a ghostly grin. 'They probably won't have thought of it.' And sure enough, when they crowded at a back porthole to look, the grass behind the house was empty.

There was a hurried conference, during which it was established that none of the Pades could ride a horse solo – not counting Isla's insistence that she *could*, which was based on the one time she had sat on a tug boat's old grey mare for ten seconds – and that the Parsons' two horses could probably take the five of them a little way, at a push, since they were four and a half really, but oh *lord*, then what? But the hammering was growing louder and more insistent, and there was no time for *then what*s. Peter and Judith crept down the stairs to prepare the horses, while the Pades changed their nightshirts for fly-silks ready to dive, then hurried down after them. Isla kept the landman quilted coat thing over the top of her clothes.

As they went down the stairs, the hammering stopped abruptly, and was replaced with voices muttering in hurried consultation. This was worse than the hammering. Kelda quickened her silent footsteps.

They went along the downstairs corridor to a galley.

Glass smashed. A porthole had been broken.

'Go,' whispered Kelda, to no one in particular, 'Go, go, go . . .'

Judith had left the key by the door, but it seemed to be giving Abe trouble. He struggled and swore at it. Behind them, they could hear the glass being smashed open wider, then the thuds and grunts of somebody dropping through. Judging by the cracking of more glass and the little cry of pain, they had shoved themselves through a gap that was nowhere near big enough.

'Oh, River, come on, come on,' muttered Kelda.

The second person climbing through seemed to be having more difficulty. But the first was not waiting. There were footsteps in the corridor.

The key turned, and the cool night air hit them.

Aeron Jupp was in the galley doorway, lunging towards them, bloodied from his hasty scramble through the porthole.

Abe and Isla were out first, and it was Kelda Aeron caught by the wrist, his face suddenly looming close in the half-light. It was like a nightmare: the familiar long nose and earnest silver eyes, but marred with rivulets of blood; the long careful fingers, the ones that used to tug her sleeve to show her frogspawn or salmon redds, digging painfully into her skin. Aeron Jupp breathing heavily, pupils huge in the dim light.

All this was just a moment's wild rush of feeling for Kelda: there was no time for thought. She swung her free fist, which caught Aeron cleanly on one eye, and he let her wrist go with a cry. Then she brought up a knee which made him double over, and drop something to the floor. She ran.

As she ran, she registered what she had seen him drop. Isla's map. The map Uncle Abe drew her. The map with the address of Camberley Cottage written on it.

She drew level with the others at the stables. Uncle Abe hoisted Isla up behind Peter on one of the horses; then as Aeron appeared in the garden, now with two more cloaked figures, Abe got up behind Judith on the other. Kelda took the other side of Isla.

'Hold on to me,' called Peter.

'Stop!' yelled Aeron. 'Kelda! *Kelda!* Aberforth! Think about what you're doing! In the River's name . . .'

He was still shouting as the horses galloped past him. Then the sound of their drumming hooves swallowed his shouts, and the Pades and the Parsons were away – charging past the houses with the saccharine names, wreathed now in early morning mist – then turning further inland, and plunging on through a landscape that meant nothing at all to Kelda except that it put land behind them, safe hard dry land, land on which their pursuers were second-class creatures, only equipped to cross on foot.

But she didn't feel relief. She was a little preoccupied by an important discovery: she did not enjoy riding a horse. At all. It was like a rollicking storm had been bundled up inside an animal, which had duly gone insane. She hung on to Peter for dear life, sandwiching Isla between them.

There was an inquisitive *quaaark* from in front of her.

'Isla,' she managed between jolts, 'did – you – bring – Robin – Hood?'

'Yes,' said Isla, 'in my dressing gown. Isn't this *amazing*?'

'Ngggh,' said Kelda.

'I *love* horses.'

'Ngh.' Kelda did not. Judging by the gakkering coming

106

from Isla's gown thing, Robin Hood didn't either. Kelda felt a new-found affinity with the duck.

They rode for what felt like hours, across flat field and farmland, the mist clearing as the sun rose. Every muscle in Kelda burned from clinging on for dear life.

Several times they crossed water – mostly canals and drains, and once the River Aire – but the Parsons rode on. Wherever they were going, the Aire apparently wouldn't take them there.

It was strange to cross over on the topside of the bridges. Kelda thought they were beautiful places. With the sun newly up, the water that stretched away on either side was a rich indigo, paling here and there to a lighter blue where the current slowed.

At long last, when the River Wharfe came in sight, Peter and Judith slowed the horses to a stop. Everyone dismounted, with varying degrees of grace. Uncle Abe looked as sick as Kelda felt.

'Rest,' said Peter. 'Well done, everyone.' And he patted his horse, directing the bulk of his *well done* to the terrifying creature. Which was fair enough, but Kelda nodded her thanks from a safe distance. She still found the horse a bit alarming, even now she wasn't sitting on it.

For a moment they all caught their breath, and smiled weakly at each other. But Isla just stared ahead. Now that the exhilaration of the ride was over, she looked suddenly deflated.

Kelda put her arms around her. 'All right, little one?' she whispered.

'I'm hungry,' said Isla. There was a wild desperation in her voice, which made all too plain what a poor substitute *hungry* was for all the feelings she couldn't name. It hurt Kelda to hear it. She pulled away.

'Is the water fresh?' she said. 'Shall I get breakfast?' And without waiting for an answer, she dipped her elbow in to check, then plunged her whole head into the glorious water.

'I'll take that as a yes,' said Abe, when she brought her head back up. 'I'll get a fire going.'

Kelda had never been so happy to dive.

11

Until they had cooked and eaten their fish, no one spoke. Then they discussed plans. Judith and Peter would not hear of leaving Isla to travel to the Mercy Cave by river. Too slow with her diving, and too dangerous while silvermen were looking for them. After a lengthy discussion of the work they still needed to do on the Trent's groundwater defences, which lost Kelda entirely, it was settled: Peter would continue with Isla on horse to the Cave, a little inland, while Abe and Kelda travelled silverside. Judith would turn back, and see to the salted river.

'Well, it's for the best, but I must say I don't like to leave you all,' said Judith. 'I'll get up to Maggie's as fast as I can. Take care of yourselves, please, I want all persons and limbs present and correct at the lighthouse – you go straight there once you've picked up Lyn and Murphy from that godforsaken Cave.'

'And *you* be careful at the cottage,' said Abe, uncharacteristically anxious. 'Isla aside, I don't think those particular silvermen will take kindly to the discovery of the Land Weard's seat.'

'I shan't stay long – the well guards there are already strong,' said Judith. 'You'll see me in Scotland in no time.'

Abe refused to be cheered. He ran a three-fingered hand across his face, and sighed. 'We've brought so much trouble to your door. I'm sorry.'

'That's quite enough of that, Aberforth Pade,' said Peter, clapping him on the shoulder. 'This is part of the job!'

Judith nodded. 'Lord, I'm almost excited. I was beginning to believe nothing dramatic would *ever* happen on our watch. How do you suppose they found us?'

'Isla had a map,' said Kelda.

At that, Abe groaned. 'Of *course*. Then it *is* my fault.'

But Judith and Peter would not hear any more apology. They fussed kindly over Abe, and plied him with more fish, and talked relentlessly over any attempt at worrying.

'Uncle Abe,' said Kelda, when he had been persuaded to stop shaking his head and muttering, 'what's this Cave place?'

'I don't know much myself,' said Abe. 'It's a sanctuary, known to a few of us who flirt with the wrong side of the Lore . . . There's some sort of secretive group there who'll see you're fed and watered and safe, if you have to stay off the waterways a while. And that's all I know. It's always been the plan, if anything happened, that we'd all head there. It seemed like a good idea,' he added sadly, 'because it wouldn't bring any danger down on our friends.'

'Enough, Abe,' said Peter. 'And you needn't be so precious about our feelings, you know. That's not the only reason. We know perfectly well that Lyn would never come to Camberley again.'

And this was so clearly true that no one knew what to say. Judith knelt forward and began heaping dirt onto the last of the fire, and Abe stretched unconvincingly. 'Those horses of yours,' he said, changing the subject. 'They really are something else. A full gallop, all this way! You'll like this, Isla – Judith and Peter here are the proud riders of the only kelpie-blood horses left in the country.'

Isla *ooh*-ed appreciatively, but Kelda looked round at the horses in alarm. Kelpies were white-water spirits, and demanded a headless sacrifice if you wanted a ride anywhere. The two horses were busily tearing up grass, and one gave an odd whinnying whicker, that may or may not have been a sneeze. They didn't *seem* like they were demanding a sacrifice.

'It's all right,' chuckled Peter, 'the connection is very slight. They're normal animals, really. But they're devilish strong. I hope you girls aren't feeling too sore – quite the introduction to riding, galloping at full speed all that way.'

'Now, even at their speed, we should—' began Judith, but she was cut off by Isla's loud enthusiasm for the horse riding.

For her part, Kelda made do with a vague polite nod, and said, 'So the horses are – part spirit?'

'A tricky question, Kelda!' said Peter, his face lighting up. 'What would that mean? What *are* the white-water spirits, if not animals? That's the real question. Personally, I'm not confident that grouping shape-shifters together makes much sense – kelpies seem to be something else entirely, while for selkies, I wonder if it's simply a matter of infection—'

'Peter,' said Judith, laying a hand on his arm. 'Time is getting on.'

He paused, and smiled ruefully. 'Ah, quite right,' he said. 'Well, then. In happier times I hope you will come and visit me and my library, Kelda, and we can talk more.'

This suggestion felt utterly unreal, but Kelda thanked Peter anyway. She liked him – and Judith too – and she found herself wishing she could stay with them. It seemed a bad omen, to lose the first of their number so soon.

When they had cleared away the fire, Judith hugged Peter, then Uncle Abe, then Kelda – which wasn't a very silverman gesture from a new friend, but Kelda found she liked it. 'Look after yourself!' Judith said. 'It's been a pleasure, Kelda Pade. I look forward to meeting you again.'

'Are you going to be all right? What if they're still there?'

'You needn't worry about me,' said Judith, 'I'll be quite all right. I'll see you at Maggie's soon.' Which didn't really answer the second question at all. But Judith moved on, kneeling down for a goodbye with Isla.

'It has been a tremendous pleasure to meet you, Isla. I'll see you in Scotland.'

'Can you bring your horse? We could go riding together.'

'Wonderful idea.' She hugged Isla too, and said, 'I will do my very best.'

Then she got into a protracted discussion with Peter about reeds and knots and herbs, which lost Kelda entirely. And all too soon she was mounting her horse, and Isla was being hoisted once more onto Peter's huge black mare – apparently called Echo, but Kelda could think of other names – and they were waving goodbye.

Judith galloped away first. Then Peter turned Echo away from the riverbank, and called, 'See you at Foxup Beck!'

'Safe journey,' said Abe, and they trotted off. Kelda felt a wave of panic, watching Isla be carried off into unknown territory by a barely-known landman on a mad animal. She stood and stared after them.

Abe touched her shoulder. 'She'll be fine, Keldie. Let's dive. Unless you want to talk about anything first? Or rest?'

'Thanks,' said Kelda, 'but I just want to get on.'

Abe nodded. 'Understood. Let's go.'

A long journey lay ahead. River Wharfe, River Skirfare, Foxup Beck. Then overland, and finally the River Lune, all the way down to Morecambe Bay, where they would find the Mercy Cave. Kelda would normally have taken the longer route, rivers and canals all the way, without the land crossing – but now they had no boat to worry about, and it felt safer to travel on the letter-used waterways. She had only seen the Skirfare once or twice, and never Foxup Beck; they were thin rivers, leading nowhere.

The Wharfe, however, she knew. They were far downriver here, where the water barrelled over soft sand, deep and strong. This was the Wharfe's busiest stretch: they shared it with chub, dace, and barbel, bream, pike, and perch – and slipping amongst them on the bed, the secretive eels, strange citizens of river *and* sea. With mer-sickness rife, Kelda kept a cautious distance.

She let Abe kick off into the lead. For a moment she hung

suspended, feeling the current press against her, always trying to take her back to the sea.

Then she kicked, and swam.

It was rare for her to spend a whole day travelling silverside. Normally she had to check for landmen before she went diving, and come back to the boat when she had fetched whatever she had been sent for. The freedom was glorious. She sank down to the thalweg where the current ran fastest, just to feel it rushing over her skin as she pushed on upstream.

At first there were bridges overhead, some of them thundering with trains and their trails of smoke, but these thinned away after the first hour or so and the world grew quieter. Then the only interruption to their journey came from the river itself, which here and there broke and braided its waters, splitting into smaller channels, and once or twice dividing into so many rivulets that Kelda and Abe had to stand and walk through the shallow water.

The undulating light from topside grew steadily brighter. After perhaps three or four hours, Abe signalled to some brown-filmed rocks, and Kelda nodded. They began to feel gently in the seam of slower water that clung to the rocks' sides.

Kelda found a trout. She cupped her hands around it very slowly, careful not to alarm it, letting it get used to this new bend in the water. Then, fast as mackerel, she snapped shut.

She looked at Abe; he was still hovering, hands wide.

A sudden memory: Abe teaching Firth to fish on his sixth name-day, Kelda 'helping'. When they shot upwards into the air, he had been so appalled at the despair of his little fish that he had hurled it back into the river, then sobbed for two hours straight. It had taken a lot of coaxing to convince him that fishing was necessary. After that, he would do it, but he was pedantic about doing it exactly by the Lore, as though this absolved him of the horror.

What had happened to that little boy who couldn't even bring himself to kill a fish?

Abe's hands came together too. He glanced over at her, and jerked his head upwards; they broke into the sunlight above, and swam to the shore.

Abe was his usual self as they built the fire and grilled the fish, humming obscure songs and making stupid jokes. But when they settled to eating, he suddenly turned serious, and said something that made Kelda choke on her trout:

'Dee told me about you and Aeron, Kelda.'

Thanks to the choking, Kelda's attempt to say 'Told you *what* about me and Aeron?' came out more like 'teeechhum-ach-ach-ach-aeron', which Abe sensibly ignored.

'That's hard luck. Aeron *and* Firth. I just wondered – if you want to talk about it.'

Kelda recovered, but she had gone right off the rest of her lunch. 'I don't know what Dee told you,' she said, 'but I do *not* care about Aeron Jupp.'

He looked at her kindly, but not like he believed her. 'She told me about you two going together at Equinox.'

'To talk about Isla.'

He just looked. Kelda could feel herself flushing, which

115

didn't help. But it was just because he was making her embarrassed, and angry, with his stupid gossip. Whatever she *might* have started to feel, it was irrelevant now.

'*What?*' she said. 'Are you serious, Abe? He wants to kill Isla!'

'You weren't to know that,' said Abe gently. 'You didn't do anything wrong.'

'I didn't do anything, full stop. We talked about Isla. That was it.'

'All right.' Abe nodded, and this time, he looked like he *might* believe her. 'Well, let's talk about Firth then. We're all heartbroken—'

'I don't care about Firth either,' Kelda snapped.

'Now that,' said Abe, 'is a lie, young lady.'

'Don't call me that. I'm not Isla.'

Abe just inclined his head. A corner of Kelda's mind felt bad. He was only trying to help. But the rest of her mind was occupied with wanting to pummel something. Preferably Aeron's face. Or Firth's face. Both faces, one for each fist, in an ecstasy of pummelling.

'Delicious,' said Abe after a moment's pause, licking his fingers. 'We're making good time – we'll be at the Skirfare in a few hours. Have you ever been?'

'I think so,' she said. 'With you, when I was little. We were looking for crayfish.'

'Ah, yes, of course.' He smiled at her. '*Skir* is Old Norse for *bright*. Well named. One of my favourite rivers.'

She smiled back, and tried to put away the pummelling mood. None of this was Uncle Abe's fault. He was trying his best. 'Maybe we can pick up some crayfish for dinner,' she said. 'Isla would like that.'

She thought there was something sad about the way her uncle smiled at her then. But all he said was, 'Yes, I'm sure she would. Good idea.'

Before the Skirfare there was the Strid.

For landmen, this stretch of the River Wharfe is deadly. For silvermen, it is a strange, other-worldly thrill.

The river narrows very suddenly, and for a brief stretch, *the current flows vertically*.

Kelda lay in the up-down tug, with no past and no future to it, just a roaring steel-strong now-now-now. She wanted to stay there forever.

But they had to go on.

The river dwindled; the sand turned to gravel which turned abruptly to limestone; they left the teeming world of fish behind, and swam now through the quiet domain of fly nymphs, clinging on to rocks against the flow. The water grew cool and dark. It was dusk by the time they turned into Foxup Beck, and waded up a stream that would not even exist in high summer.

Then they left even that little water behind, and walked a way inland, to where Peter and Isla were waiting.

Kelda's heart lifted at the sight of Isla, safe and kneeling beside Robin Hood in the grass. She was weaving something out of reeds, leaning against Peter. Echo was tied up a comforting distance away, apparently asleep on her feet, and a pile of firewood with trout beside it was already waiting – which was good, because Kelda had forgotten all about the crayfish. Rainclouds and night were both gathering in, and there was a shadowy peace over everything.

Peter waved cheerfully, and Kelda found herself waving back. All desire to pummel things had been left behind. Isla looked up and proudly gave a landman salute, a new gesture she must have learned from Peter.

'Hello,' called Abe. 'Oooh, dinner.'

'Isla caught it,' said Peter, beaming at her. He seemed delightedly bemused to have her curled up against him; Kelda had the distinct impression that Isla being a six-year-old was more alien to him than Isla being a silverman. Isla herself did not look up, engrossed in her reeds.

'Looks great,' said Kelda, ruffling Isla's hair, then flopping down beside her. Now that she was out of the river, her muscles shook a little with the day's exertion. 'What you making?'

'Peg-a-lantern net,' said Isla, pausing briefly to show Kelda the tangle of reed, mixed with something darker green, in a pattern that was almost-but-not-quite like guardian knots. Peter beamed at it approvingly. Then she returned to weaving.

'Um,' said Kelda, 'that's – er, well done.'

Peter chuckled. 'I don't believe your sister will have seen one of these,' he said. 'You might need to explain.'

'It's for catching peg-a-lanterns but it has baneberry leaves in it to lure them in so we don't have to run after them as much. But baneberry is poisonous so I have to wash my hands afterwards. And stop Robin Hood eating it.'

118

'Right,' said Kelda. Then, 'Do we *want* to catch a peg-a-lantern?'

Isla nodded. 'To get to the Cave.'

There was a sudden spark of light, and then a curl of smoke: Abe had started the fire. 'No one knows the way to the Mercy Cave,' he explained. 'You have to get a peg-a-lantern to take you there.'

Kelda didn't know the Lune mouth very well, but she was pretty sure she knew that this was mad. 'Aren't they on salt marshes?'

'That's right.'

Salt marshes were not good, and nothing that inhabited them was good, and no good idea in the world started with catching a peg-a-lantern. 'Are we talking about the same thing? Bogs and creeks and getting pulled under by quicksand? Peg-a-lanterns that drown unsuspecting landmen? Those saltmarshes? *Those* peg-a-lanterns?'

Abe nodded. 'But you forget, we have the Land Weard and his Lore. We won't have to go chasing across a bog. They'll come to *us*.' He smiled at Peter. 'Peter's a regular will-o'-the-wisp-whisperer. He taught your dad a fair bit, too, in case of need.'

Peter smiled back, and carried on tying his own net – a much neater version of Isla's. 'Ah, we're just fancy herbalists.'

'Well, sure, and we're just frogs with silver toys,' said Abe. 'But your Lore is much prettier.'

Kelda wondered if she could find a way to ask the question that had been niggling away at her ever since Camberley. It didn't feel rude inside her, but it was in danger of coming out all wrong. She knew she wasn't good at this kind of thing.

'About that,' she said, 'the Lore, I mean, and – and the Weards, and . . . Well. It's just. I always thought the Lore was rubbish.'

It hadn't come out brilliantly. But Peter laughed, face upturned in pure delight. 'Spoken like Abe's niece through and through,' he said. 'Well, it's a good question. Do you know your sailing knots and guardian knots?'

'Yes.'

'And do you believe in Jenny, and fuathan, and lavellans?'

'Of course.'

'And do you catch Jenny in a silver net and burn it, and arm against fuathan if you see blind mist, and kill a lavellan with a knot-bound arrow?'

'If I have to. Better take another river,' she said – quoting, without even realising it.

'River Lore, ninth stanza,' said Peter.

'Well, yes. But that bit's just – facts.'

'Exactly!' declared Peter, delighted. His enthusiasm was infectious – it lit up his whole face, and his long arms were recruited for wild gestures. 'Facts preserved in the Lore! There *is* a great deal of nonsense, you're quite right – notably the anti-landman prohibitions, which you might be interested to know didn't appear until the sixteenth century. And they were originally far more elaborate . . . But let's not go into that; I'll start rambling on again. Alongside the nonsense, there's a great deal that's true, too. And we may as well make use of what's true.'

'Peter and I disagree about the ratios,' added Uncle Abe. 'I think there's a lot more nonsense. Maggie's wasting her time with this Sea Lore business, for a start.'

'Ah, maybe so. But we need any help that we can get, with tides like the other day.'

Uncle Abe had no argument with *that*. For a minute they just watched the wood smoke curling up into the heavy grey evening, and Isla and Peter plaited their reeds, while Abe hummed something lilting to himself, and began to prepare the fish. Kelda knew that they were almost certainly safe here, so far from any navigable river; but she couldn't quite catch the evening's calm. She picked a blade of grass absent-mindedly, and began shredding it. She wanted Mam and Dad. And despite herself, she missed Firth – and she couldn't help thinking how much these sensible, knowledgeable people could have helped him. If only Mam hadn't shut them out.

'Did that answer the question, Kelda?' said Peter. 'I'd gladly answer more. I should warn you, though, I can be tremendously boring on this subject.'

Kelda would have laughed, on a kinder evening. She settled for smiling at him. 'I do have one more,' she said.

'Be my guest.'

'Are we actually catching a peg-a-lantern? You weren't joking?'

The flickering lights inhabiting the wetlands of Britain go by many names: ignis fatuus, will-o'-the-wisp, hinkypunk, Jack o' lantern, Friar's Lanthorn, Kit o' the candlestick, walking fire, spunkie, Gillian Burnt-tail, elf-fire, Robin Goodfellow and – in the Lancashire wetlands – peg-a-lantern. Unwary travellers foolish enough to follow these lights are led astray among quicksand and fast-changing tides, and drown.

In modern times, this phenomenon is understood to be a chemical reaction: the spontaneous combustion of methane, resulting from animal or vegetable decomposition.

This is correct, but not especially useful. It's much more useful to know that, if caught, ignis fatuus will lead you safely across the wetlands wherever you need to go; and that the surest way to catch one is with a reed-net lined with baneberry leaves.

For the correct guardian knots, and advice on finding fresh baneberry, see the fourteenth stanza of the Land Lore, lines 12–15.

12

Before they could go hinkypunk-hunting, there was another long day of travelling, beginning with several hours overland. Isla and Peter went ahead on the tireless Echo, but Abe and Kelda had to trudge. It was exhausting and dispiriting work. Kelda began to wonder if there was something in the landman idea of shoes, after all. The aching in her legs didn't help, either – her morning on Echo had stretched muscles she hadn't even known she had.

For the last hour it rained, which was a relief. Then they slipped into the Lune, and the rain became ripples overhead while the current took them downstream. Kelda hardly had to swim. Sometimes she even lay on her back and let it carry her, watching the raindrops spread circles across the water's skin above, thinking about Mam and Dad and Peter and Isla. The fear in her was a constant drumbeat, a wrongness to everything. But tonight, her family would be together again, and that at least would be right.

They went back topside well ahead of the brackish water, partly for safety, and partly because the water here began to thicken with landman dirt: sawdust and cinders and sewage.

Dirt hung in the water like a haze, but much worse was the telltale ache of invisible poisons, creeping in through Kelda's pores. It took a long time for her skin to stop feeling heavy and itchy once they were topside again.

Isla and Peter were waiting at the appointed place. It was a contraption of wood in a field, that Abe said was called a kissing gate – although it didn't look much like a gate, and Kelda didn't know what kissing had to do with it. Isla was overflowing with news.

'We went to *Lancaster*!' she said. She sounded more like her old self, but slightly manic, as though she had been wound up too tightly. 'It's so big, there were so so many people. And we saw a castle *and* a cathedral, and there was this stable place with loads and loads of horses where we could leave Echo just for now till we come back, and they'll look after her. And Peter bought me a little wooden horse to have while she's gone' – Isla waved aloft a toy, not much bigger than her palm. 'And we got you shoes!'

There were indeed two pairs of shoes at Peter's feet. They weren't leather – they were something shinier, and green.

'There's saltwater on the marshes,' said Peter. 'I thought you two ought to have wellingtons. I had to hazard a guess as to your size – I erred on the large side, we can stuff them with something if needs be . . .'

The wellingtons were unbelievably clumsy things. Kelda had to sit on the kissing gate and wriggle and heave just to get one on, and even when she had succeeded, it didn't seem to bear any particular relation to her foot. She wished it had been leather shoes. She'd always quite liked the look of those.

This reminded her of the landman in the forest, with his soft leather boots, and she paused with the second wellington in hand. 'Oh! Peter, I keep meaning to ask you. I met a landman in Sherwood Forest, and he knew all about us – I think he must've been one of your friends. About my age, with red hair?'

Peter frowned. 'Well, I don't know who that could have been,' he said. 'The Kingsleys have a boy, but he's much younger, ten or eleven . . .'

'He was in these brown trousers. With a white shirt.'

'I'm afraid,' said Peter, 'we change our clothes with a regularity that would astonish you. And almost every male landman will own brown trousers and a white shirt. We're not the most imaginative creatures.'

Kelda didn't know how else to describe the stranger, but she was desperate to make Peter remember him. She had felt so much happier about their meeting, thinking he was one of their friends. 'About an inch taller than me, maybe,' she said. 'Eyes grey, like us.'

Peter's smile grew a little crinklier, and he looked sideways at Kelda. 'Well, whoever it was, he sounds dreamy.'

Kelda rolled her eyes, and began tugging on the second boot. 'I'm just worried – he knows about me and Isla now. I thought he'd be one of your lot.'

'It's strange . . . But then, I imagine I don't know everyone who knows.' Peter looked thoughtful a moment, then shrugged. 'Well, whoever he was, he can't do any harm now. The worst already happened, and we survived it.'

This was true enough. Kelda took out her unease on the second boot, ramming it on to her foot. Then she stood unsteadily. The green tubes gaped around her calves. Abe had been wrestling with his boots on a tree stump, and now rose equally uncertainly.

'Wonderful,' said Peter, nodding. 'You look like regular country folk. Ready?'

Everyone nodded.

Peter picked up two long sticks leaning against the kissing gate. The reed nets from the night before had been fixed to the ends. He handed one to Isla.

'Right,' he said. He took Isla's hand. 'Let's go hunting.'

The marshes, mudflats and sands of Morecambe Bay are treacherous.

Twice a day, the tide rushes in, and reclaims the bay for the sea. Then it retreats, leaving the land heavy and soft with water. Some parts become quicksand. The surest way to find out *which* parts is to step on one of them.

Travellers at low tide must be sure they know exactly where they are on the featureless flats, and where the sea will be when it returns. It does not forgive mistakes. Mist and fog are deadly.

The Pades and Peter waited near to the bank of the Lune for night to fall, while Robin Hood retreated to the river, and the marsh's own birds flew home for the night with ragged cries. The sky burned a fierce sunset across the flats, turning the creeks and the pools and the distant sea to gold.

Then it was dark.

*

There was wind that night. The distant sea was restless. The Pades and the Land Weard waited.

They waited some more, the wind numbing them. Every time someone shifted their weight, the mud squelched.

Peter kept checking his pocket watch: if they didn't spot a lantern in time, they would have to wait until tomorrow. They needed to set out a couple of hours before the tide returned, if they were going to cross safely.

Kelda's nervous excitement faded slowly to discomfort, and cold, and a jittery sort of boredom. Abe had squatted down long ago, and she joined him, struggling to stay alert. The strange thing about the flats was that there was nothing to make looming shadows in the dark – no trees, no houses, nothing. The night felt empty.

The little flare of light came quite suddenly: a burst of blue, that turned to white-gold and hovered there, flickering in and out. Instinctively, Kelda put a hand up to her silver pendant.

Peter was checking his watch, but looked up when everyone else gasped. 'Oh,' he said, uncertainly, 'it's a little late . . . I was just about to suggest we might turn back for the night.'

Abe squinted up at the stars. 'Nonsense. Plenty of time.'

'Well, we'd have to catch it very quickly.'

'Better start then.'

Peter thought a moment longer, then put his watch away, and said, 'Right then.' There was a squelch, as he shifted position in the mud; then he looked down at Isla, and saluted. 'Ready?'

She saluted back. 'Ready.'

Kelda and Abe waited safely by the bank. As Peter and Isla moved towards the little light, it darted further back, off to the right. It seemed impervious to the wind.

'This way, Isla,' Kelda heard Peter say, and they tramped forwards, but to the left. Peter had said the lantern was like a mirror guide: it wants to lead you off course, so you should always go the opposite way – but stay close enough to hold its interest. Isla was not always good at believing instructions the first time, but she had clearly placed whole-hearted trust in Peter, and she followed him faithfully, net aloft.

The light flickered, almost indignant. It drifted a few more inches to the right.

There was a flare from a match – a dull thing compared to the little lantern – and then an acrid smell. Peter was burning some baneberry. Then the match went out, but the light of the lantern seemed to double. It hovered, confused.

'Nets ready, Isla,' Peter murmured. 'Come on, little Peggie . . .'

The lantern hopped a few more inches to the right; when they didn't follow, it split itself in confusion, one half-light hopping right again while the other leaned back towards the smell of burning baneberry. For a moment, the stress of the split extinguished the light altogether; then it reappeared, a whole foot closer to the waiting shadows of Peter and Isla.

'Good,' murmured Peter. 'Good. Ready . . .'

Kelda was forcibly reminded of fishing. Peter and Isla held their nets forward very, very slowly, hovering either side of the little light, but not moving. At the smell of baneberry in their nets, it glowed brighter.

Then Peter said, '*Now*!', and the nets closed.

It should have caught fire. Kelda flinched instinctively, starting forward to help. But although the lantern reared up through the reeds like a torch head, there was no smoke, and no spreading blaze. Just the little flame dancing, a searing blue once more, casting a pool of cool light large enough to pick out Peter and Isla in strange silvery shades. With the wind whirling her dressing gown, her face solemn, Isla looked oddly impressive.

She slipped her stick into Peter's hand, so that Peter could hold the whole trap aloft. It shook and trembled, but the knots held.

'Well *done*, Isla!' Peter said. 'Splendid work!' Then he called up to the lantern. 'The Mercy Cave, please. I'll free you at the Mercy Cave. Understood?' He lurched forward, then steadied himself. 'Well,' he called back to the others, 'it certainly knows the way. Ready?'

Abe and Kelda squelched cautiously over to Peter, Robin Hood bringing up the rear with hurried smacks of his webbed feet. The little peg-a-lantern was tugging at the net.

'Now,' said Peter. 'Follow my footsteps *exactly*.'

Kelda didn't need telling twice. If Peter veered slightly, she veered slightly. If Peter took a longish stride, she took a longish stride. Sometimes the sand sucked at her a little, and her breath caught; but then her wellington would come out again with a *shluck*, and she would hurry to keep up, trying not to think too hard about anything but placing one foot in front of the other. Outside their little pool of light, the marshes lay in abysmal darkness.

For a very long time, none of them spoke, intent on the lantern and their own footsteps. The wind and sea were the only sounds.

It was Isla, of course, who grew confident first. She began to hum something to herself – it must have been a landman song of Peter's, because he joined in, whistling. Which was comforting, in the darkness.

'It's so *pretty*,' said Isla, gazing up at the peg-a-lantern.

'It's a little trickster, outside that net,' said Uncle Abe. 'Don't get too fond of it.'

'Can we keep it?'

'Absolutely not.'

'Why not?'

'It's a night creature,' Peter called back. 'It will disappear in daylight. And if you take it away from its marshes, it will never reappear.'

'Oh.' Even Isla couldn't argue with this superbly good reason. She fell quiet, and shlucked on through the darkness in their silver-lit parade. They must have been walking towards the sea; it was growing steadily louder as they went on. Kelda was cold to the bone.

She didn't know how long the silence had lasted when Isla broke it again. 'There'll be white-water spirits in Scotland, won't there?'

'Oh, plenty,' said Peter. 'Kelpies and selkies and all sorts.'

'Kelpies are like your horses, aren't they? Can I keep one of *them*?'

He laughed delightedly. 'Certainly not! They're not horses, they're shape-shifters. And they're dangerous.'

'What if I used guardian knots?'

'Ah no, you can't hold a spirit. Only appease it. And the price for that is not generally something you'd wish to pay.' The net tugged urgently. 'Oof – left here, troops! Careful!' They all meandered around some invisible danger, and Peter went on: 'My advice, Isla, is to leave the white-water spirits alone. They're not like the creatures you're used to – they're trouble. Maggie says there are even wyrms in the lochs.'

'Woah.' Even Isla didn't want a wyrm for a pet. There was a moment more of contemplative silence.

The sea seemed to be getting louder faster now, although they had not changed pace.

'Is it . . . ?' said Kelda.

'Yes, it's coming in,' said Peter. 'We'll reach the Cave before the tide does, though. Keep steady now.' But he didn't sound entirely confident.

It was definitely getting closer. Kelda squinted at the darkness, but the wet sand played tricks under the stars, and she couldn't make anything out.

And then, quite definitely, a film of sea was visible: a sheet of wrinkled darkness in the very-dark, rolling towards them with the steady speed of a river current.

'Peter . . .' she said.

'I know,' said Peter. 'Stay close.' The little lantern was pulling urgently now, turning fiery white with its efforts.

'Should we turn back?' said Kelda – then, twisting her head, she saw that the sea had already rushed up a creek behind them, turning it into a salty river. There was no way back.

'Stay with us Kelda!' said Abe. 'See those cliffs up ahead? I think that's where we're going.'

'But it will be cut off in a few minutes!'

'Yes, exactly,' said Peter. 'That's why it's a refuge. Your kind can't get to it at high tide. Hurry, now.'

After that there was no more talking, just their redoubled footsteps shlucking across the sand, then splashing as the sea water rose. Kelda repented every negative thought about her wellington boots as she waded through the sea, miraculously dry and safe. The water had risen well above her ankles when they reached the cliffs.

The lantern knocked itself against the limestone, as though it was trying to crack open the net. By its light, Kelda saw the hole in the rock face, round and jagged and high up above the sea. Below, a pile of rocks offered a way to scramble up.

'Thank you!' said Peter. He parted the nets. 'Off you go, little friend.'

There was a blaze of silvery-blue light, and then the lantern was off with a rush. It seemed to suck all the world away with it.

'Right,' came Peter's voice. 'Well done, everyone! Kelda and Abe up first. I'm here if you slip.'

So while Isla gathered up Robin Hood from the water, Kelda felt for a foothold in the dark, and began to climb. The boots made her unsteady, but she didn't slip. She clambered into the Cave, and left the sea behind.

She blinked. The Cave was a new kind of dark, but at the far end, a fire burned. Two figures at its edges stood, and came forward.

'Mam!' Kelda ran, boots flapping, and she and Mam held each other tightly. They squeezed as though they were trying to crush the breath right out of each other, and they only let go when Isla barrelled in for a hug of her own. Then Kelda drew away, and turned to Dad.

Except it wasn't Dad.

It was the stranger from Sherwood Forest.

13

The boy was half-silhouette against the fire, but it was unmistakably him. His red hair caught the light, and his eyebrows arched in greeting.

'Hello,' he said.

'What's going on?' said Kelda. She had to shout slightly to be heard over the pounding of waves on rock below. 'Where's Dad?'

Mam shouted back, over Isla's head, 'Out on the Lune, looking for you girls. In case you were on your way.'

'Why didn't he wait here?'

'He was worried. Restless. You know your dad.'

'Restless' was Mam's code-word for 'angry'. Kelda felt her own anger rising. 'Did you two *fight*?'

'Well – yes.'

'What about?'

'Not now, Keldie.' Mam held out an arm and pulled her close, sandwiching Isla between them; then spoke more softly, right into her ear. 'Please.'

So they hugged, and the waves pounded the rock, and the silhouette of the stranger went to tend to the fire, and everything was wrong wrong wrong. She couldn't *believe* Dad had gone wandering off. He would have to cross the marshes all over again to make it back, and until then, Kelda would have to put up with the knot of anxiety in her stomach. All she had wanted in the world was all of them together again.

Except Firth.

Mam pulled back at last to clasp Abe, then nod awkwardly at Peter, who was shouting an explanation for his presence over waves.

'Yes,' said Mam. 'I see. Well – thank you.' And she sort of dragged her face into a smile. She had to, because the Land Weard *had* saved her daughters, but her furious disapproval of everything he stood for was obvious. That annoyed Kelda too: Peter was so utterly good. She suddenly wanted to bawl over how *wrong* everything was.

She took herself a few paces back, and breathed deeply – but the breath was full of salt tang and dank. This didn't feel like a sanctuary. It felt like a cold, dark hole carved out of a colder, darker void, which it was. She leaned against the Cave wall, and shut her eyes.

There was a touch on her arm. It was the boy from the forest.

'Dinner?' he said. 'You look set to keel over.'

Kelda couldn't fathom what she was supposed to do with dinner in a cold dark hole in a colder darker void, and for a few seconds she just stared at him stupidly.

'Come on, sit,' he said. She let him lead her to the back of the Cave, because it was warm and light, and Kelda's brain had apparently been reduced to a moth. Or a wounded animal. Something with only instinct left, anyway.

He gave her a grilled trout without speaking, and she wolfed it down. As she ate, the others came to join them; the stranger apparently had a whole pile of fish, because he set to grilling dinner for everyone, leaving the family to trade news at a frantic pace. There was a jar of fresh water too, made of something cool and shiny Kelda couldn't name.

It was a little easier to talk back here, although the pounding sea underlay everything like a drumbeat. They talked about the destruction caused by the strange tide, and Mam and Dad slipping away down the Ouse in the confusion on Willig's alder boat. They talked about Isla and Kelda finding Camberley, and the attack in the night. No one talked about Dad. They had never talked about his moods before, and apparently nothing had changed now, even here at the edge of the world.

'And the girls met Douglas on the Maun!' said Mam brightly. She was working overtime to be normal in Dad's absence. 'We realised it must have been you two . . .'

'It was in Sherwood Forest!' said Isla. 'Like in Robin Hood.'

Kelda was silent. So Mam had been sharing all their secrets? What was this, a cosy boat-crossing gossip? They were supposed to be hiding. Strangers, however friendly, were a liability.

Douglas. A water name – *dubh glas,* a dark stream.

'It was thanks to Douglas the girls found you,' Mam explained – directing the comment to Abe. Since thanking Peter, she had not spoken to him again.

Peter was doing his best to pretend he hadn't noticed this. 'Oh, this is your landman friend?' he said to Kelda.

'Er,' said Kelda, 'I mean, I – he's the one I met, yes.'

'Ah – we've heard all about you,' said Peter.

'Is that right?' Douglas spoke for the first time, eyebrow-smile raised in Kelda's direction.

Embarrassment made Kelda blunt. 'I was worried about whether we could trust you.'

'Fair enough.' He considered this. 'And now I've turned up again, and you're even more worried?'

'Well – yes.'

Mam quickly said that they were all under a lot of pressure and very tired, and Peter added that anyone who could grill a fish this perfectly was clearly a saint as far as he was concerned, and Isla announced that she and Robin Hood thought he was brilliant. But Douglas just looked at Kelda, not offended in the least. His eyes really did have a silver edge in the firelight.

When all the nervously polite interjections had died down, he said, 'I was in the forest looking for the lavellan. I thought it would go hunting at Equinox, but it looks like it turned back west before it got there. I'm tracking it here now.'

'Someone sick?' asked Abe. Hunting the water-rat was wildly dangerous, but the sap from around its heart could cure almost anything.

'My dad,' said Douglas. 'Back home in Inverness.'

'Oh, I'm sorry. Scotland? You've come a long way.'

Peter said, 'You think the lavellan's in Morecambe Bay?'

'I think it's somewhere this way, but it's more that there are people here who can tell me. The people who brought this fish.'

'All this food just *appeared*,' said Mam, 'while I was asleep. The people who do it are very secretive, apparently. But,' she added hastily, 'very *good* people.'

'Who are they?' asked Abe.

Douglas shook his head. 'Sorry – not my secret.'

'How did you get here so fast?' asked Kelda, frustrated by all these diversions. Everyone seemed to just be accepting the presence of this lavellan-hunting landman as though it was perfectly natural. 'You don't have a horse?' *Silverside*? she thought.

Douglas broke his earnestness at this, and his eyebrows went back up. 'Well, there are these creatures called trains that breathe out smoke . . .'

'Ah,' said Kelda, eyebrows rising in return despite herself. 'In the mysterious land of England.'

'That's the one.'

She was still deeply uneasy, but she couldn't think of any more questions – except, *But are you telling the truth?*, which didn't really count. She realised she was staring at him, and looked away. Peter had been wrong about the clothes: he was still in the same brown trousers and white shirt as before, although he had put on the leather boots now. His skin didn't shine at all. But what kind of landman hunted a giant vicious water-rat which they were supposed to believe was just a myth, and spent their nights in a silverman hide-out, grilling trout?

Isla yawned hugely, and Peter cuddled her to his side, which made Mam's lips twist in annoyance. 'It's late,' she said. 'You girls should be in bed. We should *all* be in bed.'

'I applaud the sentiment,' said Abe, 'but what exactly *is* bed here?'

'Oh, there's another cavern,' said Mam. 'There are blankets stored in there. And it's a little warmer.'

So they put out the fire, then Mam showed them all the crack in the rock that led to a second cavern. If it *was* warmer, Kelda couldn't feel it, but the sound of the sea was at least more muffled here.

There were not quite enough blankets, so Kelda and Isla shared. The darkness here was absolute, and the cavern was crowded with all of them. Kelda found a patch of rock that didn't seem to contain a human of either species or anything slimy, and tugged at Isla's hand, squatting down. She was relieved that Robin Hood seemed to have wandered off to find his own bed; for now, Isla was content to clutch the little wooden horse toy tightly.

Eventually everyone was settled under their blankets. There was a few seconds' quiet.

'When's Dad getting back?' said Isla.

'Soon,' said Mam, from somewhere to the left.

'I want him to be here.'

'He wants to be with you too. He's off watching for you on the Lune. But he'll be back.'

Isla snuggled back against Kelda, sighing, and squishing the cold silver of Kelda's pendant against her chest. Kelda's skin seemed extra-awake in the pitch black, as though it was making up for her eyes. She felt every iota of warmth from

Isla; the faint pulse of her heartbeat; every bump and ridge in the rock; the cold where the blanket didn't quite reach her toes. And she could hear everything extra-clearly, everyone's breathing – Mam's tight shallow sleep-breathing, Abe's familiar heavy snorts, a new soft snore from Peter. Kelda had a feeling Douglas wasn't asleep.

And under it all she heard the steady pulse of the sea, knocking against the rocks, pounding to come in.

She slept lightly, and woke to footsteps. For a moment the darkness was still full of hooded figures, a bloodied face, a hand on her wrist; and this mixed confusingly with other dreams, dreams she didn't want, of Aeron tugging her away along the riverbank into the night and leaving the revellers behind – hidden between oak trees – *We've got a bit of time still, I think . . .*

She willed her heart to slow. The footsteps were going *away*. Leaving the cavern. Not an attack.

Silently, she eased away from Isla, and stood to follow. She couldn't quite have said why, except that it was unbearable for there to be any mystery in that darkness.

In the entrance to the main cave, she blinked, adjusting. Dawn had turned it a sombre grey. The smell of the sea was sharper out here, and the waves were much calmer than before.

At the Cave mouth, Douglas was squatting down, perfectly still, watching. Waiting for something. Kelda realised that she was going to see them – the people who brought the fish. Were they landmen or silvermen? Why did they do it? How did Douglas know them?

Suddenly there were two hands on the lip of the Cave, one

clutching a sack. Somebody heaved themselves up, and threw themselves bodily into the Cave mouth.

'Douglass,' they said. There was a slight hiss to the way they said *glas* – as though their voice was a wave, retreating.

Bile rose up Kelda's throat. It was a woman, and she was infected with the mer-sickness – so heavily infected that she must surely be dead.

But she was alive.

14

Kelda half-believed she was still dreaming. The sickness had taken this woman's whole body from the waist down, and crept up half her torso too, and one of her arms. Where she wasn't scaled she was pallid, and naked; she looked helpless here on dry land, wriggling next to Douglas on the rock to try and find some purchase. The scaled arm was limp, flopping beside her.

And she had come from the *sea*. This was, to Kelda, most terrible of all. She kept very quiet, and waited in the shadows.

'Morning, Mariana,' said Douglas. He sounded perfectly calm.

The woman, however, seemed agitated. 'Why have you returned?'

'It's lovely to see you too.'

'This is no place for you, Douglass.'

'It's no place for anyone,' he agreed. 'It's miserable sleeping in there.'

'Why do you seek us?'

'Oh, for a chat. How've you been?'

The woman hissed, eyes wide. 'You mock me.'

Douglas had his back to the Cave, but Kelda knew by now the arch his face would have taken on. 'Mariana,' he said, 'I do not.'

'You mock our ways.'

'Outrageous allegation.' Douglas shifted. 'Look, I need help.'

There was a silence.

'Is that all right?' he said. 'Will you help me?'

'We help the pure of heart,' she said, 'beset by a sick world.'

'Yes, right,' said Douglas. 'So that's me, I'm very pure. I'm after the lavellan that's woken up. What do you know?'

Mariana was silent. Kelda wished she could see their faces properly.

'It woke from sleep in its caves inland,' she said at last.

'Yes,' said Douglas, 'I know, but it's not there any more.'

'It woke to feast at Equinox.'

'Right. But it didn't make it that far east.'

'It now stalks here along the safety of our western coast. We have seen the signs. The fish flee its presence.'

'Mariana, I *know*,' Douglas said, 'I got that far. But there are four rivers here. Which one?'

Mariana didn't answer this. Instead, she announced, 'It runs from the beast.'

'Surely it *is* the beast?'

At this, Mariana hissed in earnest, leathered stump writhing. 'You know nothing of beasts! The sea alone holds true terror!'

'I think I know *something* about beasts, Mari,' said Douglas, unimpressed.

'Not of this,' spat Mariana. 'Not even you.'

'All right. So the lavellan's running from this thing. But where is it?'

She cocked her head. 'Why do you seek it?'

'Why do you think?'

'There is no cure for you.'

Douglas shrugged. 'Now, now, it's not good merfolk form to speak of what can't be known.'

'You are not sick, Douglass.'

At that, Douglas just laughed – but it was a bitter laugh. 'Are you going to tell me or not?'

Mariana shifted her weight with an uncomfortable thud, breathed heavily from the effort, then spoke again. 'It was resting in the Lune mouth. It began upstream again tonight. But you should not seek it.'

'I know, I know. Big scary rat. Thank you, Mari.'

'No!' said Mariana. 'I do not speak of the might of the lavellan! That is nothing. The beast at sea is near too, and gathering its strength. The Lune will flood.'

At this, Douglas leaned forwards. 'What do you mean? Another of those tides?'

'Tomorrow. It will try its strength at first tide, and push again at second. It will take the Lune.'

'Take the Lune?'

'The river will be salt.'

'Right. More massive tides. Well,' said Douglas, 'that's not exactly a problem for me.'

'It is a problem for us all! The River turns, and all evil follows.'

Kelda could hear Douglas' arched smile again, as he replied, 'Aren't *we* evil?'

'You joke too much, Douglass.'

'You joke too little.'

'The tide will turn. And silvermen are approaching, in great numbers. You should flee this place.'

'Gladly. When I have what I came for.'

Mariana shook her head. 'You are too stubborn, Douglass. I have given you my warning. That is all I can do. I must go.'

'Well,' said Douglas, 'send the others my love. Thanks for the help. And, Mari . . .'

She looked at him.

'Be nice to the family here, will you? They're good people. Definitely the pure of heart.'

Mariana nodded curtly, then heaved herself to the edge of the Cave. For a moment the sunlight caught her damp leathered skin, and she was a blinding silver, and beautiful. Then, without looking back, she hurled herself at the sea.

Kelda was so enthralled that she forgot all about retreating. As Mariana dropped from the Cave, Douglas turned.

'Oh!' he said.

'Oh, um,' said Kelda. 'Sorry. Er – good morning.'

For the first time since she had met him, Douglas looked unsettled. 'How long were you there?'

Kelda was not a good liar. She didn't say anything, but guilt must have been written across her face, because Douglas said, 'River and moon.'

'Keldie?' came a voice from the cavern next door.

'Coming!' said Kelda, relieved; and with a sort of bobbing apologetic nod at Douglas, she sped into the cavern, away from his accusing stare. She would have felt bad for eavesdropping, under normal circumstances, but there was no room in her head for that right now.

'I had a bad dream,' said Isla. She still seemed half-asleep.

Kelda slipped under the blanket. 'Well, it was just a dream.'

'I was in the alder and spinning and spinning and you weren't there and then fuathan came . . .'

'I'm here.'

'You always always will be.'

It was not a question, but Kelda replied anyway. 'Always always.'

They lay, not speaking, and Kelda felt Isla's half-sleepiness growing heavier. That was fine by her; she had no desire to get up again yet. She needed time to think. She had been so overwhelmed by the very existence of the mer-sick woman, she had barely given thought to what had actually been said.

So Douglas really was looking for a lavellan. But not for his dad – *he* was sick. Or not sick, Mariana thought.

And then there was this beast thing at sea. As far as Kelda was concerned the best policy with any dangerous creature was just to avoid them, not to spend time worrying about them – but if it was going to keep terrorising the waterways, would Isla be blamed? And what would happen to them all, if it didn't leave?

She pushed this thought aside, since there was nothing she

could do about it. The most serious news was that silvermen were coming this way. They needed to get away, as soon as possible. She would have to get Mam to talk about when Dad might be back.

She lay there as the others woke. All she wanted to do was lie and hold on to Isla, in peace, before another day of running for their lives. One by one the others stood and left the cavern, until it was only the two of them left in the dark, two heartbeats together.

Isla was moaning slightly in her sleep. She had never done that before. Whatever this thing out at sea was, Kelda hoped it came charging up the Lune and ate every last silverman, starting with Firth.

Then she stiffened, struck by a sudden realisation.

The Lune. The Lune was going to be flooded by saltwater.

Dad was on the Lune.

When Kelda and Isla emerged into the Cave, the fire was already lit, and breakfast was cooking.

Before she could even say good morning, Douglas had her arm, and was steering her back to the cavern. 'Can we talk,' he muttered – but it wasn't a question.

Kelda nodded, which was irrelevant since they were already squeezing through the crack. The light barely reached in here. They faced each other, shadows.

'The merfolk are a secret,' he whispered. 'That's really, really, really important.'

This wasn't quite what Kelda had expected. 'I understand,' she said, whispering too.

'Promise?'

'Promise. I mean, we've got Isla. I know about secrets.'

'If people knew they were here . . . They're all supposed to have been killed once the sickness spreads, you know the Lore. Your lot used to just slit throats. They risk a lot helping out runaways.'

'How did they survive?'

'It doesn't always kill you. Not if you're bitten below the waist and you stop it before it spreads too far – vital organs are more of a problem. *Most* people die.'

'And the others live in the *sea*?' Little Fossy Jupp came unbidden into Kelda's mind, and she pushed the thought away. She felt irrationally glad the girl had been found belly up. The thought of a life in salt was horrifying.

'It's the eel bite. Eels can live in both. And they're safe from silvermen, there.' Douglas said this fast, impatiently; then, 'Kelda, do you swear? If they're found . . .'

She nodded, then realised he couldn't see her. 'I get it. I won't say a word. But—'

'No but! But is bad!'

'Listen, we have to tell the others about the Lune,' she said. 'My dad's out there, and he doesn't know. If he's silverside when the tide turns . . .'

There was a moment's silence, as Douglas took this in. Then, 'Oh, no. Oh, that's bad.'

'So we have to tell them. And about the others heading this way.'

She had a feeling that Douglas was doing in-the-dark nodding too. 'Right. We tell them that I spoke to the people who run this place, like I planned, and they told me. No need to give anything else away.'

'Thanks.'

'Thank *you*. Look, Kelda – I know you're afraid of everyone right now. I get it, really. But I'm not here to spy on you, and I'm not going to tell anyone about Isla.'

Kelda was still uneasy, but there was nothing to be done about it. And at least they *both* knew secrets now, which felt safer.

'I'm sorry I spied on you,' she said. 'It just sort of – well, I didn't realise it would be so private. I won't tell anyone about the folk. Or . . .' – she didn't like to mention non-existent sick fathers out loud – '. . . the rest.'

'Thank you.'

'Why do they talk so weird?'

'They don't talk much at all, normally. And they're very formal about it when they do. It's a pride thing . . . keeping apart from the rest of us.'

Isla's head poked through the cranny. 'Uncle Abe says it's done and he's going to eat it all if you don't come.'

'All right,' said Kelda. Then whispered, 'You'll tell them now?'

'Yes. Let's go.'

Back in the Cave, everyone else was gathered at the fire. No one looked like they had slept well. Kelda took a plate of the patties, and Douglas told everyone what he had learned.

When he had finished, there was a moment's appalled silence. Mam put her face in her hands.

'He definitely headed to the Lune?' Abe asked her.

She nodded into her hands, and whispered, 'To watch for the girls.'

'He might still come back in time,' said Peter. 'Did he say how long he'd be gone, Lyn?'

Mam shook her head.

'Right,' said Abe. 'Then I need to find him.'

'We'll all come,' said Peter.

Abe shook his head. 'No. There's Isla to think of too; it sounds like we need to get her out of here, if our lot are heading this way. Lyn, Peter, get the girls on a train to Scotland and out of danger. Murphy and I will meet you there.'

'Some of us should come with you,' said Kelda, 'and help search. There's both banks to cover, and silverside. It doesn't make sense for *everyone* else to go to Scotland.'

There was a moment's silence. Then Abe spoke again. 'Peter, I know you want to help Murphy, but I think you'll have to go with the Isla party. That will need landman money, and someone who understands trains . . .'

Peter nodded. 'You're right, Abe. Quite right. I'll take Isla.' And he gave her another of their salutes.

But Isla was scared now that the time had really come – fear always made her look younger, suddenly, and liable to melt like a candle – and her new friendship with Peter was quickly forgotten. She looked up at Abe, and said, 'I want Mam or Kelda.'

Abe nodded. 'Of course. Either Mam or Kelda goes with you. And one of them stays to help me.'

Kelda and Mam looked at each other. Kelda was desperate to help find Dad and desperate to see Isla safely to Scotland.

Neither task was safe, with the hunting parties after Isla, and the strange tides here, and the lavellan at large. How would they choose?

Mam cleared her throat. 'There is some possibility,' she said, in a very small voice, 'that if Murphy sees me, he won't actually stop to talk.'

Kelda stared at her. Only once in their whole lives had she ever seen Dad jump silverside when Mam was trying to talk to him, during one of their worst fights, when Dad went silent on her for two full weeks. 'Mam,' she said, 'what *happened* between you two?'

'We were so frightened,' said Mam. 'We said such stupid things.'

Abe put an arm round her. 'Don't dwell on it now, Lyn. Plenty of time to kiss and make up once we're all safe and sound. That settles things then. Me and Kelda up the Lune for Murphy; Peter and Lyn and Isla off to Maggie's.'

Mam did not look at all happy about this. She hugged Isla, studiously avoiding Peter's smile of assent in her direction. Her pointless objection to the Land Weard irritated Kelda. If they had all been encouraged to be a little less orthodox – if *Firth* had been encouraged – things might have been so different.

Douglas cleared his throat. 'I'm looking for the lavellan on the Lune, so I can keep an eye out too. If you like.'

Abe smiled at him warmly. 'Tremendous. Three hands to the Lune, three to Maggie.'

Peter leaned forwards. 'Douglas, can you ride a horse?'

'Sure.'

'Take mine. I can't take her to Scotland, and it will speed the search. We'll pick her up in Lancaster – find another livery yard for her when you've finished, and we'll go back for her when we can. I can give you money.'

Douglas nodded, and Abe clapped his hands together. 'Right,' he said. 'That's all settled, then. We'll go after breakfast.'

Within an hour, a crocodile-line of six humans and a duck was snaking across Morecambe Bay in the early morning sun, casting long shadows across the sand.

Heading inland was a much simpler business than finding the Cave, but there was still the danger of quicksand. Douglas led the way: he knew the flats well, he said. No one asked why.

Kelda was concentrating on moving forward, and didn't look back until they were some distance from the sea. By then, she was only just close enough to make out the cluster of pallid bodies on a rocky outcrop in the sea, watching them go, singing softly to themselves.

15

Kelda had ventured into the occasional town before Isla was born, with Aeron and the others, Firth tagging behind wide-eyed. But she had never been to a city. Lancaster horrified her. She put on her wellingtons as protection against the crush of people and horses and carriages, but the boots gave her poor purchase on the cobbled streets, and she stumbled along in bewilderment. (Peter had bought her and Isla skirts, too, drab things in pale blue cotton. She hated them.)

The strangest thing about landman settlements was the way that she could pass through them unnoticed. To *her*, the silver eyes and slight shine of a silverman were obvious. But to them, she was just a girl, grey-eyed and unimportant. It seemed as though the people swarming around her didn't even see her. If anything it was Douglas who drew attention, with his bow and quiver. When he bought a newspaper from a young boy with enthusiastic lungs, the boy actually backed away, even as he took the money.

There was relative calm in the livery yard, although it was full of the smell of hay and manure and the sound of snorting and whinnying and stamping. Looking around at the other horses, Kelda thought they seemed almost like toys after Echo – oddly small, and drab. Peter, Douglas and Isla went to fetch Echo; Kelda waited with Mam and Abe.

'Have a look at this,' said Douglas, handing the newspaper to Abe as he left. 'It's worse than we thought.'

So the three of them squatted on the livery yard floor, and spread out the paper. The inside front page was a map of waterways, ludicrously incomplete, with spiky dotted lines showing those flooded by the peculiar tide. Kelda had not imagined anything like this. The tide had extended all the way across the south and the east, and had spread right inland to the little knot of canals at the centre. The Wharfe was already salted; they must have been only just ahead of the spread.

Mam read out loud in a tight almost-whisper. ' "Flood levels have been mitigated by the low rainfall this winter, but the damage is still severe in places, and an emergency relief effort is being discussed in Parliament today. Of even greater urgency is the state of the affected waterways. Salinity levels are remaining high, and indeed the saltwater has encroached further inland, for reasons that are not yet clear. A special commission has been assembled to study the phenomenon, but chairman Dr Oliver Keynes declined to comment at this stage. In the meantime, dependency on spring and well water . . ." ' She scanned the page – 'It's all landman business after that. Oh! Where will everyone go?'

Kelda was wondering the same thing, but not with the same empathy as Mam. The other silvermen would all have been forced off the Ouse and Trent, and their nearest obvious candidates for safe water were the Mersey, or the Lune and the Lancaster Canal. Mersey was closer. But the River Mersey was a foul soup of soot and pollution, and no silverman spent time there these days if they could help it.

The smell of horses and manure and the sound of Mam's worried muttering was suddenly all too much. 'I'm going to wait outside a minute,' said Kelda.

'You all right?' said Abe.

'I'm fine. I'll be right back.'

Outside, the swirl of the crowd was at least something else to think about, and felt comfortingly far away from silvermen. Most people seemed to be here to buy things from the shops, but some things were sold in the street – an old woman opposite Kelda was waving flowers at people aggressively, and the small boy with the newspapers was shouting at the top of his lungs about landman politics. Quite a lot of people bought papers, but no one bought flowers.

Kelda was admiring a young couple in superlative hats when the paperboy suddenly swore loudly. She swung her head to look, along with half the street.

'OI!' he yelled. '*Thief!*' And then he was off, scrambling through the crowd, sprinting after a running figure.

Kelda turned cold all over. The running figure wore a woollen hooded travelling cloak.

A few seconds later they rounded the corner, but it had been long enough to be certain. No one else on this street was dressed like that. And why steal a penny paper, except for the very good reason that you didn't own any currency?

They were already here.

Kelda rushed back into the livery yard to tell the others what she'd seen. Abe put a hand on her shoulder.

'Right,' he said, 'let's all take a breath. This is fine. Isla's going to be on a train out of here any minute now. I'll ask Peter if they can all go in one of those horse cab things to the station, just to be safe.'

The others were approaching now, Douglas leading Echo. Abe quickly explained the situation to them all.

'Right,' said Peter, uncharacteristically grim. 'I'll hail a hansom. You wait in here. With a bit of luck, we can catch the midday train.'

And just like that, it was time to say goodbye.

Kelda knelt down to give Isla a string of instructions, all the while hugging her fiercely. Isla just nodded into her chest, not saying a word. She was holding the little wooden horse tightly; it dug against Kelda's ribs.

Then she said, from inside the hug: 'Don't come to Scotland.'

Kelda drew back to look at her. 'What?'

'Don't come. You should be on the waterways. It's a crying shame, I heard Uncle Abe say so.'

Abe's face melted. 'Oh, Isla, I was just . . .'

But Isla wasn't listening. 'There isn't anyone else we know in Scotland and the rivers are too tumbly to be waterways so you can't have a boat, and then you can't have a normal life and we'll grow old there and it will just be us.'

'That's what I *want*, silly goose,' said Kelda.

'But you'll be cut off from all the waterways, and you can't marry, and—'

'I don't want to. I don't care. Where's all this coming from?'

Isla had her stubborn face on. 'I don't want it to be my fault.'

'*Nothing* is your fault. Look, I couldn't now, even if—'

'I saw your boat designs. You should have the red one. It was nice. And you should have lots and lots of children because you'd be such a good mam.'

'Isla . . .'

'I heard Firth and Trent saying how Aeron Jupp is in love with you, did you know? You could be his love-match, he's nice. And have the red boat. I don't want it to be my fault.'

'I do *not* want to marry Aeron Jupp,' said Kelda. 'And if that *is* how he feels, he's . . . he's got an odd way of showing it. Anyway. I'm coming to Scotland.'

Isla shook her head, then suddenly launched herself at Kelda and bawled into her shoulder.

Peter came hurrying back into the courtyard. 'I've got us a cab! Ready? We may be in time for the early train, but it's a close thing . . .'

Isla was shaking her head into Kelda's shoulder, and she just clung even tighter at this. Hating herself, Kelda scooped her up, and carried her over to the cab despite her protestations. Mam climbed in first, then she put Robin Hood down on the seat, and Kelda passed Isla over into her arms.

'I'll see you in Scotland,' she said. 'I *will*. No more of this, young lady!' And she kissed her, and kissed Mam, then stepped aside for Peter to get in the cab.

There should have been more. There should have been something she could say, something that would see Isla safely to Scotland, and stop her crying. But there wasn't anything: the door shut, and the cab rattled away. Kelda watched it go until it was out of sight.

Abe put an arm around her. 'Well done,' he said. 'Well done. She'll be safe now.' He squeezed her shoulders tightly, then said, 'Douglas. How do you go about getting food in this nightmare place?'

Ten minutes later they were walking the tidal stretch of the Lune upstream, out of the city, Douglas leading Echo. The horse seemed not at all sure about her new leaders, and they had to stop several times to plead and coax her onwards. For the first time, Kelda wondered whether it wouldn't be easier to have a normal-blooded horse after all.

Douglas had found them eel pies from one of the street sellers, and they ate while they walked. Kelda was mildly surprised to learn that landmen knew about eels – you could never be quite sure *what* they knew, their scholarship seemed so patchy – but she didn't have time to dwell on it. She was constantly scanning the streets, on the lookout for woollen cloaks.

She didn't see any. Instead, all through the outskirts of Lancaster, she saw landmen scurrying about with huge sacks of something heavy, stacking them up against the river – in case, she presumed, of more strange floods. Here and there they would pass clusters of men wading in the river itself, with nets and vials and measuring instruments and worried expressions. Kelda gathered that this was landman river expertise at work; it was quite touching in its uselessness.

As they left houses behind, a smaller stack of the sacks continued, but the landman presence petered out – apparently they were happy with their defences here. Kelda wondered what Peter would have made of it.

'Right,' said Abe, coming to a halt once they had gone a few minutes and seen no one. 'Tomorrow's first tide is in the wee hours – not much past midnight. By my calculations, we've got time to go up the Lune on one bank and down the other on this beast before then' – he indicated Echo, who was currently taking a stubborn interest in some nearby clover, and snorting to herself – 'And of course we'll need to check silverside. Now, Kelda, I know we both hate riding, but for your own good, I'm taking the river. We don't know how many of our people are about, and I'd rather you were inland. I'll meet you both at the head of the river – and if anything goes wrong, make your way back to Lancaster, and get up to Maggie at Moray Firth. Ask for the lighthouse, you can't miss it. Douglas, you understand the trains?'

Kelda began to protest, but Abe cut her off. 'I'm putting my foot down. Isla's safely away. From now on, you are my littlest niece again, and you're going to keep *yourself* safe. Douglas, go as far inland as you can with the river still in sight.'

Douglas nodded. He wasn't saying much.

'If you see the hemlock,' said Kelda, 'you'll need to follow it, won't you?'

He shrugged. 'We don't have long. We've got to find your Dad.'

'But you've come all this way.'

'I'm – my dad's not going to die if I don't get it,' said Douglas. 'And I can always go back and pick up the trail again.' Kelda didn't argue, but she felt bad. This was good of Douglas. None of this was *his* fight. She hoped fervently that they would find Dad soon, and Douglas could go on and find the lavellan to cure his whatever-it-was. Preferably before the lavellan found *them*. Water-rats had keen noses, and they were silverman hunters.

They parted ways at the aqueduct. 'Keep well inland, remember,' said Abe. 'And if you see any of our lot, gallop east as fast as you can go. Don't try and do anything heroic. I'll take care of myself.' And only when they had agreed, then promised, twice, did he slip silverside. His shadow shot off upstream, and was gone.

Douglas exhaled heavily. 'Well. Do you want a breather before the horse?'

'We should get on.'

'Yes,' said Douglas, 'but do you *want* a breather?' He sat down on the grass. 'I think I'm enforcing one. You've only had half that pie. Sit, eat, get some water. We'll go in two minutes.'

So Kelda knelt on the banks to cautiously splash her skin, the water still heavy with dirt; then she sat, with some relief. She took off the hated wellingtons, and the blue skirt too now that they were out of town, and abandoned them on the banks. Douglas sat too, and they ate. There was a minute's silence, apart from the heavy breathing of Echo.

'So, who's this Aeron then?' said Douglas.

Kelda scowled. 'The boy who's trying to kill my sister.'

'Oh.'

'Let's go.' Kelda stood, dropping the last of her pie and wiping her hands on her fly-silks. 'We haven't got much time.'

She hated the horse. She hated the horse so much. Echo didn't love having two full-sized riders again either, and bucked horrifyingly if Douglas tried to take her too fast. Kelda knew she should be full of gratitude and admiration for the big, patient mare. But she was a little busy feeling sick, and trying not to fall off. It didn't help that she had to sit nestled against Douglas' chest, his arms around her to hold the reins, which was adding a muddling embarrassment to the whole ordeal.

Where trees obscured the landscape, they took a meandering path to take in more of the bank; where there was a clear view of the distance, they trotted straight through. It was all Kelda could do to stay upright, so she had to trust Douglas to keep an eye out. Twice he brought Echo to a halt and pointed out a distant walker to her, but it wasn't Dad.

Then the hemlock trail began. Hemlock is poisonous, unless you happen to be a water vole – or a lavellan's sister, as silvermen call them. It was trailing up the Lune, along their path; there was no difficult choice, no need for Douglas to make any noble sacrifice.

For the first time, the possibility of meeting the lavellan became real to Kelda. Lavellans were too rare to really worry most silvermen. But if you knew one was in the area, you ought to leave, fast – they could track down a silverman over large distances, and a bite would be venomous, and fatal.

The patches of woodland thinned as they went upstream, and after the first hour or so they were crossing moorland, yellow with thick gorse, the hemlock trail lying across it like a scar. But there was no lavellan – and no Dad. The landscape hid itself from them here and there in the folds and undulations of the valley, but each time they crested a hill, the newly revealed land was empty.

Whenever Douglas halted Echo and paused to look about them, Kelda found herself wanting to turn to Isla, and tell her it was going to be all right. It was bizarre to have no one to tell.

About an hour after the hemlock trail had begun, Douglas reined Echo in next to a small circle of wire fence, oddly perched in the middle of the landscape. Below the horse's hooves, the gorse had been strangled entirely by hemlock. Echo skittered uncertainly.

'Dismount,' Douglas whispered.

Kelda did so clumsily, and he followed with a more elegant drop. Echo was breathing heavily, but beneath that, Kelda could hear a new sound: a furious hissing, spitting sound, like something frying. Douglas snaked under the wire and squatted there, looking down. Kelda saw an angry fissure in the rock, overgrown with moss and ferns.

'Lavellan?' she whispered. It looked like an ideal hide-out for the underground rat.

'Mm-hmm,' Douglas murmured. 'Definitely.' He picked something out of the ferns, and held it up: a cracked pair of glasses, with a leather band attached – in the silverman style, for diving. They were horribly familiar.

'Oh,' said Kelda. '*Dad.*'

Silver stupefies brackish creatures. For the larger ones, which cannot be easily caught under a net, the aim should be to stupefy the heart.

Where creatures have tough outer skins, simple weapons may break. The proper guardian knots should be used in their construction to ensure that they will hold. See the nineteenth stanza of the River Lore.

A spear can be used on nymphs or grindylow, but for more dangerous creatures, a bow and arrow is preferable. This will allow the attacker to keep a safe distance.

If the first attempt strikes the creature but misses the heart, retreat.

16

Douglas opened his satchel, and produced two lengths of rope. He was prepared. It was strange to Kelda to think he had been anticipating doing this entirely mad thing, all this time – she thought that if she had ten more seconds to think about it, she might find herself turning and running.

He tethered Echo to one fence stump, to the mare's intense displeasure, and attached the second rope to another. Then he squatted down, assessing the cave entrance.

'It's going to be tight. You coming down?'

'Of course.'

He didn't try to change her mind. 'Right. I'll go first, then you can haul it back up.' As he spoke, he was tying the rope around his waist, so there wasn't time to think this through; she just nodded. There was something business-like about Douglas that was reassuring – it reminded her of her family.

He touched his cap in a mock-salute. 'Good luck!' – and with that, he was wriggling into the shadow in the earth.

Kelda didn't watch. She had a feeling her body might rebel if she gave it too much of a preview.

There was a gentle splosh far below, and a few seconds later he called softly, 'All yours.'

She hauled the rope up and knotted it around herself into a harness, then once more for safety, then once more for extra-certain safety; then she began.

There was barely room to slip through the opening. She had to turn her head sideways, and when she bobbed down into the total darkness, there was a moment of pure horror. But after that, the shaft got wider. She steadied her feet against the rock and worked her way down, further and further from the light. The hissing and spitting was louder down here.

Then she let her feet fall into the water at the bottom, and untied. Douglas waited, his head cocked towards the tunnel behind her.

'It's that way,' he said, nodding in the direction he was looking. 'I think I hear your dad too.'

He was alive, then. He was alive, he was alive.

Then Kelda heard him too, and all the relief disappeared. The sound was very faint, and it wasn't clear if he was calling for help, or just yelling out in pain; but either way it tore her apart to hear it. 'Yes,' she said. 'That's him. Let's go.'

'Hold on.' Douglas put a hand on her arm. 'Let me get ready to shoot. We don't want to give ourselves away too soon.'

This was sensible, so Kelda waited while he strung his bow. But when Dad yelled again, it took all her strength to stay still and quiet; a hundred times harder than resisting the peg-a-lantern.

'Right,' whispered Douglas. 'Let me squeeze past. I should lead, for a clear shot.'

This was sensible too. Kelda was glad *someone* was feeling sensible. The cave filled her with abject horror. The water at her ankles was cold, and felt very old, and somehow hostile. There was only just enough room for Douglas to edge past her, and as they stepped away from the shaft, she had to stoop her head slightly to avoid hitting it on the rock. It was hard to be sure in the darkness, but it looked as though things only got narrower and lower ahead.

But Dad was in there.

It was impossible to move silently through the water, but they went as quietly as they could, moving their feet in slow motion. It *was* getting narrower. At one point, Kelda had to turn sideways to fit through. And all the while, they could hear the lavellan rasping and wheezing to itself. They did not hear Dad again.

Then the tunnel widened out, before suddenly dropping out beneath them; Douglas almost toppled down, and Kelda only just snatched him back in time. They stopped to listen. In the darkness, Kelda saw Douglas nod. It was down there.

Very, *very* quietly, he lowered himself through the hole. It was not deep; his feet touched the bottom before his hands lost their grip.

Very, *very* quietly, Kelda followed. But she was not quite as tall. She had to drop the last couple of inches, and she landed on moss and slipped, careening into Douglas, who fell in turn; and they were bumping and rolling down a sloping tunnel, dislodging stones as they slid, landing at the bottom with a thump and a clattering of rocks and a skittering of arrows and a loud landman swear word from Douglas.

The hissing intensified.

Douglas scrambled to his feet. 'Oh, *salt*, the bow, I've lost the bow . . .'

Kelda could feel, rather than see, that they were in a wide cave now. And she could hear and feel and smell that the lavellan was in it too, or close. She gagged.

'Back,' Douglas whispered. 'Back, back, get out.'

'No . . .. Dad . . .'

'We don't have a weapon, Kelda. I can't find my arrows . . .'

Kelda patted the ground around her, finding only moss and slime and rock and puddles – then her hand met something long and cold, ridged with knots.

'Here,' she said, handing it to him, then returning to the search. 'I can't find the bow . . .'

'Maybe I could use this like a spear. Riskier – I'll have to get close.' He was breathing heavily, and for a moment, Kelda was sure he would turn back. But then she felt his hand pressing something into hers. 'Matches. We'll need a light. Could you . . . ?'

Kelda struck a match. The flare showed them a small cave, dripping stalactites. It was briefly beautiful. An opening in the wall led through to another cave.

There was a colossal snout in the opening, questing, quivering.

Then the match went out.

'Another, another,' said Douglas, no longer bothering to keep his voice down. The blind rat would be able to smell them by now, anyway. There was an angry hiss, as it squeezed its fluid body through the opening. By the time a second match

167

flared, it had reverted to its usual shape, although something of its snake-like quality was still evident; little muscular twitches caused ripples and undulations all along its great length as it snuffled at the dank air.

Kelda had known it would be big, but she had not been prepared for this. It took up half the cave. Its nose hung enormously above them, quivering. And in that brief flare of light, she saw that it was wounded: a great gash, starting on its face, running all the way down the length of its side. Its ears, too, were horribly mangled; she suspected their efforts at silence had been unnecessary. It certainly didn't seem to know quite where they were now.

'D'you think that's a silver wound?' she whispered, as the light died. 'It looked bad.'

'I think so,' breathed Douglas. 'It's confused.'

It was. Its great head waved about almost feverishly, scenting them, but it didn't seem to know which way to attack. It lifted and put down a paw, and Kelda rolled out of the way just in time. She felt a faint hope: if it was already half-stupefied, they were truly in with a chance, even without the bow.

'One more match,' said Douglas. 'I'm going to aim for the heart.'

A whisker brushed past Kelda just as she struck the match, and she yelled in shock. The light flared. Douglas plunged.

Kelda's yell was nothing to the lavellan's. With a sound like metal on metal, it squealed in outraged agony. The rasping breaths grew loud and fast, as though the creature was grating its own gullet every time it inhaled. There was a full minute of the awful squealing, and blind stumbling; Kelda and Douglas backed up into the tunnel, out of the way of the blindly crashing paws, the wildly swinging snout.

At last it fell. The squealing stopped: the breaths continued.

Then, after a long, long minute, the breathing stopped, too.

The humans waited another minute more. The darkness seemed to wait with them. Then Kelda said, 'Think it's dead?'

'Think so.'

'Right, then.'

'Yes.'

'Good.'

'Right.'

Kelda took a steadying breath, which stank of the lavellan. Then she raised her voice, and called: 'Dad?'

The sound bounced around the cavern. But in among the echoes, from the cave beyond, came the unmistakable reply, faint and astonished: 'Kelda?'

'Dad!' She was scrambling up, squeezing past the still-warm body of the lavellan, the stench and the horror forgotten. Something warm and oozing smeared her sides as she pushed by.

'Kelda,' said Douglas, from close behind her. 'I'm just going to get the heart-sap.'

She'd forgotten all about that. 'Sure. I'll go on.'

'Right. Here, take my matches.'

Kelda took them, but felt her way to the hole in the rock in darkness, saving the precious light. Only once she was through the hole, and could hear ragged breathing, did she light one.

This cavern was larger than the first, and even more

beautiful. The stalactites and stalagmites here were elaborate, and somehow stately; in the match-light, the wet walls glistened and shone. And there, slumped against one wall, most beautiful of all, was Dad: alive.

The light died. Splashing and slipping, Kelda hurried over. 'Dad. Are you hurt?'

'My little girl.'

'Are you hurt?'

'Yes, yes. Bit me. Little Kelda . . . where's your hand? Where's your hand?'

Kelda felt around for his hand, and squeezed it. 'Dad. I've got a friend back there. Together we can carry you out. Understand?'

'Kelda. There's things . . . I want – to tell . . .'

'Save your strength. You can tell me when we're out.'

'No, no, too late now. Bit me. Tell your mam – I'm sorry. I said so much . . . I love her. Tell her I love her.' He gripped her hand painfully tight. 'Promise? Please . . .'

Without consciously deciding to, Kelda took her hand back from his. She would do anything for her father, except listen to his defeat. 'Douglas!' she yelled. 'He's wounded, it's bad. Can we carry him?'

She heard the sounds of someone feeling for the entrance hole. 'I'm all done here,' he said. 'Where are you? Light a match!'

The climb that followed would recur in Kelda's nightmares for years. Going back up the sloped tunnel was hardest: it proved far too low to stand, and they had to push-and-pull Dad up it, bumping him along the stones. Then they carried him between them like a piece of timber along the tunnel

170

above, jolting and jostling him each time one of them slipped or tripped, and with every bump he would cry out in agony. It seemed almost worse down here without the hissing and spitting of the lavellan; its silence filled the tunnels instead, in awful reproach.

At the entrance, Douglas went up first, then threw Kelda the rope for Dad.

'You have to use your feet, Dad,' she said. 'You're going to have to push against the rock.'

'Go,' he said. 'Too late.'

'Look, we *are* going, this is the way out. Come on, here you go . . . feet here . . . got it? Douglas!' she yelled. 'Ready!'

She supported him with her hands as far as she could, but he ascended the last couple of feet like a puppet on a string, wafting his legs ineffectually at the wall and bumping against the rock as Douglas hauled.

Then the rope came back for Kelda, and she was over the top at double-speed. Douglas was kneeling by Dad, examining the wounds. In the daylight, it was awful. The bite was on his arm, discoloured and oozing. But he looked beaten and bloodied too, which didn't make any sense. They hadn't bumped him *that* badly on the rock, and lavellans didn't give black eyes or smashed jaws.

'Dad. What *happened*?'

Dad replied, but his words were too slurred now to understand.

'What do we do,' whispered Kelda. 'What do we do?' For a moment, she had an overwhelming urge to put her mouth over his and breathe. But that wouldn't work this time.

At Dad's side, Douglas was uncorking a bottle, smaller than his palm, and pouring something honey-coloured on to the bite. It took Kelda a moment to register what it must be. He had emptied the bottle.

'Douglas! Is that . . . ?'

'Only thing that will work,' he said.

'*Thank you*,' she said. It was inadequate. She was sorry she had ever doubted him. She felt a sudden vertigo at the gap between her feelings and reality. Firth was a traitor. The stranger from Sherwood Forest was saving her father. How were you ever supposed to know who to trust?

She held Dad's hand again, tightly. 'There, Dad. We've got the lavellan's sap. You're going to be all right.'

'Too late,' Dad muttered.

'Keep talking, Kelda,' said Douglas. He had gone to the fence wire, and snagged at his shirt sleeve; now he was tearing it off, for a bandage. 'Keep him with us. He's only got to hold on a minute, then this should set in.'

'Did you hear that, Dad?' Kelda knelt close. 'You have to stay with us. Then you're going to be just fine.'

'It hurts.'

'But it's doing you good. Isla's going to Scotland, Dad. We can all go too. We're going to live on the Caledonian Canal and see the lochs and the shape-shifters. It's going to be beautiful.'

Douglas tied the bandage tightly – a guardian knot, Kelda noticed. 'This is going to hurt a moment, Mr Pade, but you have to push through it. You've got a wife and three children who need you to live, remember that.'

Dad said something, but it sounded more like an exhalation than anything else.

'What? Dad, rest . . . it's all right now . . .'

Dad tried again, grimaced, and managed, 'Two.'

'What?'

'Two children.'

Kelda nodded fiercely, and squeezed his hand. 'I know. But don't think about Firth now. Think about the future.'

'No,' said Dad. 'Not Firth. Firth's . . . mine.' Then a look of utter peace swept over his face, and at the same moment, his cheeks flushed. 'Oh,' he said, 'That's better. That's better.'

Douglas let out a heavy breath, and sat back.

'Much better,' said Dad. And with a sigh of suddenly-perfect happiness, he closed his eyes, and fell into a deep, healing sleep.

17

Douglas went on to meet Abe while Kelda watched over Dad. It started to rain. She lay on her back and let it sing on her skin, which bloomed and faded with every drop.

Since Isla wasn't there, she told *herself* about how it was going to be all right. Abe would be there any moment now. The train was safely on its way to Scotland. Nothing to be scared of, little one. Then she concentrated on the smell of damp gorse, and watching Dad's peaceful breathing.

Douglas was back on Echo sooner than she expected – he had spotted the shadow of Abe silverside, not far ahead – and Abe followed shortly after, emerging from the Lune clutching salmon. Still it rained. Douglas had put on some kind of waxy, hooded coat, and it made him look oddly small.

There was no hope of a fire, but they could have the salmon raw. Douglas set to gutting it as he explained what had happened, and Abe cleaned some of Dad's mysterious other wounds with water from the Lune. When Douglas had told almost everything, Kelda picked a piece of gorse, began to shred it, and completed the story.

'Uncle Abe. Just before the sap took hold, Dad said he only had two children.'

Abe didn't look up from Dad. 'Cutting off Firth already?'

'No. I thought that. But he said that's not what he meant.'

'Ah,' said Uncle Abe. 'Lyn must have told him back at the Cave, then. I did wonder.'

Kelda sat up. 'Told him what?'

Still Uncle Abe did not look at her, and still the rain sang. 'Told him *what*?'

'Well, it's not really my place – but you have a right . . .' He sighed. 'Murphy's not Isla's father. I mean, he is in every sense that counts, obviously. But technically, she's Peter's.'

'*What*?'

'It was surreal seeing the two of them together. He's always known about her, but they've never met . . . She's grown so much like him. The curly hair – and the smile, have you noticed?'

'How can you possibly know that?' said Kelda. She found she was half-shouting. Isla was pure silverman: it was a foundational family creed. And here was Uncle Abe, pulling it out from inside her like fish guts as though it was nothing.

Uncle Abe ignored the shouting, and carried on as normal. Just occasionally, his everything-is-fine peacemaker act could be infuriating. 'Your mam told me, after she saw what Isla was. She was worried, didn't know what to do. And I think it says a lot about your mam that she kept the secret. I really thought she might choose the Lore. But she chose Isla.'

Kelda was not in the mood to start praising Mam right now. She didn't want to hear another word about stupid secrets and affairs, or even *think* about it: Isla's purity was all that mattered. 'How can Mam be sure?' she persisted. 'Couldn't she be wrong?'

'No, Kelda,' said Abe. 'Isla's half and half. What other explanation could there be?'

'She's just different. Maybe it's a sickness . . .' But even as she spoke, Kelda knew she was wrong. She was remembering, now, the way Mam studiously avoided Peter; the way Peter beamed at Isla, full of wonder; the cosy little companionship between the two of them, with their stupid salute and the stupid wooden horse . . .

'There's nothing wrong with her,' said Abe. 'She's half-landman. Your dad always suspected, I think, but he didn't *want* to believe it.' Abe looked at his sleeping brother sadly. 'He wasn't there, on that visit to Camberley – he stayed to look after you and Firth – but he thinks *I* was. The truth is I went away for a couple of days with Judith to see one of their springs. I never told him that. I wanted him to be . . . easy, in his mind. To be happy.' He shook his head. 'I'm not sure I did right. Lyn begged me . . .'

'Begged you to lie to us? How *could* she? River!'

Douglas had been focusing on the fish with fixed concentration, trying to retreat into his hooded thing and be as not-there as possible. But just then, Dad stirred, and his head snapped up. Abe leaned forwards at once, a hand on Dad's chest.

Only Kelda didn't jump to attention. She was still reeling from this revelation, and she had just been blindsided by a sudden, new thought. *Nothing wrong with her.*

You are not sick, Douglass.

There was an obvious, simple explanation for Douglas, the landman with silverman ways. If Aeron had found one other like Isla in Willig's books, how many more might there have been who were kept a secret? And surely if there *were* others, they might well have hidden in the Mercy Cave, before fleeing to Scotland – just like Isla?

Abe spoke softly. 'Murphy. Murphy, it's me.'

'Aberforth.'

'Little brother.'

Dad blinked up at him. He looked oddly naked without his glasses. 'It bit me, Abe.'

'That's healing now. You'll be all right. Can you sit? You should eat.'

Painfully, Dad sat, and Abe handed him the first piece of salmon, which he wolfed down. A second piece later, he was coherent, albeit in pain. It was his other injuries that seemed to bother him now; there had only been enough lavellan sap for his arm. He turned his face to the rain as though for a blessing. Kelda had so many questions for him – about what he knew, about what he had always suspected, about what he wanted now – but she didn't want to hurt him any further.

'You're looking better already,' said Abe. 'Here, have another piece. What happened, Murphy?'

Dad took the fish, and said, 'Our lot.'

'*Silvermen* did this to you?'

'Punishing the traitor.'

'*What?*'

'A bunch of them spotted me and came after me. Then

they got distracted when the lavellan attacked, and when they'd wounded the thing and left it mad with pain' – he tore a hungry bite from the fish – 'they fled and left me to it.'

Kelda was not sure she had ever seen Abe angry before. He was angry now. 'That's not Lore. That's not how we punish people. By what right—'

Dad shook his head, then stopped when it hurt. 'They're reverting to old Lore now – they've declared a new Weard. The full twelve-man council. They're scared by this business with the tide, really scared. Everyone's up ahead on the river, travelling together, alder boats and silverside only – had to get here quickly, no time for houseboats. Something's gone badly wrong.'

'Everyone?' said Douglas sharply. 'On this river?'

'Yep.'

Kelda just felt tired at this news. She wanted to leave them all far behind her. But Douglas was suddenly agitated.

'This river's turning tonight,' he said. 'The saltwater's coming.'

Dad stared at him. 'How do you know?'

'I was told. By people we can trust.'

'That's why we came looking for you,' explained Abe. 'Oh, River. Are they close, do you think? How long ago were they here?'

Dad shook his head. 'I can't . . . it's a blur.'

Douglas was on his feet. 'We can get to them before high tide, if they're still on the Lune. It's barely dusk.'

Kelda looked up at him in amazement. 'You're *helping* them?'

'Kelda,' said Abe, a hand on her arm, 'Firth is there.'

'I don't care.'

'Kelda—'

'I don't care, I don't care, I don't care!' Kelda could feel tears starting. She knew she was behaving badly, but she couldn't stop it; she wanted to roll on the gorse and beat it with her fists, throw a wild tantrum, pour down on everyone like the rain. 'We've come all this way and Camberley wasn't safe and then the Lune wasn't safe and then we found Dad but we had to fight a lavellan and now we've rescued him and we've rescued Isla and we are all going to Scotland. I am not rescuing the people who did this to us. I am not, I am not. It isn't fair.'

For a moment after this speech there was silence, besides the rain.

Then Dad said, 'Kelda, I understand. But – my son.'

'Who tried to kill your daughter!' yelled Kelda. 'Or does she not count any more?'

'Of *course* Isla counts. But so does Firth.'

'And the rest,' said Abe. His eyes were wide, looking at Kelda like he had never seen her properly before. 'You wouldn't leave hundreds of people to die, Kelda. Willig helped us. Others would have helped us, gladly. There are good people.'

'That's not my problem,' said Kelda. Even she could hear how mulish the words sounded. She wished Abe would stop looking at her that way – like she had done something shocking, and faintly revolting.

Douglas didn't speak. He looked paler and smaller than ever in the folds of his hooded coat. A small, quiet voice of reason reminded Kelda that if her guess was right, he must have silverman family.

'I'll go,' he said. 'Too risky for you all' – and he jerked a head at Dad, in case they had forgotten exactly what the risk was.

'Nobly pronounced,' said Abe, 'but I don't think they'll treat an interfering landman too well right now, either.'

'Firth would listen,' said Dad. Kelda rolled her eyes, but he went on, more reasonably: 'Willig. Dee. There are plenty who would . . .'

'I'll have to come with you,' said Abe to Douglas. 'Murphy's right, but you won't know which of them are safe.'

'Abe, no,' said Dad. 'Look what they did . . . I think they'd have killed me, if the lavellan hadn't come.'

'Since when do silvermen *kill* each other?' said Kelda, appalled.

'Since always,' said Douglas. 'Look at Isla. Look at the mer-sick.'

'Right, but – I mean . . .'

'Oh, sure. Other than the ones who don't count.'

Abe cut in quickly. Kelda had to admire the dogged survival of his instincts. Here on the hopeless moor, with his brother in pieces beside him, he still spread his hands out wide and tried to smooth over somebody else's argument. 'The Lore is cruel,' he agreed, 'but the old Lore was worse. Anyone of age can be killed for hiding or helping an outcast – and for a host of other things. It wasn't just exile, back then.'

'Then you *can't* go,' said Kelda.

'I'm going, Keldie.'

He was firm, and his faint revulsion was there again,

rebuking her. She wanted to stop feeling angry, but it had her in its grip now. She knew she was really just wildly afraid for Uncle Abe, but it alchemised to rage before she could get it out into words. There was nothing to do but stomp away from them across the moor until she had control of herself again.

She stomped. She realised, as she stomped, that some of the rage was for Mam: she tried, with an effort, not to think about that. There was no time. The rain hummed against her, calling her back to herself, reminding her what she was. She turned her face to the sky.

After several minutes, she stomped back again.

'When do you come of age, under old Lore?' she demanded.

The others, deep in conversation, looked up. 'Seventeen, same as now,' said Abe; while Dad, quicker on the uptake, said, 'No, Kelda.'

'Well, then,' said Kelda, '*I'm* going.'

'Absolutely not,' said Uncle Abe. Dad tried to sit up to say another more upright *no*, but this was a mistake, and he just said 'Ow' instead.

'I'm not of age. They'll kill you if they catch you. They won't kill me.'

'Only if they're keeping to the rules,' said Douglas.

'Of course they will,' said Kelda. 'They're *obsessed* with the rules. It's the only sensible option, you know it is. I'll go with Douglas to point out the right people, and he can be the one to go and speak to them. We should set out right away.'

Abe put a hand up to her elbow. 'Kelda . . .'

'What? I thought we had to rescue Firth! I thought we had to charge off and rescue everybody and save the salted day!'

'Yes, but—'

'Then let me do it. I got us this far, didn't I?' She looked at Douglas. 'Get Echo ready.' Then she looked at Dad, still crumpled in all the wrong places, and all her anger became something bigger, quieter but stronger, no longer trapped like a wild thing in her body but filling up the whole world like a steady drumbeat. She knelt beside him and kissed him. She couldn't think of anything big enough to say, so she said the only thing she could think clearly.

'I'm going to *kill* Firth if I see him.'

'Of course you are,' said Dad. He wheezed, and it might have been a laugh, or just pain. 'You're his big sister.'

18

E cho was reluctant to ride again, and wouldn't be hurried. It took Douglas and Kelda two hours before they reached the others, but when they did, it was not hard to see them. A chittering was underway, and they saw the flame of the oil lamp from a long way off. They dismounted, left Echo tied up at a bankside oak to eat and rest, and crept forward on foot.

The rain had stopped, but there were heavy clouds, obscuring the moon. As they drew closer, they moved into a thicket of trees lining the riverbank, and edged forward quietly. On the river, Kelda noticed, lines of alder boats had been left bobbing alongside the banks.

The trees thinned a frustrating distance from the chittering, and they were forced to stop. They were down-wind of the gathering, and could hear snatches of voices, but Kelda wished they could have got just a little closer.

She could see now that the ring of squatting figures was enormous, and many rows deep, but didn't seem to be everyone – and as her eyes adjusted to the torchlight of the meeting, she saw more shadows huddled in their own groups further off, attending to their own business, stretching off well beyond the available light.

She looked back to the chittering. It was Trent speaking, one of the oldest of Firth's crowd. Trent was stocky and square-faced, with hard little eyes. Kelda had never liked him much. She strained to hear.

'. . . spreading fast. The landman papers report it in all the southern and eastern waterways, and southwest across to the Tamar. True fresh water is now limited to the very upper reaches on all of these – on most of our home.' He paused. He seemed ill-equipped for the news he was delivering. 'That's all we know,' he ended, abruptly; and he doused his own oil lamp, and lit the next. 'Call on Aeron Jupp,' he added; and he disappeared back into the ring of squatting shadows. Following him with her eyes, Kelda saw him stop to relight a torch, and someone from the back ring stood to tend to another – and as they moved towards the light, Kelda saw the telltale hedgehog-hair of Firth. Her stomach squeezed. She kept her eyes on him as he crouched back down, a tiny figure between two much larger ones. So now she knew where to find him, if she wanted to.

While the torches were lit, Aeron had stepped forward.

'Thank you, friend,' he said. He seemed taller than ever, viewed from this distance; the flickering gold cut strange shapes across his long face. 'Well, brothers, sisters, we will have to keep to our safehold here in the west a while longer. The first question is food. If all households fish their fill at once we will soon bleed our sanctuary dry. I propose a delegation dives tonight, and the New Weard will oversee a coordinated—'

'We can't *fish* for ourselves now?' came a voice. Dee Marshman had stood, but she had not waited to be called. 'This is going too far, Aeron.'

'Sister,' said Aeron, 'it's only for a short time. We're fighting for our lives.'

Dee was stalking away from the circle, but Aeron didn't waver. He was so confident, so self-assured. His old earnest intensity, which had been awkward on the deck of the boat or among trees at the Humber, was finally appropriate.

Kelda was so intent on listening that she hadn't noticed Douglas move closer, and jumped when he whispered: 'Very dreamy, in fairness. Fiery preacher-boy type.'

She could *hear* the arch in his eyebrows. She was beginning to suspect that he joked most when he was most nervous, and if she had guessed correctly about his past, then this must be an overwhelming scene for him; but still. 'Shut up.'

'Flashing eyes. Tall, dark and handsome. I'd say he's a catch.'

He was breathing right against her ear, and Kelda didn't know if it was him or Aeron or fear that was making her heart gallop, and it was an altogether unnecessary diversion. 'Would you *concentrate*? They're planning to dive.'

'I sort of imagine the sea water might just turn right back round again at his handsome righteousness.'

'Shut *up*. We need a plan.'

'Well luckily, while you were raptly listening, I came up with one.' And when she turned to look, he was wearing a woollen travelling cloak. It was a shock to see him looking so silverman.

'How—?'

'It was on one of the alder boats. I reckon I can get away with going out there, if I'm quick. Have you seen anyone we can trust?'

Dee Marshman was lost to the darkness. Kelda looked at the shadow of Firth. It was hard to believe he would betray them again. But it had been hard to believe the first time.

'Just my brother.' She pointed. 'Hood down, between the two tall ones . . . see, just by the lamps? But I don't know . . .'

'A gamble.' He considered. 'Well, look, he doesn't gain anything from telling everyone you're here, does he? *You're* not a cursed child bringing unholy sickness to the waterways.' And before Kelda could comment, he added, 'Anyway, we don't have much time. Have to risk it. Give me your pendant.'

'What?'

'As a sign for him. So he knows I'm with you.'

Kelda hesitated, then untied the cord around her neck, and handed it over. 'Be careful. If he raises the alarm—'

'I'll run. I'm fast. See you.' And with that, he slipped out to join the chittering, hood up, silver in hand.

The next moments were agonising for Kelda, as she strained to see his shadow moving along the rows – then crouching by Firth – then pausing. For a moment they both seemed to be still. But then they stood, and left the circle. A couple of neighbouring listeners glanced up, but took no real interest, and soon returned to listening to Aeron. Still, Kelda stepped far back into the trees, well out of sight.

Footsteps and the snap of twigs followed her in, then Douglas appeared between the trees – with Firth.

Firth took a step towards her.

'Kelda,' he whispered, 'What are you . . . ?'

'Doing here? Rescuing you. And if you move a *finger* to give us away, Firth Pade, I swear to salt I will kill you right here.'

'Hi,' said Douglas. 'I'm Douglas.'

Firth blinked at Kelda. 'Rescuing me?'

'The weird tide's coming up the Lune tonight. You need to tell everyone to stay out of the water.' She turned to Douglas. 'There, done. We can go.'

'Kelda, wait,' said Firth, forgetting for a moment to keep his voice low. 'I'm – is Isla safe?'

Kelda just snorted. 'Come on, Douglas.'

Douglas did not come on, and Firth caught Kelda by the arm. 'Please,' he muttered. 'You have to wait, I need to tell you something. Dad – he's around here somewhere, I heard they left him to a lavellan, I got away to look for him but I had to get back before—'

'We know. We saved his life,' said Kelda, 'Douglas and me. When we had finished saving Isla's life.'

'Oh, thank the moon,' said Firth. 'Oh. Oh, thank *River*.' He took a deep, shuddering breath, while Kelda thought: *No. Thank me.* 'Mam? Abe? Everyone's all right?'

'Good of you to remember us all. Aren't you needed at the chittering? You must be on this holy new Weard?'

'I'm not of age.'

'Well, you can tell your wise leaders about the tide. Is Aeron in charge now or something?'

'It's a council of twelve,' said Firth, 'like in Old Lore. You're sure about this tide? How do you know?'

'Can't tell you.'

'What?'

'Firth, she's telling the truth,' said Douglas. 'You have to tell them. It's urgent. It'll happen at high tide tonight.'

Something in Douglas' tone got through to Firth. He looked at him as though it was a surprise to find him there, and he nodded slowly. 'Right. So . . . right. River, this is . . . I'll need a reason. To give the others. It's not like I'm a water scholar . . .'

Kelda shrugged. 'Tell them a kelpie told you. We're far enough north.'

For a moment Firth spluttered his outrage at the thought of *lying* about white-water spirits, but Kelda used one of her fiercest I-will-pummel-you looks, and it worked as well as ever. He fell silent. Then: 'It's a lot to ask them to believe,' he said. 'And besides, I'd have to have offered a sacrifice . . .'

'That's for getting a ride on one, not for prophecies.' Horse-spirits will sometimes deign to carry mortals, if you happen to have a blood sacrifice whose head you're willing to cut off. But they can talk for free – very occasionally. Firth still looked doubtful.

'Aeron will love it,' Kelda insisted. 'It's very holy warrior, I bet he's been just *waiting* for something like that to happen. Say it came to you because of your great and noble sacrifice over Isla. Or you can just let everyone dive in the saltwater if you like. There's not a lot of time left, Firth.'

Firth nodded silently. It was one of his desperate moody silences, where he seemed tied up in too many thoughts to untangle himself. But still: it was a nod.

'Go on, then,' said Kelda, jerking her head at the chittering. 'Off you go.'

'Kelda. I'm so sorry.'

Kelda said nothing. Firth stood just looking at her, staring out at her from all his tied-up thoughts. He seemed to have forgotten Douglas entirely.

Sometimes, when Kelda was in a good mood and Firth was in a staring one, she used to try and coax him back into the real world. But now she just turned to leave. She was surprised at how blank she felt.

'Bye, Firth.'

Douglas refused to leave their hiding place until they had heard Firth deliver the message. Kelda knew that every moment they lingered was rash, but deep down, she wanted to see it too. And they had been lucky, so far, and their little stretch of riverine trees was beginning to feel like a charmed place. It would surely hold them a while longer.

Firth was not a good orator, and gave his news with dismal understatement – Kelda could barely hear him. But as she had predicted, Aeron pounced on the arrival of a spirit-guide, and made a rousing follow-up speech. The whole company was all but ordered to keep to the banks until the night had passed; and the New Weard, it was declared, would convene to discuss the next move. After that the chittering dispersed, and the night beyond the trees was a mayhem of babbling voices and busy figures making camp.

Kelda was ready to leave. She had no desire to stand around looking at her own world from the outside in. But Douglas lingered, peering out at the mass of silvermen with an unreadable expression.

'Douglas,' she murmured, gently. 'It's not safe here.'

'I know. I know.' He tore his eyes away. 'Right, let's go.' He set out, hands in pockets, suddenly wildly casual. 'Has anyone ever told you, by the way,' he said, 'that you look just like your brother?'

Kelda didn't even tell him to shut up. She couldn't imagine what it must have been like for Douglas. Had there been anyone to help him, or was he cast out on his own? Had he been Isla's age? Younger?

It hurt to think of Isla; she wrenched her mind back to the present. She tried to focus on something kind to say to Douglas. 'Turns out that doesn't count for much. Family's not everything, you know – truly.'

He looked at her sharply, and she wondered if she'd been too obvious in her effort to be comforting. But all he said was, 'You seem pretty devoted to *yours*.'

And since this was true, there wasn't much else to say. Kelda wanted to be able to say *something*, or do something, to help him, and she missed Isla painfully. The two feelings merged into one, somehow.

After a moment, Douglas said, 'Let's hide out further downstream. We'll be plenty far away enough from everyone then. Just, I want to wait for the tide – someone might have missed the news – I want to see that everyone's safe.' He sensed her hesitation. 'Please. Otherwise I'll never know for sure.'

Kelda nodded. Then she realised she was doing in-the-dark-nodding at him again. Tentatively, she placed a hand on his arm. 'Sure. I understand.'

They sat on a tree branch overlooking the river's edge, a cautious distance away. Upstream, out of sight, massed silvermen watched from treeless banks.

The great tide was a wonder.

It came carrying reeds and rocks and gaping, helpless fish. It whipped the startled current into a frenzy of eddies and wavelets, whirling and lashing in wild rebellion. The river groaned with its weight.

The banks could not contain it. It spilled out on each side, churning and heaving, grasping at the earth.

It was a long time before the water calmed again, and the creatures of the Lune settled – some to bob at the surface, and some to carpet the riverbed. The midstream current flowed on, but it was empty of life.

The river was salt.

There were no cries, no shouts, no human bodies among the debris on the water. As far as they could know, everyone was safe. A song of mournful thanks rose from the banks ahead, hundreds of voices strong, brought in snatches by the wind. Kelda felt a wave of homesickness.

'All right,' said Douglas. 'Time to go. Thanks.'

'Of course.'

They dropped from the tree, and walked a few moments in silence, back towards Echo.

Kelda broke it first. 'I don't look *that* much like Firth.'

'Oh, you really do. You've both got that same fierce look. It's something in the cheekbones.'

'Fiery-preacher fierce? Are you soft for Firth too now?'

'Oh, no. The Pade fierceness is much more – practical. Soldierly.'

Kelda snorted. 'Thank you? I think?'

'I mean, you can probably keep saying thank you every day forever, seeing as I saved your dad's life.'

'Forever's a lot of days. What about when you're not around? Do I send sweet thank yous on the wind?'

'You're going up to the east end of the canal, aren't you? That's where I'm from. Inverness is right on the water – just before Moray Firth.'

'Oh!' Kelda was taken aback.

'So,' he grinned at her, 'no excuses.'

Kelda was glad. And she was glad Firth was safe, she realised. The darkness seemed kind now, and the singing in the distance was a welcome sound, despite everything.

They had left the trees behind when Kelda noticed the first tendrils of inky black in the air. They hung suspended: darker than the darkness, a blind scar across the night. She froze.

'Douglas. Look.'

'What? – *Oh*, River.'

It was coming from in front of them. They would have to retreat – back upstream – immediately.

AN EXTRACT FROM 'MICROBIOLOGY' IN:
THE WATERWAYS: ESSAYS ON A HIDDEN WORLD

....

Landman stories misclassify fuathan as water spirits. They do, after all, appear to come from nowhere, blank-faced and gossamer thin, before slipping back to nothingness. But they are certainly not spirits.

To be fair to landmen, they are not quite flesh, either.

When the water changes, so does the life it holds. Fresh and saltwater each have their own fish, and their own plants – and their own teeming microscopic bacterial world, the most powerful life, supporting the rest. This is easy to forget, but also easy to see, once you know where to look: it lies in a slick film over rocks and riverbeds, and coats the surface of still water with slime. And when a river is healthy, that's where it stays.

When the river is unhealthy, a cloudy night or a new moon can be fatal. Fuathan like the dark. The filmy coating on the water peels away, one clammy coil at a time, and the faceless creatures drift inland – hunting. The first sign of danger is the blind mist, which they exhale with every breath: outrun it if you can. If you can't, find something silver: it normally repulses them. If you can't do that: stay very still, and pray to the moon and River.

19

I t only took a few minutes for the darkness to be complete.
It made the night that had come before it seem like day.
It was so dark it pressed against Kelda's mind: it was impossible
to say which direction she had just come from, and it took all
her concentration just to keep track of where her own limbs
were and stay upright. She lost Douglas almost immediately.

She could still hear, though, more sharply than ever.
Judging by the commotion, the silvermen were here too. Either
she had run towards them, or they had run towards her, or
both; there were footsteps and cries on all sides.

Silver jewellery and trinkets and the occasional hastily-
grabbed weapon shone like stars, the only things still visible.
The lucky people who had silver were calling out for the people
they loved, trying to hold on to them; judging by the sound of
scuffles, plenty of other people were just grabbing on to the
nearest silver-holder they could find.

Kelda's hand went to her neck to untie her pendant – but
it wasn't there. It was still with Douglas. So she stood very
still, and prayed to the moon and River.

To her left, there was a cry. It was a shout of pure anguish.

Within a moment it was muffled hideously, like a fly screaming into spider silk.

Then it stopped.

Even though it was a bad idea, Kelda was running again. Twice she stumbled, her balance weak in the mist; then there was some sort of root in the earth, and she fell. From here, getting up again was unfathomable. She was very unclear what *up* would entail.

Feet pounded past her, but no one trampled her. She was lucky.

Something winked at her, a way off to – well, to *that* direction, whatever it was. Silver. Someone else on the ground, holding silver. With a concentrated effort of will, she forced her body to understand the direction it needed to go, and rolled.

To her surprise, she didn't find a warm body – only the silver. Somebody had dropped it. It was a moon-shaped pendant on a long cord: small, cold, wonderful. With her hands around it, her head cleared a little.

She stood unsteadily. It was still unfathomably dark, but she could think now. And she was a little safer.

Should she call for Douglas, hold on to him and combine their silver? But that meant raising her voice, surrounded by silvermen. It would be rash.

She heard her voice calling out anyway, before she had decided to.

'Firth? Firth Pade?'

All around her the calls continued, punctured here and there by the awful muffled screams.

'*Firth!*'

She stumbled on, calling for Firth, no longer thinking at all, not pausing for breath until she hit a tree face-first, and stumbled backwards. She steadied herself and turned away, any other way, to try again.

'Cordie!' Someone near her with a large silver arm-band on cried out: they had found their person. Kelda gathered herself, and tried again: 'Firth?'

'No, it's me,' said the voice, and there was a hand fumbling for her arm; then Kelda was being pressed against a warm chest by shaking arms.

The pendant. Kelda was wearing someone else's pendant, and this silver-banded-person was confused. *Cordie.* If only the darkness in her mind would clear, she was sure that meant something. She knew the voice, too. Instinctively, she felt glad to be near it. And she felt something else, something harder to put in words – like rain on her skin, but inside.

She could feel the voice in the man's chest when he spoke again; she could hear a heart beating too. 'We're all right,' he said. 'We're all right.' And one long hand went to her head – and stopped.

Kelda knew the answer to all her questions in one horrible, eternal second. Aeron Jupp felt down the thin, straight plait that clearly did not belong to Cordelia Elver. Then his hand went to her cheek, free of leathered skin, and he was pressing his thumb along the lines of her face, urgently, as though he could read something there.

'Kelda?' he whispered. His grip didn't loosen.

Kelda didn't say a word. She seemed to be frozen.

'Kelda. It *is* you, isn't it? How . . . ?'

She said nothing.

'Oh, Keldie,' he said, 'I'm so, so sorry this had to happen.'

Sorry, sorry, sorry. It was Firth all over again. Except that it very much wasn't.

'I forgive you, of course. You know that?'

Kelda couldn't speak. She could hardly think. And then to her horror he was kissing her, and it was nothing like her half-remembered night-time dreams. It felt how the muffled screaming around her sounded – and her heart was hammering against her chest and she couldn't breathe, but she couldn't seem to pull away either – and all she could think was that with some weak, soiled corner of her mind she had *wanted* this.

When he finally pulled away, it was as though the spell which froze her had broken. She wriggled and twisted to get away from him. He tightened his grip.

'Wait,' he said. 'Listen to me. You're not of age yet. We don't have to hurt you. You can come back to me – to us. But we have to know where Isla is. Look around you. *Look* at what's happening. For Fossy, Kelda. Where's Isla?'

Kelda couldn't get her arms free to hit him. She spat in his face.

His grip tightened. 'River, why won't you *listen* . . .'

They both felt it at the same moment: the cloying coldness of barely-there membrane. Where it touched her, Kelda's skin recoiled, and she could *feel* it trying to shrivel itself back into her body, the muscles beneath desperately contracting against the bone. The fuath began to expand, reaching out with something like limbs.

197

Kelda twisted away to slash outwards with her silver. This time Aeron did not resist. He kept an arm around her waist, but he let her turn, outwards to the fuath. It recoiled slightly at the silver, but kept trying to embrace them both. Kelda felt a webbed expanse grasp for her neck, and her windpipe tightening.

'Let me go,' said Kelda. 'We have to fight it . . . Use your silver . . .'

He let her go at last, and they both tugged at the enclosing membrane. Holding it made Kelda's fingertips shrink back against their nails so forcefully it hurt, but she didn't let go. Thanks to the pendant and Aeron's band, they were an almost-even match.

Then suddenly, it sensed easier prey behind them. With a terrible sucking noise, it withdrew. The blood rushed back into Kelda's limbs. Someone else screamed.

Kelda slashed the pendant wildly behind her, towards the source of the screaming. But then the screaming stopped, and there was nothing more she could do. She had to get away.

Aeron had already run.

Kelda ran too now, ran who-knew-where, bumping into people and trees and stumbling onwards. After a minute she found her voice again, and began croaking for Firth. She had lost all control. It felt as though her splintered mind had finally broken, and now she was just left with shards of feeling – blind panic – Firth, lost – Aeron's heart – fuath against skin – Dad, half-dead – Isla, Isla, always and always.

After a while, it seemed to be getting easier to run. It was still black, but the blackness was less unbearably heavy.

Then she realised she could *see* some of the running shapes.

She looked up. The clouds were dispersing. Around her, other running shapes were stopping to look upwards too.

Moonlight. They were safe.

After the blind mist, the great gibbous moon felt like a search light. Kelda kept running, but now with purpose, following the Lune downstream and leaving the silvermen far behind before the mayhem settled. She had no idea where Douglas was now; she had to hope he would do the same thing.

She was well away before she let herself slow to a walk. Beside her, the black surface of the Lune was newly pockmarked with riffles and eddies, its currents writhing and twisting in confusion around the new piles of debris beneath.

Kelda cried as she walked. She wished above all else that she could hold Isla. But Isla was far away, and Kelda had let her go; and she had tried to rescue Firth – and she had let Aeron kiss her – and everything was wrong. She wished she could jump into the river and get clean, clean, clean, and let it carry her away, to anywhere at all.

But the river was wrong too. So as the night dragged on relentlessly, and the embittered Lune roared past her, Kelda walked on overland, with a weary feeling that she had always been walking, and was never going to stop.

20

D ouglas must have been further downstream than Kelda when the blind mist had lifted, because he was already with Dad and Uncle Abe when Kelda arrived. And he had brought Firth.

Amid the shouts of relief at her arrival, Firth offered nervous explanations about wanting to see Dad. Kelda was too exhausted to protest. She joined in the general thanking of the moon at all of them being alive, hugged Uncle Abe, and sank down on the moor beside Douglas. It was Dad she wanted really, but he was propped up against her brother.

'I tried to find you,' said Douglas. He handed over her pendant. 'I still had your necklace. But I lost you right at the beginning.'

'I found some silver,' said Kelda. Cordelia's silver. Treacherous silver. Perhaps the kiss wasn't exactly her fault, but why hadn't she pulled away? She tied her own pendant back around her neck, gladly dropping Cordelia's in the grass.

Dad and Firth were deep in conversation again; lower, Douglas added, 'He followed me when the mist cleared – he was desperate – had things he needed to say to your dad. And there wasn't time to lose him, anyway, I was just trying to get away . . .'

'It's fine.'

'I'm sorry. I don't think he's a risk, but I'm sorry if it's hard for you.'

'I'm fine. Really.'

His eyebrows went up. 'Well, of course you are. Have you ever not been fine since Isla was born? Or were you like this before her too?'

'Like what?'

He considered, then grinned, and looked pointedly from Firth's face to hers. 'Soldierly.' He opened his satchel, and rifled through it. 'Have you ever tried chocolate?'

'No?'

He produced something wrapped in foil, peeled back the end, and snapped off a piece. 'Take some.'

Kelda took it uncertainly. It was hard, but turned slightly gooey at the surface where it met her fingers. She sniffed it: sweet.

She saw Firth looking at her in faint horror, and immediately made up her mind, and put the whole piece in her mouth.

'Oh, *salt*, that's good.'

Douglas laughed out loud. 'You look like you've seen a kelpie.' He offered the chocolate round the group. Abe took some eagerly; Firth and Dad declined.

'Douglas,' said Abe, licking chocolate off his fingers, 'you are a hero and a marvel. Chocolate! And I haven't thanked you yet,' he added, 'for saving my brother's life. That was a wonderful sacrifice you made. I'm in your debt.'

Douglas didn't seem to know what to do with this, and just nodded. When Dad and Firth joined in the thanking, he kept up the nodding for much too long, bobbing about awkwardly.

'What are your lot going to do, Firth?' he said at last, changing the subject. 'Where next?'

Firth, briefly united with everyone else in thanking Douglas, looked a little crestfallen at this reminder of his separateness. 'Scotland, I think,' he said. 'The eastern end of the Caledonian Canal. That was the back-up plan.'

'*What*?' said everyone at once; including Dad, who tried to twist round to Firth to say it, and followed this up with noises of earnest regret.

'What?' said Firth. 'Is that bad?'

'Why there?' Kelda demanded.

'It's in some of the histories. We've been studying some of the really ancient ones, trying to understand what's happening. You know the more famous ones, right, about our kind sheltering in Scotland? By the Crescent Bay . . . Aeron's been all for going there since day one, he thinks this is a sort of repeat of the blood rivers, but he only got the rest of the Weard to agree to it as a sort of plan B – if the western waterways turned bad too.'

'River and moon,' said Kelda. 'What a waste of time. It's just *stories*.' Isla was singing in her head again: *Spring tides hold sway, the Crescent Bay will turn to waters thick and red! All Caledonia, red!* Kelda felt a rising horror. That particular history had been quite specific about the need for sacrifices of the unworthy.

202

No one else spoke. Firth looked from face to face.

'Isla's there, isn't she?' he said heavily.

'Yes,' said Uncle Abe, before Kelda had time to think of a suitable lie. 'And your mam.'

Mam. Kelda wanted to tell Firth everything, to share it with the only person in the world who would hurt the same way. But Firth was already preoccupied with the news about Isla. He had put his head down on his knees, and curled up his spine, as though he was trying to fold himself away entirely.

'Why there?' he said.

It sounded more like he was pleading with the universe than really asking, but Abe answered anyway. 'A friend of ours is there,' he said. 'She shares Aeron's fascination with the old histories, although for rather different reasons.'

'Don't tell them, Firth,' said Dad.

Firth's shoulders began to shake.

'You don't have to do it. None of this is her fault – our fault. None of it.'

Firth looked up at that, and pleaded, 'How do you know?' – and Kelda was back on the deck of their own boat again, debating Isla's future at the camp fire. *How do you know?* She had never tried to answer the question, not for a second. Some people just believed the Lore, and some people just didn't. She couldn't think of anyone besides Firth who couldn't decide which way to fall; who *worried* about it all the time.

'I'm just so scared,' he said, 'that she might actually be part landman. Sorry, Dad. But I can't see how else . . .'

'She is,' said Dad.

Firth looked at him in horror.

'It doesn't matter,' said Dad. He seemed to mean it. 'She's still our Isla.'

'But then . . . it *is* her . . .'

'No; the problem's out at sea,' said Douglas. 'It's nothing on the River. There are people who know the sea well, trustworthy people – they told me. If this is in the Lore at all, it'll be the Sea Lore.'

'Really? How . . .'

'Our friend by the canal is working on it,' added Abe. 'You can meet her in Scotland, Firth. She might be able to tell you more. But you know, she probably can't prove to you either way that it isn't somehow still Isla's fault. No one can. You're never going to get a final answer.'

Firth's eyes widened with hurt at that, as though his uncle had actually kicked him. Abe spread his hands.

'At some point, Firth, you're just going to have to be all right with not being certain.'

'But we *have* to know.'

'Firth, there is no good reason on the wide waterways to think that Isla is somehow capable of sickening the water, except that somebody wrote it down once. I feel no guilt about ignoring that possibility entirely. But I don't have any proof for you. And if there was a way to prove once and for all why the River gets sick, if the big questions were all that easy, then clever people wouldn't still disagree. You're a smart boy, but you aren't going to be the one to personally discover the truths of the universe by worrying about them.'

'But . . . we can't just . . .' he began; then tried again. 'The things that are happening . . .'

'Yes. It's truly terrible. But the world has always been full of terrible things. There were terrible things before you were born, and wonderful things too, and there'll still be terrible and wonderful things when you die. It's not your fault, Firth; it's not a test.'

'I know, but . . .'

'I don't think you do. Otherwise you wouldn't always be on the lookout for something you're doing wrong. At some point,' he leaned forward earnestly, 'you *must* just accept that you *don't know*. And you might be wrong about how the world works. And you might cause bad things without knowing it. You just might.'

Firth continued to stare, as if Uncle Abe had announced that he might be a goat, and that this was just fine.

'Does it make any sense to you that Isla's existence is killing the River? Forget the Lore and your friends for a moment. Do you actually *believe* it?'

'No,' he said. It was a half-whisper. 'I've tried to, and I just can't. But if I'm wrong . . .'

'Then you're wrong. Accept it, Firth; that's the only way out.'

Firth put his head back on his knees. Kelda couldn't fathom what he might be thinking. It was like his first fish all over again. He had curled up like this then too, and she had just watched him, mystified. She remembered bringing him piles of aster drops and persuading him to eat them all, one by one, baffled that any number of them didn't seem to help.

Whatever Douglas might think, they were not alike. Firth was her oldest friend, but she still didn't understand him.

There was silence. Dad painfully put an arm around his son. Douglas passed Kelda more chocolate.

'If our lot are going,' Kelda said, turning back to things she understood, 'we have to get there first, to warn Mam and Isla. It'll be all right as long as Isla stays . . . inside.' She had almost said *in the lighthouse*, then checked herself. She found she wasn't furious with Firth right now, but he still couldn't be trusted, and now that she wasn't furious this hurt like salt.

'They'll never take the train, right?' said Douglas. 'Dirty landman ways, and besides, they'd need money. We can easily get there first by train. Let's get back to Lancaster tonight.'

'I don't know,' said Abe. 'The flooding tonight was like nothing I've ever seen. I doubt Lancaster's defences held. The line might have taken a hit.'

Douglas considered this. 'You're right. Not worth risking the lost time. If we take the Eden up to Carlisle and get the train there, we'll still be well ahead of them.'

Abe nodded. 'Murphy can't travel yet,' he said. 'I'll camp out here with him until he's well enough, then we'll follow. You can manage the trains, Douglas?'

'Sure.'

Kelda felt tired. More people peeled away. First Firth; then Judith, Peter, Mam, Isla; now Dad and Uncle Abe. It was like peeling herself away a little every time.

'Well, then. You and Kelda go on ahead. Send a telegram to Maggie from Carlisle if you can. Firth, you should get back to the others – we could use someone on the inside. Keep their trust, all right? If we see you there, you have my full permission to act terribly. We need you – we need to know what they're up to.'

Kelda looked at Firth. Uncle Abe was assuming an awful lot here. 'Are you on our side, then?' she demanded. 'Or are you going to tell them about Isla?'

In the silence that followed, the Lune was the only sound: flowing on and on, unstoppably out to its end.

Dad tightened his grip on Firth. 'Don't, son.'

'I won't,' Firth whispered. It was Kelda he was looking at. 'I promise.'

Kelda and Douglas left straight away. There was no time to lose if they were going to catch a train within the day, and Kelda couldn't have slept anyway. She hugged Dad and Uncle Abe goodbye, and they set out, Firth walking with them for the first stretch. They retrieved Echo from her oak, where she had been mercifully downstream of the Fuath; she nuzzled at them with a relief that even Kelda found touching. Then they said goodbye to Firth.

As she watched Firth walk away, in her head, Kelda began telling Isla about how they would all be fine. But she didn't believe herself at all now, so she stopped.

She and Douglas rode inland. Once they were far enough from the riverbank he turned Echo north, and they rode through the night, leaving the Lune behind.

21

They reached the River Eden in the grey before dawn, and gave poor over-worked Echo time to rest, while they caught some hasty sleep themselves. Kelda was growing used to the mare. She even patted the great muzzle in thanks. Echo whinnied indifferently, which was fair enough.

Then, when the sun was up, Douglas remounted, and Kelda slipped silverside.

There was a slight mist over the water, and the sun turned it to gold. Beneath the surface, it was liquid light. Rivers are busy with life in the morning, and the vibrations of the myriad fish mingled with the currents and danced against Kelda's skin as she swam.

The Eden, unlike most of the waterways, flows north. It isn't navigable by boat, and leads nowhere that a silverman has reason to go. Kelda had never been here.

It was not an easy swim. The riverbed was full of surprises, tumbling down in a sudden drop here or piling high with boulders there, carved here into a lurching weir by landmen, narrowing here at the banks without warning and forcing the water faster. Kelda lost herself in the joy of navigating that water. By the time the sun was strong overhead, she had passed the Eden's confluences with the Eamont and the Lowther, and the river had swelled to something mighty, and a little calmer.

She broke the surface, and called out to Douglas, who was taking Echo at an easy trot alongside her shadow.

'Breakfast?'

'*Yes.*'

It didn't take her long. She had spotted a hole in the bank, and with expert deftness she roused the sand martin inside, and whipped her eggs out. She dived back under and emerged at the other bank to find Douglas had tied up Echo and left, presumably scouting for wood.

They were in a red-stone gorge lined with hazel and sycamore. Although the overhead sun was bright now, gilding the ripples on the water, the land here was cool. Somewhere among the leaves, Kelda could hear the chitter of a woodpecker.

'The Eden's pretty nice,' she said, when Douglas returned with his finds.

He grinned. 'My favourite. Welcome. You're in white-water country now.'

Kelda wasn't sure if it was the effect of the water on her skin or the beauty of the gorge, but she could *feel* that this was true. She felt unbelievably calm, as though the night before was a bad dream; or rather, as though this was a good one.

When they had both gathered enough wood, and Kelda had found them a flat rock to fry on, and two more to spark a light, they began to build the fire.

'I love it here,' she concluded.

'Me too. I hope we're not still here if it turns. I don't want to see that.'

Kelda was taken aback. 'You think it might?'

'I think they all might.' He sat back and considered their handiwork, then reached for more kindling. 'We've got about an hour until high tide at the Eden's mouth. You should stay topside till then, to be on the safe side.'

'What makes you think it could happen?'

'What makes you think it couldn't? Whatever this thing out at sea is, it seems pretty bent on taking the whole of Great Britain so far.' He set to work grinding the rocks for a spark.

'But . . .' Kelda suddenly felt like a little child, oblivious to dangers, appalled to learn of their existence. It hadn't really occurred to her that the tides might just keep coming, even in white-water country. 'But – all of them? Then where would we go? Where would anything go? Wouldn't the landmen die too?'

The fire sparked to life. 'You've got enough on your mind with Isla,' said Douglas. 'Let's just get home. We can worry about the rivers when you don't have to worry about all of this.'

'Douglas, I'm not *fragile*—'

'No. I didn't mean it like that. It just – it won't help. And I want to hear from Peter's sister first – she might know how to fight whatever this thing is; or maybe it's already finished with us anyway.' He stretched out a hand. 'Pass the eggs?'

She passed them. 'What d'you think it is?'

'No idea. Something brackish, I guess?'

'Surely the sea is *too* salty for anything brackish.'

He shrugged. 'This is why we need to hear from Maggie. We can scratch our heads all day, but it's obviously something we've never heard of.'

'I wondered about a wyrm.'

'That's not what a wyrm does.'

'That's what Peter said. But they're pretty much just pure evil, aren't they? And I can't think of anything else that bad.'

'Well, that's very offensive to wyrms,' he said, eyebrows aloft. 'And just because we can't think of it, doesn't mean it doesn't exist.'

'That's cheerful.'

'I know. Don't tell Firth, he'll never recover.'

The eggs were soon sizzling, and they were perfect, golden and delicious. The wooded gorge was perfect too. Douglas looked fairly perfect himself as he squatted over the fire, one sleeve rolled and the other torn, red hair glorious in the sunshine. But all the perfectness was a charade. A nice dream.

'I haven't asked you yet,' said Douglas, 'in the blind mist – were you all right? I mean, you came out alive obviously, but it was horrible in there. I keep having these awful memories . . .'

Kelda was suddenly tense. 'I was fine.'

'Well, of course you were. But what happened? Did any of them get you?'

'There was one.'

'Ugh. But after you'd found silver?'

'Mm-hmm.'

'What did you have?'

211

'A pendant.'

'Huh. Not much by itself against a fuath.'

Kelda was sure her face must give everything away – that it was turning scarlet – that her lips were somehow scarred. 'Well, it was enough, obviously,' she said, far more tartly than she meant to. Douglas looked at her, surprised.

'Sorry,' she said. 'I'm – I just don't really want to talk about the fuath.'

'Fair enough. Have an egg instead,' he said, sliding one off onto a stone for her.

'Thanks.'

'You're very scary when you're annoyed, you know.'

'Well, don't be annoying.'

He laughed again. It was good to make him laugh.

'Note taken, soldier.'

By mid-afternoon the Eden swallowed the Caldew and the Petteril, swelled, and rolled into the floodplains of Carlisle. They both covered the last miles to the city on Echo as landman settlements grew, and the river turned foul. Kelda should have left the water sooner. The ache under her skin seemed to be seeping down into her muscles, weighing her down.

Kelda borrowed the stolen travelling cloak to hide her skirtless silks. The first time they passed some landmen, Douglas stopped to ask about directions for stabling Echo somewhere until their return. Kelda had forgotten about that. She was surprised to feel a little sad about it.

After the Eden valley, it was a rude shock to be in another landman city. Carlisle's streets were wide and, to Kelda's dazed brain, chaotic; the golden morning had turned into a warm day, and it felt choking in amongst the crowds. A great red chimney dominated the view, while everywhere from smaller chimneys smoke was unfurling upwards. But when the wind blew, there was an oddly sweet smell underlying it all. It put Kelda in mind of the chocolate, or the feeling of being half-awake and knowing you can go back to sleep – something sweet, and comforting.

At the livery yard, Douglas wasted no time bargaining, and agreed to a wildly high price. Kelda knew it must be high, because the yard owner looked startled, then almost ashamed as Douglas handed over the little metal coins.

'Bye, Echo,' said Kelda. 'You were very good to us. Sorry we made you work so hard.'

Echo did not show any sign she had heard, and the ostler led her away. Just like that, another goodbye. It made Kelda tired. But, she reminded herself, *this* goodbye meant that the long, long journey was almost over. She was going to Isla.

They just had to catch a train first.

The train station felt like a fortress. But she and Douglas were allowed to walk right in, and once he had handed over some coins, they had two pieces of paper that entitled them to actually sit on one of the enormous machines, and be taken all the way to Scotland – to Edinburgh first, where they would change for Inverness. Kelda felt a stirring of excitement, despite everything. She had a feeling this would be a lot better than riding a horse.

Then they went down the road to a building called the post office, where Douglas wrote out a message for the telegram to

Maggie and the others. He spent a while crossing things out and trying again, because apparently they were paying by the word, and some of the more obvious sentences he wanted to use would have cost all their money. But he finally settled on SILVERMEN YOUR WAY STOP CAREFUL STOP, and they handed over the money, and were back at the station with time to spare.

'We've got a while,' said Douglas. 'Hungry?'

He led Kelda through yet another crowd of people, to a sign saying REFRESHMENT ROOMS in bold white paint. The REFRESHMENT ROOM turned out to be a pink room with lots of little tables in it, each covered in a red-and-white chequered cloth and sporting a shorn flower in a bottle. At first they thought all the tables were occupied, but then Kelda spotted an empty one nestled in the corner.

'Tea,' said Douglas. 'Lots of tea.' So he went to hand over the last of the money, while Kelda pushed through the chairs and the chatter – which was mostly, she gathered, horrified gossip about the waterways. She sat down at the table, and watched Douglas.

He seemed at home here. It was odd – she had got used to thinking of him as one of her kind, when they were in the river valleys. Here, he was transformed by the crowds and the foreign signs and strange rooms. He was a landman again. It made her feel slightly panicky, as though he was slipping away, and might fall through the cracks into this other world and disappear.

He leaned easily on the counter full of meaningless food, chatting to the matronly woman at the till, making her laugh.

When he came back, he was carrying two impractical china cups with tea in, each on a plate with two round light brown things.

'These,' he said, as he set down the plates, 'are what you've been smelling. You're craving them right now and you don't even know it. Go on, take one.'

Kelda picked one up and bit into it. It was crumbly. It was sweet, but milder than the chocolate. It was the smell that came when the wind blew.

'Good, right? Biscuits. There's a factory here, the smell is everywhere. I can't pass through Carlisle without buying biscuits. Dunk it in the tea, it's good.'

She did. It really was.

'So,' said Kelda, 'is your house in Inverness full of chocolate and biscuits?'

'Ever heard the landman story about a gingerbread house? I live in one of those.'

'Seriously, though, what's it like?'

'Delicious. Perfect for catching unwary children in the woods. A bit sticky, though.'

Kelda folded her arms. 'Tell me properly. Is it nice? Do you miss the waterways?'

He gave her a *look*, with his eyebrows all the way down.

'What?' she said. 'Are we just not going to talk about it?'

'I was hoping so.'

'Why not?'

'But on the other hand,' he countered, 'why?'

'You really don't want to talk about it? I grew up with *Isla*. Of all people, I'll understand.'

215

Douglas reached for one of the biscuits. 'Let's talk when we get there. Deal?'

Kelda took another bite of biscuit. It was delicious. When she lived on the Caledonian Canal she would eat chocolate and biscuits at Douglas' house any time she wanted. And she would grow old with Isla, and never fight fuathan or lavellans or Jenny ever again. She might even learn to forgive Firth properly, given time, and stop feeling like there was grit against her heart whenever she thought of him. The other silvermen wouldn't stay forever, and the rivers surely couldn't just stay salted indefinitely. The journey was almost over.

She smiled at Douglas. 'Deal.'

Kelda adored the train. She sat with her nose pressed to the porthole like a child as England swept past in a wild cascade of green and became Scotland.

Whenever the train passed water, it was tumbling over rocks and knotting itself in rapids, and she felt she could have reached out and grasped a kelpie or a selkie without even trying. It took her breath away.

After a while, exhaustion blurred the world outside the window into dreams, and she was never sure afterwards which scenes were real and which were only imagined.

They arrived in Edinburgh too late to catch a train to Inverness that night. Douglas led Kelda through sloping streets of crowded soot-grey stone, to the Water of Leith – a secretive river that slipped along below high walls and huddled trees.

Kelda washed her skin, then they found a weeping willow, and curled up at its roots under the leaves.

'Will you be all right without a blanket or anything?' Kelda asked.

'Sure. It's a warm night. You?'

'I'm fine. Sorry, I should have thought of it. We could have found something warm in Carlisle.'

'It's not your job, Kelda. Relax. I'm not Isla.'

'Right.'

Kelda was exhausted, and she was normally expert at sleeping anywhere, but she couldn't seem to stop feeling fidgety. She rearranged herself into a series of positions, trying to find something comfortable, without success. It didn't help that Douglas just lay there watching her. In the end she stuck with a highly uncomfortable half-upright prop against a tree root just because she was starting to feel stupid.

'What's the canal like?' she asked, because he was still just watching, and the silence seemed suddenly like a living thing.

'Beautiful. It joins up these breath-taking lochs – you've never seen anything like it, I promise. Do you mind that you won't be part of silverman life – once all this is over, I mean?'

'Salt, no. I've gone right off them.'

'Fair. But you won't be lonely?'

'My family's there. And you'll be there.'

'True.' He smiled properly, all mouth and no eyebrows, and still he didn't look away.

The feeling of rain-on-the-inside was creeping over Kelda again. Then suddenly Aeron was in her head, running his long thumb urgently along her cheek, the memory made vivid by the surge of feeling; and she felt sick with shame. She rolled over, turning her back on Douglas.

'Good night,' she said. And she did her very best impression of falling immediately to sleep, ignoring his answering, 'Good night, soldier.'

It was only a pretend-sleep for a minute. With her eyes closed, true sleep quickly overpowered her. She was dead to the world until morning.

An extract from 'Engineering and its Effects' in:

The Waterways: Essays on a Hidden World

....

Silvermen have learned to tame water creatures, but it is only landmen who have tried to tame the water itself. As well as building their astonishing railways, they built canals. This involves channels and locks, not knots; and stone, not reeds or silver. The project has been remarkably successful in getting them where they want to go, and remarkably disastrous for the life inside the rivers, destroying the wilderness of banks and the delicate balance of life they supported.

Canals and natural waterways are now heavily intertwined. Consider the Caledonian Canal: it strings together Loch Linnhe, Loch Lochy, Loch Oich, Loch Ness and Loch Dochfour, a daisy chain of deep-blue deep-quiet blooms, before running through and alongside the River Ness at Inverness, and out into the sea at Moray Firth.

As well as canals, landmen built sea walls, which was a brave attempt. But the sea is not a river, and it can't be held with stone, or silver, or reeds. It's held in place by the moon; if this fails, nothing is stronger than the sea.

22

It was noon by the time they finally reached Inverness, a landman town of red stone and clear light. The lighthouse was still a good few hours to the east, mostly along the coast where Kelda couldn't swim. She wished they were going west instead, to the canal and its lochs; Douglas had described each one to her on the train, and the water had sounded wonderful.

Instead they found a quiet bend in the River Ness for Kelda to quickly refresh her skin. Then it was time to go.

They took a route just seaward of the occasional landman villages, threading through silver birch and fir trees and bracken. Douglas insisted on walking with her until the lighthouse was in clear view. Then he insisted, equally firmly, on letting her reunite with Mam and Isla alone.

'They'll want to see you!' she protested.

'I'll come this evening.'

'Why not come now?'

He shrugged. 'They're not *my* family. It's not right if I'm there.' And he wouldn't hear otherwise. 'See you tonight. I want to head home first anyway.'

'Where *is* home?'

'Just back along the way we came. I'll show you tomorrow.'

And then their goodbyes were said, and it was just Kelda, alone. For a moment, it felt as though she might just float apart.

The sea spread out to her left. The firth was a cruel steel-grey that day, and it rocked and rolled itself in the way that lakes never did, with the strange, indifferent life of the ocean. Kelda watched it with a fascination tinged with horror. It was all too easy to believe tales of blood and sacrifice, here.

The lighthouse stood on a promontory, and as Kelda followed the curve of the land she took a path right down to the shore, through gorse and broom and sorrel, then over tufty dunes onto a small desert of stark white sand. The horror quickly overtook the fascination, this close to the sea. She hated the way the waves kept hurling themselves closer, then writhing back again. They left thin silver outlines where they had fallen, like a threat. She tried not to look, and hurried to the lighthouse.

It was a peculiar structure, even by landman standards. Kelda suspected it was peculiar even by *lighthouse* standards. It had all sorts of instruments sticking out from its red-and-white sides – some she knew, like the barometers and weathervanes, but others were a mystery. But Maggie had grown bindweed round the door, and it made her smile to see it. She rapped the knot-carved knocker.

There were footsteps, and the door was opened by a woman who looked exactly like Judith, if Judith had been stretched out with a rolling pin. She was dressed in a pinstriped skirt over a pinstriped blouse, which made her look even longer than she was.

'Yes?' she said.

'Hello,' said Kelda, slightly wrong-footed. Maggie Parson didn't smile like Judith. She didn't smile at all. 'Er, I'm Kelda. Kelda Pade.'

Maggie looked left, then right, then peered at Kelda's face. 'You look like your mam,' she said – thoughtfully, as though this was an interesting argument she was considering. Then, while Kelda was still wondering what to say to this, she said: 'Come in, then.'

So Kelda stepped inside. Maggie shut the door, and the awful crashing of the sea was instantly muted.

It took Kelda's eyes a moment to adjust to the gloom, but when they did, things didn't make much more sense. She appeared to be in a round room lined with metal circles and cylinders and wheels, with a spiral staircase rising from its centre. Maggie was already clomping away up these stairs, so Kelda followed.

She had never climbed a spiral staircase before. It was an odd sensation – like her brain was forever one step behind reality, running to reorient itself.

They passed more gloomy rooms piled high with instruments, books and dust, before reaching a bright little brick galley, lined with portholes that looked out over the sea. At the stove, her back to them, was Mam. The whole place was thick with a smell Kelda hadn't smelled in six years: bitter chowder.

'Is this Kelda?' Maggie demanded.

Mam spun, and her hands flew to her mouth. Then she threw herself on Kelda, and held on tight, her breath too shaky to speak.

'Mam?' said Kelda. 'What is it? What's wrong? Why are you making chowder?'

She felt Mam do one of her settling-breaths, the big inhale she did when she was putting her feelings away in a little box and steeling herself to keep going. But she didn't let go of Kelda. 'They're here,' she said. 'Our lot. We didn't know – we got your telegram too late.'

'What happened?'

'Peter went out for herbs, and Isla slipped out to follow him, I didn't know . . . and our lot . . . they've taken them.'

Kelda drew back from Mam's hold, as though it was the hug that was forcing this news on her. 'They've – what? Is Isla – why are you making chowder?'

Mam shook her head, and kept shaking it. 'No. She's alive. Firth came to see us last night. They're planning some kind of ritual sacrifice tomorrow night – they're waiting for the spring tide – like in the blood rivers history. Firth says a few of them came up here to see their precious Crescent Bay, and they found them on the way . . .'

'But they were on the Lune two nights ago,' said Kelda. 'It's not *possible*.'

Mam looked over at Maggie. But Maggie was looking out of the porthole – not as though she wanted to avoid the moment, but as though she was genuinely more interested in the sea.

'Well,' said Mam – then, 'maybe sit down.'

Kelda ignored this. 'What? What happened?'

'They summoned kelpies,' said Mam. The smell of chowder was overwhelming. It was the heady smell of summer herbs, of the terrible and the wonderful and the unknowable, of the gates of life open at both ends.

Kelda heard her own voice: 'Who was the sacrifice?'

'A search party found your dad and uncle on the Lune,' said Mam. 'They've brought Dad with them for the ritual up here. They killed Abe.'

After this announcement, the chowder continued to bubble, and the distant sea continued to roll, and the lighthouse continued to stand, and Kelda continued to breathe. So it couldn't be true.

Mam kept talking. She had her business voice on, but was speaking slightly too fast, wound up too tight. 'Judith got here yesterday. She's keeping watch on our lot – she's been taking it in turns with Maggie – they're back west, by one of the freshwater lochs. We're going to try and get Isla and Dad out, of course. We've got until the spring tide tomorrow night, when our lot are expecting saltwater – which Maggie says *will* actually happen, she's a sort of sea scholar, I don't understand it all . . . Anyway, they think it's going to all culminate there, like with the blood tides in the Caledonia histories, and they think that's the time to – to sacrifice . . .' Mam couldn't finish this thought, so she took a sort of gulping breath, then restarted. 'Firth should be back with news for us later, then we'll try and get them out when it's dark. So for now, I'm . . .' and here Mam suddenly faltered, as though a stray emotion had snuck in, and she gestured instead to the stove and the table. Reeds were waiting for a casket; Mam had already neatly plaited some. The misplaced fury rose up again in Kelda.

'Abe doesn't believe in this, any of this,' she said. 'This is stupid. We should be *doing* something.'

'We will. But we can't march up to them in daylight, Kelda – they'll overpower us easily, and that will be the end of it. There's no one else to rescue Isla. We only get one chance.'

'I can't believe you've been sitting around plaiting casket reeds. What's the point? We don't even have his body.' *Because*, said the feeling deep in her gut that told her how the world was, *he isn't dead*.

'We'll do an empty casket.'

'What, like he's been mer-sick or something? A hollow death?'

Mam just nodded. Kelda almost slapped her.

And then a moment later they were holding each other in a crushing hug instead, and Kelda wasn't sure how it had happened, but all her anger was gone, and she was clinging to Mam like an infant; and Mam was clinging back, just the same.

'I'm so sorry,' Mam whispered. 'I'm so so sorry. About all of it. My little love. It's far too much.'

23

The worst thing was that there really was nothing to do until dark. Mam vented this on casket-weaving, but Kelda couldn't, because that meant giving up the certainty that Abe was alive. Instead her thoughts prowled restlessly around the question of Isla. She quizzed Mam endlessly on what had happened, and Mam answered, the same small answers over and over again.

Maggie had gone out shortly after Kelda arrived, and she returned an hour or so later with more reeds in her arms for Mam. Kelda turned round in her chair, eager for fresh answers.

'Mam says the water's turning to salt here? Are you sure? Is there anything we can do to stop it?'

'I'm not sure about *anything*,' said Maggie simply. 'Here, Lyn, I hope these will do. I couldn't find any canary grass . . .'

Perhaps Maggie didn't understand. 'If it turns at the spring tide they're going to throw Isla and Dad in,' said Kelda. 'And who knows what they'll do to Peter . . .' Kelda didn't want to know what treatment this so-called Old Lore would sanction for an interfering landman. 'So,' she said, 'if we *can* stop it . . .'

Maggie nodded. Her face was impassive, but the long

untidy curls escaping her upswept hair had their own expressions – a sort of melancholic waving and drooping as she moved. She *must* feel something for her brother – and, Kelda realised, her niece. But all she said was, 'Yes. I know. Would you like me to tell you what I've worked out?'

'*Yes.*'

'Not,' added Maggie, after a thoughtful pause, 'that it's necessarily going to help.'

'I want to know anyway.'

Maggie nodded again, and put the bundle of reeds down on the table. For a moment she seemed to be distracted by the view of the sea, but then her eyes wandered back to Kelda. 'Follow me, then.'

So Kelda stood, and followed Maggie down the spiralling stairs to the ground floor, the room of circles and cylinders and wheels. With each corkscrew turn they seemed to unravel the room upstairs a little bit more, until it was almost possible to believe that Kelda had dreamed it. Here the smell of chowder was replaced by the much more sensible smell of polish, and something mildewy that gave her an itch to start cleaning immediately.

'Tide predicting machines,' Maggie said, gesturing to the strange cylinders and wheels. 'They work out when the tide is coming in at any given coast. I've adjusted some of the parameters to try and account for the brimghast.'

'The what?'

'That's what's out there. Brimghast. And if I've understood it right, it'll be taking the water up here at the spring tide, when it has the most momentum – it's saved the strongest waters for last. So unfortunately your lot will be proved right, but it's certainly not Isla's fault.' She had gone to a shelf at the wall, and brought down a slim, pocket-sized book bound in blue leather, which she held out to Kelda. 'Here. I've copied up everything that's left of the Sea Lore, from all the different scraps. It's not a lot.'

Kelda took the book, and leafed through it. The first dozen pages were full of Maggie's slanting handwriting, but most of the book was blank.

'You need the passage on brimghasts. Third page,' said Maggie, pulling up stools for them both. 'Some of it's missing, but here's what we know. They're a kind of sea spirit – *brim* is sea, *ghast* is spirit – really, they *are* the sea. A piece of the sea that's remembered itself, and started to have its own ideas. It's rebelling. I think this particular brimghast must remember being groundwater here, because it seems intent on taking the whole island back. It's been snaking around us for weeks now – they can grow tremendously long. Right now I believe it's stretched around most of the British coast.'

'You mean it's wrapped itself around the whole island?'

'That's right.'

So this was the 'beast' mer-sick Mari had told Douglas about, in the Mercy Cave. She hadn't been exaggerating. 'It wants *all* of the waterways?'

'Yes.'

'This is why the River's been sick?'

'It's why we've had the tides. And it's keeping up the push back against the current, so the saltwater isn't flushing away like it should. But if you mean the infestations all season – well, it hasn't helped to have it lurking around, but the low water levels haven't helped either, and all the rubbish being dumped by our lot in the rivers. There's more than one way to starve a river of oxygen – these things are never straightforward, you know.'

This wasn't the kind of answer Kelda wanted. She wanted it all to be the brimghast. She wanted to be able to point at the thing that wasn't Isla, and say, '*There.*'

'Of course,' Maggie went on, unhelpfully, 'it gets even *more* tangled, because the brimghast was very likely provoked into wakefulness in part by precisely those changes to the waterways – from what I can understand of sea spirits – so there isn't a neat causal line. More of a scribble, really. Have you found the passage yet?'

Kelda shook her head. She had stopped turning pages, enthralled by the tantalising promise of a proper explanation, albeit a messy one – pollution and oxygen and oceans, not blood purity and sacrifice. But she pulled her attention back to the book now, turning to the third page. There wasn't much text, but there *were* pictures of knots, with strange tiny faces at the ends.

'Oh!' – she had never expected to find knot guides in this strange book. 'They can be held?'

'Yes, in theory. You have to provoke them into condensing themselves down into something smaller first. Turn to the back, there should be some paper there . . .'

Kelda turned, and unfolded a piece of paper that had been tucked inside. It took her a moment to understand what she was looking at. She had never seen a map of the world before.

She scanned it for the familiar shape of the British Isles, but none of the great land masses looked right.

'We're here,' said Maggie, pointing at a tiny blob, with her first half-smile. 'And these,' she stabbed at crosses in the middle of the oceans, 'are bound brimghasts.' The crosses had names, in miniscule writing: *Saltstraumen. Moskstraumen. Naruto.* 'When they're near the surface we landmen know them as maelstroms, or whirlpools – they're only a danger now to any ships daft enough to cross them. That one there, off Scotland, that's Corryvreckan – the last one to come near us.'

'And it was bound?'

'Yes. You probably know the story of that? Though there's a lot of nonsense in the silverman versions, with the rivers turning to blood and so on, and the role of Sea Weards has been written out entirely in favour of a nice uncontroversial sacrifice. Anyway, its final attack was here, this is Crescent Bay – this was the traditional seat of the Sea Weard, you know, because it's the strongest coastal water – the last line of defence. So it was the last place the Corryvreckan brimghast attacked, before it was chased away by the Sea Weard and ended up being bound out west. And it looks like it will be the last again this time – as soon as there's a spring tide in this ghast's favour.'

Kelda half-listened to this; she was really only interested in the knowledge that this thing could be stopped. 'What are they bound with?' she asked. 'Silver?'

Maggie shook her head, her curls swaying in a hundred tiny, wistful little *no*s. 'The first stanza of the Sea Lore begins: Only the moon or the sea can bind the sea.'

'Then . . . what are the knots?' said Kelda, turning back to the page.

'Well, quite. The very question that has occupied me, ever since the first signs of trouble.' Maggie leaned forwards. There was a dull flicker somewhere behind her impassive eyes, a spectre of enthusiasm that made her look suddenly like Peter. 'And I've solved it. The brimghast of Corryvreckan has knotted *itself*. The sea has bound the sea.'

Kelda looked at the pictures of knots, with the tiny howling faces. 'But how do you . . . ?'

'Wyrms.'

'Er,' said Kelda. 'What?'

'Look at the knots. Look at the faces on them. This one I think is the brimghast, but these . . .' She pointed at the faces with long-fingered stabs, her hair enthusiastic in its bobbing now. 'These two look like the pictures of wyrms in the River Lore. And they're sea beasts, too, of course. My idea was, you have to get a wyrm to dance the brimghast into knots. So I went to find the wyrm at Loch Morar.'

'*What?*'

'Unfortunately,' said Maggie, 'it's a grumpy old git. Wouldn't tell me a thing for free. But I sacrificed a seal, and for that it at least told me I was correct.'

'You talked . . . to a wyrm?' This was, famously, a stupidly dangerous thing to do.

'Well, I talked to the landform, not the waterbeast – tiny old man, massive beard. And I was lucky, because it turns out it's practically dead, and in no fit state to attack anyone. Anyway. The brimghast can be bound, if you happen to know

231

a friendly wyrm. They have to attack it, goad it into following them. Dangerous job.'

'Could we – could we sacrifice to the Morar wyrm?' Sudden visions of tit-for-tat justice crowded Kelda's mind. She could think of some people she would willingly sacrifice. For a moment Uncle Abe's death was abruptly, howlingly real to her, and she had to pull herself back to the matter at hand with an enormous effort of will. Then the moment passed, and it was utterly untrue again.

'From what I could gather,' said Maggie, 'there isn't a sacrifice on this earth that would induce it to have a go. The Maree wyrm seems to be dead. I'd heard rumours of a new one at Ness, but I visited the only island on the loch, right out southwest, and it won't even come out for a talk with me.' She sighed. 'I believe it's because I'm not the Sea Weard.'

'You're not?'

'No. Look at the front – very first page.'

Kelda flipped, and read: *This is the book of the Sea Lore, entrusted to the Weard of the Sea, who shall be two in number and inhabit all dominions.*

'I only inhabit land,' said Maggie. 'A landlubber like me can set up home at the old Sea Weard seat, and set knots on the sea walls and tinker with tide machines, but it doesn't make me the true Weard. I can't compel a wyrm.' She said this heavily, and Kelda might normally have wondered how long it had taken her to reach this conclusion, and felt sorry for her; but she was thoroughly distracted.

'But that's Isla,' she said. 'And Douglas, my friend Douglas.' She spilled his secret without even noticing, she was so overtaken with excitement. 'They're two in number. And they inhabit land *and* river. Do you think Isla's meant to be the next Sea Weard?'

'No,' said Maggie. 'Nobody's meant to be the next Sea Weard – somebody killed off the last one sometime in the twelve-hundreds.'

'Right, but maybe it's *meant* to be revived again now . . .'

Maggie tutted, curls bobbing in agitation. 'Abe always said that you were the clear-headed one, Kelda. Don't be daft.' If it bothered her to mention Uncle Abe, she didn't show it. 'Nothing is *meant* to be anything. But is Isla *capable* of being the next Sea Weard? I've wondered that myself. The only way to know is to try, I suppose.' She had her looking-at-the-sea face on as she studied Kelda now. 'There's another one like her, you say?'

'Yes. Douglas. He's coming tonight. We can ask him to go – go and talk to a wyrm.' Kelda felt like Mam, furiously plaiting reeds; but it was all inside her, all that frantic movement. 'And then we can stop the salt coming – and if we can get Isla and Dad out in the meantime – and then . . .' But 'and then . . .' was a step too far for her imagination. All she knew was that there was something, something she could be doing with the awful night ahead that wasn't sitting around breathing in the chowder.

'All right,' said Maggie.

'*All right*' brought Kelda up short. Normally people protested that her plans were too dangerous. She could have handled that, or enthusiastic agreement; but 'all right' was astonishingly indifferent.

'All right? D'you mean – do you think it will work?'

'Well, it's unlikely. It's only a guess. And even if it's the right guess, we're missing all the information we need about how a Weard goes about compelling a wyrm. But it can't hurt to try.'

'But we have to be right! There's no *time*!'

Maggie considered Kelda for a long moment. 'Kelda,' she said at last, 'I think it's the best we can do. I think we may as well. I think if we don't do anything, Britain will lose its river water, and once the groundwater guards fail too, it will be well on its way to a quick and horrendous death. So yes, I think we should do it. But I'm not going to make you any guarantees.' She took the book back from Kelda, and closed it. She looked as though she was searching for the right words. 'I'm sorry,' she said, 'if you need reassurance. I know I'm not terribly good at that. But Kelda, there *are* no guarantees.'

Kelda *did* need reassurance. She had needed it ever since she had arrived, and been hugged by Mam like she was silver in a blind mist. So she just stared at Maggie, mute, turning her eyes in a desperate appeal to somebody older and wiser.

'Come on,' said Maggie, standing. 'Your mam needs you.'

So Kelda stood.

At the foot of the stairs, Maggie turned back.

'You see,' she said, 'when you've spent your life studying the ocean, it's difficult to pretend humans are in charge of anything. I've forgotten how to make *myself* believe it, I'm afraid, never mind other people. I'll do what I can to help you, Kelda; but I can't do that.' She put an awkward hand on Kelda's arm, patting it gingerly, as though she had forgotten how people were meant to touch each other. 'I'm sorry.'

An extract from 'White-water Spirits' in:
The Waterways: Essays on a Hidden World
....

White-water spirits are summoned by finding their home islet on the river or lake where they live, mixing a drop of your blood with the water, and calling for them. Once they have been summoned, asking them for help is a more complicated matter.

A selkie, the seal shape-shifter, can grant small favours of healing or information, and is the friendliest of the spirits. If you are trying to get help from a selkie you could sacrifice a bird, or maybe a rabbit; but it's also worth just asking nicely, on a good day.

For a water-bull, sacrifice a sheep or goat. They are not bright, but they are honest, and strong, and really very enthusiastic about dead sheep.

Kelpies, the horse-spirits, require human sacrifice for almost all favours – preferably, for their own obscure reasons, headless. They are merciless, but they are at least dependable, being always merciless according to the same rules.

Wyrms – known also to landmen as uilebheists, knuckers, water-dragons, beithir, or loch monsters – are much less predictable. If they don't feel like helping you, there is every possibility they will hurt you instead. If you should ever need to summon a wyrm, the general advice is: don't.

24

Judith returned. Her smile was gone, and she looked somehow rubbed out. She and Kelda hugged tightly, but it wasn't comforting; fear hugged fear, fear for a sister and fear for a brother. Kelda pulled away with a sick feeling in the pit of her stomach.

Judith had no more news, except that some silvermen had stopped to quiz her, and she thought it would be wise for them to all hide out and wait for more information from Firth now. She went to wash; Maggie had wandered off to tinker with her tide machines; and Mam and Kelda were left alone to plait reeds.

It still wasn't real to Kelda that the casket was for Uncle Abe, but the rhythm of the reeds against her palm and the nearness of Mam was a real and steadying thing. She wanted to lean on Mam and cry – but she also wanted to shout and rage at her, and storm out, and never see her again. So even that was wrong.

For a while they worked in silence: through, tug, round, under. Through, tug, round under. Then, with sudden forceful desperation, Kelda said, 'Mam . . . '

Immediately, Mam put her reeds down. She had clearly been waiting for this. 'Your dad told you why we argued.'

'Yes.'

'Kelda, I'm so sorry.'

'He told me to tell you *he*'s sorry. I forgot. He said he's sorry about the things he said, and he loves you.'

Mam's eyes widened, and for a moment she didn't seem able to speak. Then she recovered her composure. 'And you?' she said. 'Are you . . . angry?'

Kelda had hardly had space to think about it, but she knew the answer. 'I'm angry that you didn't tell us. That feels – it makes all of it feel like a lie. All my memories of the family.'

Mam nodded, one time too many, then said quietly, 'It was wrong of me to hide it. I was very afraid of losing your dad. But – it was wrong.'

She was doing her pale-and-patient saintly bit again, and Kelda wished she would stop. It made her feel that there was a whole real Mam behind it, who she would never be allowed to meet. 'Do you love Peter?' she asked.

'No,' said Mam, without hesitation.

'Then what were you *thinking*?'

Mam gripped her hands together very tightly. 'Well, we'd had a big fight – me and your dad – the worst we'd ever had. He'd been missing for a few weeks, and I didn't know if he was coming back, and . . . and when he did, he said he thought he wanted us to separate. It was . . . Abe persuaded me to go away to Camberley with him, so that you two wouldn't see the state I was in. And to give your dad time to think, he said.' Mam's hands were twisting and twisting in her lap. 'So I went away, and . . . well. The point is, when, I came back, your dad said he'd changed his mind. He was so sorry. He wanted me after all. And I couldn't tell him what had happened. I *couldn't*.'

Instinctively, Kelda put a hand on top of both of Mam's, to stop the desperate twisting.

'I'm not proud of it, Kelda,' said Mam. 'It was a moment of weakness, and the biggest mistake of my life. Although I don't regret Isla.'

'Of course not.'

'But I regret hurting your dad, very much. And I know it's been tricky sometimes on the boat, and you've done so much for Isla, things I should have done. I . . .'

'It's fine.'

'No, it's not. I've just felt so . . . Well, that doesn't matter, it's no excuse. But now there's no secrets. If your dad can forgive me, we can start again. If *you* can forgive me. For all of it.'

Kelda looked down at her reeds, and blinked several times. She wasn't sure why she was crying. She had never thought that she needed an apology for raising Isla.

'You don't want Peter, then?' she said at last.

'No.'

'You did once.'

'Well, yes, he's very – he's nice. But it's all of you I really want – really *need*.'

Kelda nodded. She could understand both these things being true at once. There was suddenly another stupid irrelevant embarrassing thought bulging in her head, and she didn't even want to talk about it, and certainly not *now* of all times; but the welling urge to say it was taking up so much space that in the end she blurted it out quite abruptly.

'Aeron Jupp kissed me and it was – I feel strange about it.'

'*What?*' said Mam. 'When?'

'In the blind mist. He thought I was Cordelia at first. And then he knew I wasn't, and he kissed me. I didn't want him to. But I didn't stop it. And I'd – thought about it, before.'

'If I ever get my hands on that boy, he is getting a *slap*. Is he quite finished hurting my children?'

'The thing is,' said Kelda, 'I . . . sometimes when I look at him, I feel . . .' *Like rain on the inside*, said her brain. She hung her head, blushing furiously. 'I don't *want* to be Aeron's love-match.'

'Then you're not,' said Mam, 'and that's that. I didn't raise you to be soft, Kelda. A feeling's just a feeling. You're sensible enough to know a feeling that you can't help doesn't tell you anything about him, or about you.' She spoke very firmly, but there was a gentleness in the way she squeezed Kelda's hand. 'I can't believe he had the *nerve* to kiss you, after all he's done. No wonder you didn't stop it, you must have been in total shock.'

Kelda took a deep breath in, and let go of a little knot of worry that had been tied up inside her, so small and quiet under everything else that she hadn't even been able to name it until now. But it felt wonderful to untie it. She breathed out, and felt a little lighter.

'Thanks, Mam.'

And Mam didn't ask if she was forgiven, and Kelda didn't

say. But they both went back to their plaits, and now, Kelda didn't want to rage any more. She just wanted them all to have time – time to relearn how to love each other. Without any more running away, and without any more tragedy.

The two of them were plaiting in rhythm now, and their reed casket grew steadily larger, as the light faded outside.

Kelda had expected Douglas before dark, but the portholes turned black, and he hadn't come. About an hour after the lamps were lit, it struck her that he was eligible for death too, if her people had found him. After that, she could hardly plait straight.

There was a knock on the door, and her heart lifted; but it was Firth. Which was, at least, something else to think about. Maggie plied him with tea, and he told them what he knew.

'We've got a dozen guards on them at all times,' he said. 'And patrols spaced out along our shore of the loch keeping an eye out, and everyone else is nearby. There's no point attacking there, they'll just take you too. But I think we'll have a chance at the sacrifice itself. They'll be putting Dad and Isla in boats, one guard each. I'd attack then – maybe out at sea if you can get a boat? I'll do what I can – they're not letting me guard them, but I'll keep close . . .'

Everyone nodded, digesting this. It wasn't much of a hope.

'Did you tell them about the Sea Lore? The brimghast?' asked Maggie.

'Yes. Some of them were interested. But some of them were furious that I was deviating from the official line. I know it's got a lot of them thinking, but I definitely haven't won

240

everyone over. And I'm not sure they bought my story about remembering it suddenly – which is fair enough.' He took a long gulp of tea. 'The Weard have had me out on patrols all day, nowhere near camp. I don't think they trust me now.'

'If I can stop it happening – if we can stop the brimghast,' said Kelda, 'do you think that would win them over?'

'Is that possible?' said Firth, wide-eyed.

'Yes. Maybe. I don't know. But do you think you could talk to them – say that if the tide doesn't turn, they should let them go?'

'I'm in tinged water already,' he said. 'But a lot of people aren't that happy with what's happening. If the saltwater didn't come . . . I think I could force a chittering then, at least. You really think it can be stopped?'

'I hope so.' Kelda didn't know. She wished Douglas would come.

Mam put an arm around Firth. 'I wish we could keep you here.'

Firth just stared into his tea cup. He looked only half-there, as though the travel by kelpie had only half-worked.

'What's it like, summoning a spirit?' Kelda asked. She knew the mechanics, but had no idea what to expect next.

'Awful. Awful. Riding here was – they just moved hundreds of us each. It was like being blown apart on the wind and put together again. And the feeling doesn't go away. It makes you feel like you're just *nothing*.'

This was not exactly comforting. Kelda regretted asking. She leaned against him, head on top of his. 'Did you see . . . when Abe . . .'

'No.'

'Ah.' Kelda was glad.

'It was Aeron and that. They didn't even hold a chittering. I didn't get a chance to even see him before – before they . . .'

Without thinking about it, Kelda put an arm round him. This made him breathe in sharply, as though it hurt him. When he breathed out again, it was all in urgent words and tears.

'I'm so sorry – about testifying. So sorry. Aeron had all that proof, from the other case like her – and he and Cordelia had done that thing with the barrel so they already had two to testify, and they wouldn't leave me alone, listing everyone who got sick this year and everyone who's been attacked and going on about all these histories where people betray the waterways . . .'

Kelda couldn't say that it was all right, so she just squeezed a little tighter, and said, 'You don't believe them any more, do you?'

'I don't believe anything. There's just – it's like there's fog in my head.'

'Wait' – Kelda drew away – 'what does that mean? Are you saying you still aren't sure?'

'Kelda,' said Mam, 'We've all—'

'No,' said Firth, 'that's not what I mean. I mean I've stopped trying to know. It's like Abe said: I can't know, I just have to choose. And they killed Abe so – I choose us. I can't help it.'

And although tears rolled down his face more than ever as he said this, he said it with utter steadiness. Kelda subsided again. He *was* helping them, so that was a start. She still didn't understand him, but it felt right to have him next to her again. Maybe *she* could just choose *him*, too, and choose to try and mend the family – if Isla survived.

And Douglas.

'They haven't taken anyone else prisoner, have they?' she asked.

It took him a moment to process the question. 'What – since we've been here, you mean?'

'Mm.'

'Not that I know, but I've been out on patrols. Why?'

'No reason. Forget it.'

She went back to waiting. When her little brother leaned against her again, she didn't push him away.

Firth slipped away, and Douglas didn't come. The casket was finished, and Douglas didn't come. Maggie went to bed first: Judith and Mam waited with Kelda for a while longer.

'I think we should try and sleep,' said Mam at last. 'I'm sorry, Keldie.'

'What if they've taken him?'

'We don't have any reason to think that, dear,' said Judith. 'There are a hundred other possible reasons. Your mam's right. Let's sleep.'

Further up the spiral staircase, Mam and Judith showed Kelda another squishy mess of fabric in a tiny circular cell of bricks, with one of the cotton dresses laid out on it. She sat down on it obediently, knowing perfectly well that she wasn't going to stay there, because if she did she would go entirely insane.

Their footsteps continued upwards, to their own beds. Kelda gave them ten minutes to fall asleep.

Then she crept down the dizzying spiral; paused in the galley to pocket Maggie's sewing needle; paused again in the room of tide machines, took the blue book, and tucked it safely in the sealskin pocket inside her fly-silks, where it would be safe from water; then crept out of the lighthouse door into the night.

25

She hurried along the shore of the firth. If Douglas wasn't coming, she would have to try speaking to the wyrm herself, and just hope it might come for a silverman more readily than for Maggie. And, of course, that it wouldn't try and kill her. Tomorrow night would be too late.

She half-ran, but still it seemed a lifetime stumbling awkwardly overland. As soon as the water was fresh in the River Ness, she slipped in, and kicked off at full speed.

The river widened into a pool of stillness at Loch Dochfour. The water here was cold and black. Kelda swam on. Dochfour narrowed, then gaped open like a wound into Loch Ness.

Here the coldness and blackness was indefinably, but emphatically, worse.

It was hard to say why. Maybe the vastness – she could feel, without needing to be told, that the loch's bed was horrifically far below her, and that the water waited around her in enormous stillness for miles. Or maybe it was the peat in the water, which clouded her vision and her skin. But none of that quite explained the sense of dread, or her sudden certainty that Uncle Abe was drifting alongside her, dead, and that every ripple of the water was Dad heaving a long painful breath into his battered body, and that somewhere Isla was crying, calling and calling for a sister who didn't come.

Kelda broke the surface with a gasp. The wide-open sky above was astonishingly heavy with stars. To her left, on the water, lay a stripe of silver from the almost-full moon, and it seemed to beg her to swim up it, all the way across to the bank, and out of the wyrm-infested emptiness.

She steeled herself, and dived back under.

Maggie had said the island was at the southwest of the loch, and Kelda had come in at the northern end; it took her the best part of two hours, pointing like an arrow through the water and pressing ahead at top speed. She kept close to the western shore, surfacing cautiously at intervals to get her bearings. The towering black hills gave her little to go by: only a ruined castle allowed her to gauge how far she had travelled. But at last, the shadow of an island was visible ahead.

When she reached it, she found it was rooted to the loch's depths by great wooden spars. It was a crannog, then – an island made by landmen. For a moment she hung suspended beside it, marvelling. Even in these desolate waters, landmen had insisted on carving out a world for themselves.

Then she drifted topside, and pulled herself up on to the island.

It was a little scrap of grassy land, with straggly conifers, and nothing else. On all sides, the water kept watch.

Kelda looked up at the smeared mass of stars, and gave her

skin a moment to recover from the unholy water. After a minute, she felt steadier, although her legs shook with the exhaustion of her journey.

She knelt at the water's edge, and took out the needle. She pricked her finger, and trailed it in the loch. It was absurdly little blood for a place this size. *All* her blood would still be absurd. And what if the wyrm wasn't here – if it was out at sea? Would it still hear her?

'Wyrm of Loch Ness,' she whispered, 'Kelda Pade begs to talk with you.'

This was answered by silence and stars. Kelda was just wondering whether to try again, when the loch erupted.

A column of water soared above her head, and for one brief moment, Kelda could make out the twisting black shadow of the wyrm inside it. Then it spun in a swift motion that felt something like the spiral staircase, and the sky around it filled with the same silvered light that the peg-a-lantern had cast, picking out every droplet of water in frozen, blinding clarity. Kelda thought she saw the shadow rear as though to strike, but had to look away from the searing light –

– and when she looked back, the light was gone, the water was thundering back into the loch, and the great shadow was collapsing in on itself, forming something human on the bank.

The something scurried behind a tree. It was hard to be sure, and Kelda's eyes were still reeling from the light, but she had the impression it was tugging on trousers.

Then it came out again, and took a step closer.

'Kelda Pade,' it said, 'I know you're brave, but even for you, this is truly insane.'

Kelda just stared at him, mouth open. He raised his eyebrows in greeting.

'Good to see you too, soldier.'

26

There was a long, long silence – apart from the sound of the loch, which continued to lap calmly against the crannog banks. The stars watched on, impassive. On their little scrap of land, nothing stirred.

'You're . . .' Kelda tried.

'A wyrm. Yes,' said Douglas. 'You know the ones – "pretty much pure evil."' He was grinning as he said it, but not quite looking at her.

'I didn't mean . . . I didn't know.'

'Well, of course not. And you weren't exactly wrong. River, Kelda, summoning a wyrm? I so nearly attacked you just then before I could pull myself together – we're not rational, not in that form, we're *dangerous*.'

She was hardly listening. She just stared. It seemed as though some of the silvery light was *inside* him now, although it was fading fast. And there was something wild about his eyes, something raw, which was taking longer to disappear. Also he still didn't have a shirt on, and she didn't quite know where to look, and it was disconcerting to be embarrassed about torsos when confronted with a wyrm.

He kept talking, too much, more wildly casual than she had ever seen him, looking everywhere but at her. 'Sorry I didn't come for dinner. This place was crawling with silvermen earlier, they've made camp by the next loch along' – he pointed back the way Kelda had come, to Dochfour – 'didn't want to send up a flare changing form and then lead them all like a beacon to the lighthouse.'

Kelda found her voice at last. 'I thought – I thought you were like Isla.'

'Well, in a lot of ways, I am.' He looked at her at last. 'Ready for a secret?'

Kelda thought it was a little late for this question, but she nodded.

'Wyrms are silvermen in exile, too. We're just sick.' He sat down by one of the trees, gesturing for her to do the same: she stayed standing. 'I got mer-sick, and Dad was away from home – he was my only family, and he was always getting called off for emergencies – so I didn't get any treatment. If I had, the spread would have been halted, and I'd be stuck halfway – merfolk if I was lucky, more likely dead. But it turns out that if no one's there to stop it – if it takes you entirely . . .' And he gestured at the loch, and the wild swirl of water still seething where he had erupted. 'That's why we used to slit people's throats. To stop them turning into monsters.'

I think I know something *about beasts, Mari.*

'It probably can't be reversed now,' he went on. 'I've gone beyond sick, to something else. But you don't get a chance for lavellan sap often – I had to at least *try* hunting it.'

'I thought wyrms were white-water spirits?'

Douglas shrugged. 'Maybe we are. No idea. How are spirits *supposed* to start existing?'

Kelda had no answer to that. She thought of Peter, and his natural history; he would want to know this. She thought, absurdly, of the invitation to spend time in his library. They would have tea, and smooshy landman chairs, and it would be warm and restful.

'You look like you might faint,' said Douglas. 'Did you swim the whole loch? Sit!'

Kelda's legs did not seem ready to follow this suggestion.

'Unless,' said Douglas, eyebrows working in manic jolly overtime, 'You're utterly repulsed, of course. If you want to leave, or slay the foul beast or something, I understand. Very natural.'

'No!' She managed to regain a grip of her body. 'No, of course not.' And she made herself sit down beside him, and tried to find the right thing to say. She wanted to make this all right by the sheer force of her own words – to will away the strangeness, and the last of the rawness in his eyes. But all she came up with was: 'So. You lied about the gingerbread house.'

'You don't know that. I might have one in the loch.'

The thought of the loch appalled Kelda. 'Do you mind it? Living in there?'

He shrugged. 'Nope. It feels right, in my other form. And it's a good place for me; it means I'm not near anyone I might hurt. But I'd go home in a heartbeat if I could, obviously.' There was a short pause, then he added, 'You know, I chose Ness specifically because it's in one my dad's old lullabies, listing all the old white-water places . . . *Bright shining Ness, oh, so deep and so darling* . . .' he sang; his voice was surprisingly melodious. Then, in his normal voice, he added, 'You know my Dad. Irvin Willig.'

'You're *Willig's* son?' Kelda exclaimed. His little boy – the one who died of mer-sickness.

Douglas nodded. 'He was away healing someone else. He tried everything he could when he got back, but it was too late. He refused to throw me overboard – I did it myself, I don't really remember it, there's a sort of feverish hour when it all gets a bit blurred.' He was talking fast, falling over his words: Kelda supposed she must be the first person he had told this story to. 'Lucky for me we were on the Lune when it happened, and if you grow up with a heretic like my dad, you know about the Cave – just in case. The folk were good to me. Looked after me much longer than they normally would – years, until I was getting too big for them. Stopped me trying to get back to my dad, too, when I was little and scared.'

'They *stopped* you?'

'They had to. I could have got him exiled – I didn't die like I was supposed to.' He pulled at some grass. 'It's bad news for him, this Old Lore stuff. Now he could be killed.'

'But he saved Isla. He's so *good*.'

'Yes. He is.'

'It's all so back to front.'

Douglas sighed, and leaned back against the tree. 'Yes. It is.'

There was another of those living-thing silences, but this time, Kelda didn't try to end it.

'Why did you come?' Douglas asked, at last.

252

'Oh.' She had almost forgotten her task in her amazement. Now, she didn't quite know how to go about it. Bargaining with a terrifying beast was one thing, but simply asking Douglas was a different matter entirely. She tried to make her thoughts line up.

'So,' she said. 'Right. Well, first you should know that they've got Isla. And Dad, and Peter. And Uncle Abe's dead.'

'Oh, Kelda,' he said. He looked at her now, really looked at her, but the look in his eyes hurt. If he looked at her like *that*, then that must mean it might all be true after all. She quickly looked away.

'So, they're going to sacrifice Isla and Dad when the tide floods the canal, which will be tomorrow night, Maggie says. It's because there's this thing snaking all round Britain out at sea, a brimghast, and she thinks that a wyrm might be able to bind it. But she thinks you need to be the Sea Weard to compel a wyrm to do it, and I thought the Weards might be you and Isla, but – obviously not. So anyway, since you hadn't come, I was going to try just – asking. And then it was you. So . . .'

She had a feeling this explanation hadn't gone brilliantly. She tried to read Douglas' expression in the darkness. 'Huh,' he said; then, 'My dad always told me the Sea Weards *were* wyrms.'

'What?'

'Two wyrms, and they were killed when they attacked some people. He knows these old poems about them, he collects rare histories – you got very weird bedtime stories, living with my dad. Why did you think it was Isla?'

'Well, they're meant to *inhabit all dominions . . .*'

'That's in the poem too. *Lord of all dominions: the rivers, land and sea.*'

'Oh. I wasn't thinking about the sea.'

'Typical silverman. Biggest dominion of them all, by a long way.'

'Have you been?'

'All the time.'

'What's it *like*?'

He looked up to the stars, as though seeking help from one inexpressible wonder to convey another. 'Sublime. I don't think I can say it really. It's . . . big.' He turned back to her. 'Kelda, I'm so sorry. About Abe. About everything.'

Kelda felt herself taking a Mam-sized steadying breath. 'Me too. But we've got to concentrate on getting Isla back.'

'Yes,' said Douglas. 'And – everything else. With the waterways. This is bad. Maggie thinks I can bind this thing, you said?'

'Apparently. And the Morar wyrm said she was right.' Kelda fished the blue book from the pocket in her silks, and found the page: 'Here. We'll need light . . .'

Douglas stood, and reached for something in the branches of the tree overhead; he sat back down with his satchel in his arms, and produced matches and a stump of candle. It confused Kelda, to see him with his satchel. It had been *almost* possible to think of him as a wyrm, out here on the water; but now, he was just the stranger from Sherwood Forest again. Willig's little boy.

He lit the candle, and held it carefully in one hand, book in the other. He read.

'Does it make sense to you?' Kelda asked, when the silence stretched on.

'I think so . . . it looks like it gathers itself inwards for strength, and then you start dancing it . . . You know, I think I've seen a bound one. Off the west coast of Scotland.'

Kelda nodded. 'Corryvreckan, Maggie called it.'

'I looped myself through it once, when I was going through a stupid reckless phase. Nearly didn't get out. I could *feel* its body – like mine, really, but pure water – I can see how this would work. I'll need to memorise the knots . . .'

'Will it be dangerous?'

'Of course.' When Kelda was silent, he added, 'I hope I'm not going to get a cautionary tale from the girl who just *summoned a wyrm*.'

'No. I know. River, I'm just so sick of feeling anxious for everyone I care about.'

There was a longish silence, in which Douglas studied the page earnestly – or at least, looked like he was. Then he blew out the candle, and leaned back.

'I'm not sure it's possible.'

'Oh.'

'It needs two. There were two wyrm faces in those diagrams, which makes sense – there's always meant to be two Sea Weards. Did you say Maggie asked Morar?'

'She did, and it was a no. But if you asked . . . ?'

Douglas laughed, but it was joyless. 'He hates me more than humans. He's half-dead, anyway. Doubt he could even get out to sea any more.'

'Are there any others?'

'Not in Britain. Not these days. They're mostly in the southern hemisphere. Well – I'll just have to try.'

'But – if it's really so dangerous . . .'

Next to her, she felt him shrug. 'If we don't do anything, things are pretty bleak for all of us.'

'Not for you, lord of the sea.'

'No. But for everyone I care about.'

'Right.' Kelda studied the stars earnestly, or at least, looked like she was. Perhaps a minute passed in silence. Then she made up her mind.

'If you bit *me*,' she said, 'how long would it take for me to change?'

'What?'

'You can infect me too, right? Would it happen quicker than an eel bite, if it came straight from you?'

'I don't know. Probably. But no way, absolutely not.'

'We have to.'

'I'll just try going by myself. It might work.'

'But it almost certainly won't. This thing is enormous. We *need* both of us.'

'We need me, and one other. It doesn't have to be you.'

'Who else is it going to be?'

He leaned forward, agitated. 'Kelda, *no*. This last trip was the longest I've been human, it wasn't like my normal life – you don't know what it's really like. You couldn't live with silvermen any more – first, because they'll want you dead, and second because you'll be liable to want *them* dead any time you're transformed in the water, and you have to go in water every month or so at least just to survive. You can't even live with the other merfolk in case you attack them. I can't let you exile yourself. You've done everything to keep your family together.'

'I've done everything to keep them *alive*.'

'Listen to me. It's so hard. Wyrms aren't really human any more. Half your life you're this other thing, this thing you can't quite control.'

'You've survived it.'

'I've had to.'

She knelt up, turning to him. 'I'm serious. Please. It's the only way. What else can we do?'

He was silent.

'If all Britain's waterways turn to salt,' she said, 'I'm dead anyway. You realise that?'

'Yes.'

'So?'

The stars and the loch and Kelda waited, conspiring with bated breath to compel a wyrm as best they could.

'Salt,' he said, 'this is the worst idea I've ever heard.'

'But you'll do it?'

He was doing in-the-dark nodding at her again, but this time she could just about make it out by the moon.

'Thank you.'

'Don't.'

So she didn't. But then there was nothing else to be said.

'So,' she said, 'how do we . . . ?'

'Can we wait? A minute? I need a moment.'

'Of course.'

Kelda didn't need a moment. She needed there to be no

moments, zero moments in which to contemplate Douglas' warning, or the feverish pain of the mer-sickness, or the cherry red boat with white trimmings, or the dismal loch. Already her certainty was ebbing, pushed back by panic. She balled her hands into fists, and willed herself not to let her doubt show.

'Kelda?' said Douglas.

'Mm?'

'I don't know if you're interested in me kissing you at all, but if you are, can I do it before I turn into a wyrm and bite you? It just seems rude the other way around.' He raised his eyebrows to maximum-joke position, but he didn't turn to look at her, addressing himself to the night air.

Kelda felt like rain-on-the-inside more than ever. Which didn't, of course, mean it was a love-match; but it was a start.

'Yes,' she said. 'Probably the correct etiquette, I agree.'

He continued not looking at her.

'Like – now?' she asked.

He did in-the-dark nodding. When that had gone on too long, Kelda reached out, and turned his face. '*Now* now?' she said.

By way of reply he kissed her, and the rain was everywhere inside her, and her heart and skin were at last outpacing her mind. And when they broke apart a little, he pulled her back again, closer; and for a minute the islet on the water was a world unto itself, with secrets of its own.

When they pulled apart at last they stayed as close as possible, foreheads and noses still touching.

'You're sure you're sure you're sure?' he asked.

'Get in the water.'

'You realise you'll have to put up with me for company, right? The Morar wyrm is no fun at all.'

'Do it now before I slay you for being an evil monster of the deep.'

'I'd like to see you try.'

'Go.'

'Aye aye, soldier.'

They stood, and went to the water's edge. Kelda sat on the shore, legs in.

'Look away,' said Douglas, 'I have to – ' and he gestured awkwardly at the trousers.

Kelda turned away. For a long moment she waited, and almost wondered if he had changed his mind. Then she heard him slip silverside.

A second later the loch erupted once more, and a wyrm towered into the air, reared, looped downwards, and struck; and a blinding pain was the last thing Kelda knew before the whole world turned black.

27

What happened next was harder to remember
            or rather, all too easy, but in pieces, with jagged
edges that didn't fit together,
    She didn't have legs any more. She was just heavy where it
should have been legs and she was not going to walk again
            'Please don't die. Please. Oh, River.'
    and a fever, but not in her head, somewhere in her gut; and
the nausea was in her head, so that was all back to front; but
that must have happened first because she still had legs then,
and they were full of fire
        'You can't go in yet. You're not ready. Kelda, you'll drown'
    her whole torso tightening, her lungs
            dragging Dad up a cavern tunnel, much too tight –
                    Firth sobbing because he hurt a fish
                    Kelda didn't want to hurt any more
                        Why did everything have to hurt?
            'I'm so sorry, I'm so so sorry'
    her face heavy too now, buried under mud, buried alive
                    under lips – 'I forgive you, of course'
            'Stay with me, Kelda'

                      'Come back to us – to *me*'

and the need for space, much more space, why were arms always pinning her

                'You can't go in yet. Please.'

She was a storm bundled up inside an animal which had duly gone insane, and she wasn't strong enough to keep carrying two of them, not for all that way, it wasn't fair, but they kept riding and riding and riding

and she didn't have any legs, oh, River, and it hurt

28

When she came to, the sun was overhead, and Douglas was beside her.

She had her own body again, apparently intact, although she had never felt so tired in all her life. She propped herself up on her elbows, and the indigo waters of the loch lapped at the crannog in orderly fashion, as though nothing had ever been amiss. She lifted a hand, and it was her own hand – although without the slight sheen to the skin.

She noticed that she seemed to be wearing spare clothes of Douglas'. Some very far-off part of her felt that this was embarrassing, if she stopped to think it through, but it didn't seem remotely important right now.

'Did it work?' she asked.

'That's one word for it.'

'I'm hungry.'

'I've made lunch.' He pointed to a great pile of not-quite chara cakes beside her, the same things he had given her in Sherwood Forest. 'Eat. You'll need to get your strength back.'

'So – I'm a wyrm now?'

He nodded.

'Did I transform?'

'You don't remember?'

Kelda shook her head, as much to clear it as anything else.

'Yes,' he said, 'you very much transformed. And you did not appreciate some basic caution on my part. You know,' he said, pressing a cake into her hand, 'you're now very, *very* scary when you're annoyed.'

'Well, don't—'

'Don't be annoying, I know, I know. *Eat*, please, I'm scared you're going to slip off this mortal coil any second.'

Food had never tasted so astonishingly wonderful to Kelda. With each bite she felt her strength come back; and when she felt back to normal, she kept eating, until she felt *better* than normal, pulsing with a new strength that was almost too much to contain.

'I think,' said Douglas, 'we should probably get you in the water soon.'

'Yes. I need that, I can feel it. I feel kind of *great*.'

Douglas nodded. 'Sure. You will, sometimes.'

Kelda squinted up at the sun; it was noon already, or maybe a little later. 'I don't know how fast we are. Should we set out soon?'

'Yes.' Douglas contemplated her a moment, then moved closer. He wrapped both arms around her so that they were sat in one big knot with knees touching, interlocked. 'Kelda. This is going to be stupidly dangerous, even with both of us.'

'I know. But we don't have a choice, do we?'

'Not really.' He rested his forehead against hers. 'The other one – corrywhatsit – is out to the west. I was thinking we should go and look first, so you know what we're up against.'

'Isn't that on the other side of Scotland? Do we have time?'

That made him smile. 'You don't know your strength yet, Kelda. Crossing the canal will be nothing. Actually I think we should swim all round the coast, down south from Corryvreckan and then back up again on this side, to get a complete look at this thing – see where it's weak.'

Kelda's wild new strength approved of this plan. She wanted to swim vast, vast distances, and never stop. It was hard to bring her concentration back to the little crannog, and the matter at hand.

'Then we'll start the attack back here at the head,' Douglas was saying, 'and when we've forced it to shrink enough, one of us should move down to take the tail . . .'

'Right. I'll do that.'

'I'll stay with the head, then. You've understood the knots?'

'Yes.'

'Right.'

'Right.'

There was a pause.

'So we should go,' said Kelda.

He nodded, but the nod was all squished up against her head, so she felt it more than saw it. He made no other move. She disentangled his arms from around her, gently, and stood to go to the bank.

Then she exclaimed in surprise.

'What?' said Douglas, jumping to his feet.

'Look,' said Kelda, pointing.

Douglas looked. 'Oh! Is that . . . ?'

'Robin Hood. I'm sure of it.'

He squatted down at the water's edge for a better view. 'How can you tell? Ducks all look the same to me.'

Kelda smiled. 'On the contrary. That duck is very clearly slightly stupider than the average duck.'

He laughed. Kelda laughed too. Her heart was lifted by the little duck, beyond all reason. Surely it was an omen, a sign, a piece of extraordinary luck: a reminder that she and Isla were linked, always and always, and nothing at all could possibly part them.

She beamed at Douglas, but he was no longer laughing; only contemplating the water gravely. Apparently he did not see Robin Hood as a sign. He just saw a duck. Her smile faltered.

'Come on,' she said. 'I want water. Let's get going.'

Silvermen know little of the ocean. River Lore touches on the subject only once, and informs the reader that the ocean is 'of great size'.

This is accurate.

29

I magine if your whole body could feel how peppermint
smells: that was silverside now. The wyrm that was Kelda
uncoiled, and stretched, and *grew* – until it was one great long
rope of muscle, suspended in the water, magnificent.

It could feel so much. It could feel the movements in the
depths of the loch, of course; this was as easy as feeling a
current pushing against out-turned palms. But if it hung
suspended and still, it could feel the string of lochs reaching
out into the sea, and the sea reaching out into itself, and sense
the great circular tugs of water everywhere in everlasting
cycles: warm rushing to cold, sky travelling back to sea, and
always the endless tug of the tide, chasing the moon around
the surface of the earth.

Swimming in this new, snake-like body was easy. It was
easy to dart and dive, to whip its great spine round in
spiralling turns; it was easy to flex any of the powerful
muscles along its length; it would be so easy to use the sharp
teeth – the teeth at the jaw, and the second set too, at the
opening of the throat. It was very, very difficult to concentrate
on small, human thoughts. The second wyrm wrapped its

body around the first, nudging it onwards, keeping its wild mind on track.

They sliced through the lochs like two great knives, water parting before them and sliding from their scaled sides. The distance was nothing now. Loch Ness, Loch Oich, Loch Lochy, Loch Linnhe –

– as they neared the sea mouth, the water crackled with salt and with countless microscopic living beings, and the skin of the great wyrms grew dizzy and alive –

– and then they reached the Firth of Lorn on the western Scottish coast, and the sea.

The sea was an alien place.

They were in a kelp forest, and the stalks of dark green and brown had no names. Nor did half the fish, or the things that bloomed and bobbled and bulged on the rocks. The light was thinner here than in rivers, a gossamer light, and the pulsing movements of the water were constant and bewitching.

Beyond the kelp, soft grey dollops of animal drifted by, chasing fish. The wyrm that was Kelda had a sudden urge to strike, to take one, to eat – but the other wyrm was there, cautioning, nudging it onwards, its great grey eyes full of purpose.

Something was roaring in the distance. The other wyrm led them straight towards it.

As the roaring grew louder, the water grew frantic. The currents here were desperate to be somewhere else – anywhere else – writhing through the narrow gap between two islands – and now the rasping-roaring filled their minds, and it was hard for the wyrm to make itself go forwards.

Then it was ahead of them – a thing shaped like their own bodies, but made of pure light – tied in a whirlpool of knots, spinning and spinning in fettered rage – Corryvreckan.

The wyrm made itself swim closer still. It ran its body up the sides of this broken piece of sea, and it hurt, like the edge of splintered glass – but still it kept going, feeling the edges of the knots. It learned the thing's nature like a child learns fire.

Then they left it behind, and swam south along the Scottish coast, towards England.

The wyrm that was Kelda could sense the wrongness nearby in the ever-moving water: a vast ribbon of water that was still, and waiting. It lay all the way along the coast. The brimghast. Its tail end was here; but they would study its whole length, and understand their enemy, before they began their attack.

It lay along the edge of the shallow seabed, at the place where the ground dropped away to the deeper open ocean. The water near it sides was crushed inwards. The pressure made the wyrm's vertebrae ache.

The first time they passed the mouth of a waterway, they both recoiled. Here the thing was bleeding itself inland, up the river, pouring out liquid desperation; then pushing itself against the currents of the river to keep its hold. The wyrm that was Kelda was assaulted by memories, only some of which were from its own mind: of leaving the Trent on a spinning boat; of millennia below ground in soft, secret rock; of being in a strange bed in a strange house; of surging up violently from springs in winter; of weary journeys north; of clouds. Of broken boats and broken banks and dams and treacherous friends and blooms of liquid poison. Of wanting to go home, go home, go home.

The wyrm that was Douglas quivered in pain here, and had to be half-pushed onwards. Then there was ordinary sea again, until the next river mouth.

The thing snaked all the way down to England and around Wales, cradled the southern coast, and climbed again up the eastern edge of England. It had stretched itself thin to reach this length, in places barely there at all. The wyrms followed it, learning where it was weakest, and where it had wounded itself to claim a river. At the mouth of the Thames the memories mixed with the stench of London, and the spirit's fury and despair at the blackened water was so thick that it became difficult to swim. Further up England, at the mouth of the Humber, the wyrm that was Kelda could hardly move for the tide of awful remembering – Aeron, Willig, Firth, spinning on and on down the river . . .

They fought their way forwards up the eastern coast, back to Scotland. The head of the brimghast was almost at the firth – ready to take the strongest waters. Even now it was growing, stretching itself further north towards Moray Firth.

As they swam, the sea had first silvered, then darkened. They could feel, in the vast distance, the tide chasing the moon – coming their way.

For a brief moment, the two wyrms entwined, feeling each other's hearts thrumming with fear. Then they parted, and began.

The wyrm that was Douglas struck first. He bit, and the

thing reared. Its northern end loosened its grip on the island to quest after the offender.

When it had been led far enough out to sea, the wyrm that was Kelda bit it a second time, lower down. It coiled in pain, and there was a rush of water as its great head turned south.

The dance had begun.

The two wyrms tore with their awful mouths at the spirit's side, again and again, and it coiled and twisted in rage as it chased them both. They were nothing next to its outrageous size, but they were faster – and for now they just had to injure it any way they could, forcing it to draw itself inwards for strength, into something smaller. Then they could lead it where they needed it to go.

Once the spirit was a little weakened, the wyrm that was Kelda swam south to England to meet the tail. Already the thing was much shorter; they had expected it might retreat from its head as the Corryvreckan brimghast had done, but instead it was drawing itself inwards from its tail, giving up its earlier conquests to gather all its strength towards Moray Firth. It must still be hoping to take the firth that night, then.

The wyrm that was Kelda bit and slashed until the great tail was persuaded to enter the fray. Then, at each end, the wyrms began to lead the dance of some of the smaller knots.

Hours must have passed, but time was only measured by the swell of the approaching tide. All the while, the spirit fought back. Once its tail lashed out with such force that the southern wyrm plummeted away, out into open sea, and half-forgot itself, and a blackness was closing in, and a confused voice inside it cried for silver . . .

Then the dizziness passed, and it returned to the attack. Fear made it zealous – fear for the other wyrm. The tail was strong, but the head was worse. The wyrm that was Kelda danced the tail into Scottish waters.

High tide came: high tide passed. The brimghast would not take the River Ness that night. Still they danced.

At last the thing's tail was curled back up to its own head, by the Moray Firth and the Ness river mouth, and the other wyrm could be felt nearby again. The spirit was weak from their bites and riddled with the smaller knots. They were winning. But there were three final knots needed, entwining head *and* tail.

The wyrm that was Kelda and the wyrm that was Douglas each struck.

The thing howled soundlessly, twisted, chased them with each end as they led it away, racing across the miles – and tied itself once.

They returned, keeping their distance – then struck again, and this time darted down along the spirit's length, close to its body. This was the most dangerous of the knots. The head and tail duly followed, entwining themselves –

– but as they did, the thing threw its head against the wyrm that was Douglas, sending it reeling towards the sea bed.

It did not reappear.

The wyrm that was Kelda hissed, enraged. It tore at the spirit indiscriminately. The spirit lashed back, but it was now hopelessly entangled in itself. It squirmed, trying to shake off the knots – its tail began to work its way out of their last trap, slowly but deliberately –

The wyrm hissed, and threw itself furiously into the final knot, attacking the creature at both ends, darting back and forth – narrowly escaping the thrashing head and tail – leading it over and under until, at last, it was done, and could no longer be undone. The sea had bound itself. The wyrm that was Kelda could feel the island breathing, the fresh water rushing itself out into the sea with a roar and a tumble of wild freedom.

Suspended in the dark, a creature of pure light spun and spun in fettered rage.

(Unseen, nearer to the shore, the merfolk who had come to watch them smiled. But they kept their distance.)

The wyrm that was Kelda did not pause. It had plunged down to the other wyrm and was running itself along its side, feeling the hurt; a deep cut, made by a jagged rock on the seabed. But it felt breathing too – quite steady – and a heartbeat.

It began nudging the wounded wyrm back to shore. *Swim,* it urged, with every pulse of its body. *Swim, swim, swim.*

Half-leaning on its friend, the other wyrm swam.

It was heavy work, to swim this way, and blood thickened the water around them. As they neared Moray Firth the injured wyrm was hardly swimming at all, and the other had to heave for both of them, steering them between rocks. They would not make it to the loch like this. They would have to rest first at the coast.

The dark water was disturbed by a strip of light, which moved in a stately curve as they swam. The lighthouse: the wyrm that was Kelda could only half-remember the word, but it knew that there was a warm idea of a home, a refuge. It pushed closer.

It was just a little too far, but at least they were close. The wyrm that was Kelda threw them both out of the waves. It coiled inwards to bring its whole body on to land, and once it was there, it felt itself flare up in silver and then condense, solidify, tighten, and breathe out: human once more.

Small thoughts returned. Wet sand between her small toes. She shivered in the night air, and looked up with small eyes.

And all around her she saw silvermen.

30

The night was lit up by lamps. They stood in a line along the shore, and they clustered in a circle too, a little way inland.

The shadows of the silvermen divided themselves between these two groups of light. But now some of the shoreline shadows backed away in horror, and some of the inland shadows hurried forwards, shouting questions; so Kelda never knew, afterwards, who had joined Firth's attempts to hold a chittering, and who had stayed to guard the prisoners and wait for the extraordinary tide.

Not that she cared particularly, in that moment. She only had eyes for the shore, where a wyrm lay like a scar across the beach, and a little way off two alder boats waited on the sand with her sister and father in ropes. They had been abandoned in the scramble to run towards or away from the wyrm. Peter wasn't with them; he was clearly not intended for the sacrifice.

'Isla!' Kelda stood and started towards the boats, but within seconds, hands held her back – and somebody's woollen cloak was thrown over her, an oddly chivalrous restraint. She fought her head free of the choking fabric, but couldn't break free. It was Maxwell Jupp, and he was strong, and determined.

'No! *Isla!*'

While she struggled to reach the boats, still calling and calling for Isla, a crescent of maybe a hundred of the braver silvermen was forming around Douglas; and when Maxwell had her safely in his crushing grip, he too turned to the wyrm, wresting her along with him, determined not to let a small thing like a raging sister keep him from the action. He pushed his way through the crowd, wielding her in front as an excuse – the traitor must be brought to the centre of the ring.

But this was no chittering. This crowd was a wild thing.

Douglas lay half in the sea and half on land, and his body couldn't settle. It pulsed painfully. Every few pulses, its whole length would heave, and turn for a moment into the shadow of a man – then back again to a beast.

Kelda had not really seen the wyrm properly before, on the island. Even she shuddered at the snake-like silvered eyes, the great snout, the serrated teeth. But then it would flicker into Douglas again, just for a moment.

On all sides, people were arguing about whether and how a wyrm should be killed. The mood of the mob bent and flared like the flames, and the force of it took Kelda's breath away – or maybe it was Maxwell Jupp's arm, crushed against her chest – or maybe it was that painful pulsing, wyrm wyrm Douglas wyrm, tearing in and out of each body. The cut didn't look so bad now that she could see it properly, but he needed to be able to stay in one body or the other. And he needed something to stop the bleeding. And, above all, he needed people not to kill him while he was weak.

She tore her eyes away from him and scanned the faces, looking for anyone who might help them, who might take pity on a wyrm and still care for Isla. Where was Firth? But instead her eyes found Aeron Jupp, staring straight at her.

There was disgust in his stare, and hatred, but there was fear too. Kelda felt a surge of pride in her new form. She'd like to see him try and hold her now.

Except, of course, that she absolutely *could* be held, as long as she was on land.

She spotted Cordelia a little way behind him – she had survived too, then. Kelda was distracted, and she missed the moment when Willig stepped forward with his sealskin satchel, and knelt down. She was alerted by the hush that slowly fell, as the message carried like a wave through the ranks: somebody was at last *doing* something.

'Can you kill it, Willig?' called someone hopefully.

But Willig was not listening. He was watching the pulsing, transfixed. The next time Douglas was in view, Kelda thought she saw him open his mouth, try to speak – half raise a hand – before he was gone again.

But it was enough. Willig set to work, rummaging in his satchel to produce woundwort and knitbone and sweet flag and herbs Kelda didn't recognise. With a visible, trembling effort, Douglas held himself in wyrm form as Willig began. Behind Kelda, someone was whispering knowledgably that he was poisoning the beast.

The crowd was quiet. No one could tear their eyes from

277

the shimmering and shivering at the heart; no one wanted to miss a moment of the myth living amongst them. Only Kelda looked away when Willig began stitches – she was the only one who could imagine how it would feel, stabbing through that leathery hide.

After a while of Willig rubbing soothing sweet flag on the stitched-up wound, the wyrm that was Douglas could breathe more steadily. Willig was murmuring encouragement. With the healer's hands on its side, the wyrm heaved the rest of its body out of the water, sending up spray and cries of alarm; and with its next breath became Douglas, pale and shaking and curled up in pain, but mercifully tied to a single body.

'Dougie.' Willig was crying, and his round face was all wonder. 'It *is* you.'

'Hi, Dad.'

And then the silence of the mob became a ripple of murmuring, as everyone further away asked everyone closer, or taller or perched up on a rock, what was happening now; and guesses spread like wildfire; and no one listened when Aeron stepped forward and tried to shout for attention; and Douglas and Willig held on to each other like a guardian knot and wept.

Kelda wanted Isla. She wriggled against Maxwell, but he hadn't once let up his grip.

Aeron at last got enough hush to be heard, but half the crowd was still babbling regardless. 'Brothers,' he was shouting, 'sisters, the time is now. This evil on our shores—'

At this, Willig released Douglas, and turned furiously to Aeron. 'This so-called evil is my *son*, Aeron Jupp, and if this

278

isn't proof enough that the mysteries of the waterways are far beyond your petty—'

Aeron shouted over Willig, addressing the half of the crowd who were listening. 'The arrival of a wyrm confirms the wisdom passed to us by our ancestors. The sacrifice—'

From the babbling brook of murmuring came multiple voices at once – there was a lone cheer of assent, but someone else yelled, 'The salt didn't come, Aeron,' and another shouted, 'Leave Willig's boy alone,' and at least three people were just yelling abuse at him.

But then Aeron gave up speechmaking and began forcibly tearing father and son apart, attempting to keep hold of Douglas – and when Willig tried to push him off he punched the healer on the nose, which raised a cry of anger – and then there were hands pulling Aeron, too, and it was a confusion of tugging and limbs and punches, and it was hard to say who was trying to help him and who was trying to pull him away. The rise of shouting and jeering seemed mostly to be against him, but as much as anything it was just the baying voice of panic and relief and confusion and desperation. The crowd closed, and became a brawl.

Still Maxwell held on to Kelda, however she struggled. She lost track of Aeron and Douglas and Willig. Only when a punch lost its way and found Maxwell's face did he loosen for even a second, one arm flying to his bloodied nose. Kelda took advantage, and bit the arm hard: then as he struggled and loosened a little further, took a well-aimed kick behind and upwards, and pulled herself free as he doubled over in pain. Then she was pushing through the crowd, back out to the shore, leaving Douglas and Willig to their fight and hurrying to Isla, Isla, Isla.

The crowd had forgotten all about the boats, and the only shadow at the shore was, at last, the familiar shape of Firth. But now there was only one boat. The second was already pushing off into the black expanse of water, which rose and fell now in huge waves.

'Kelda!' yelled Firth, as she raced over. Dad, she saw, was lying at his feet, only semi-conscious. 'I got Dad untied, but Aeron got here before I could get Isla free . . .'

'*What?*'

'Trent was holding on to me, I only just got away or I'd have got them both out . . .'

'But what's Aeron doing?'

'He's going to do the ritual now, he wants her drowned by dawn either way, and he's smashed this salted *boat* so I can't salting *follow*. He's gone crazy . . .'

And that was all Kelda heard, because a moment later, she was out of the cloak and in the water again, in pursuit.

31

The wyrm that was Kelda could feel the boat's path, that was easy: a wrongness in the criss-crossed ripples of the huge waves overhead.

But what should it do? It could crush the boat, but Isla was in it. Should it take the risk, and trust that it could scoop the girl up again? But if it failed . . .

It had so little command over this body. It was all strength and no precision. Even keeping its mind on track was hard. It would be so easy, in this form, to strike the wrong person, to lose control . . .

The boat up ahead had stopped moving forward now. The wyrm found a rock, pushed up through the blackness to the air above, and threw itself with a gasp on to the rock's surface. All Kelda's own beautifully fine-grained, tamed thoughts rushed back in as her body condensed once more. She squinted through the spray, to the boat.

The waves were enormous. The little boat bucked wildly, and all around rocks rose from the water – except, more treacherously, for the ones that didn't – the ones that lurked secretly under the surface. Isla, at the bottom of the boat, was

281

out of sight. And Aeron stood, just staring ahead, his back to Kelda.

'Aeron!' yelled Kelda. 'If you throw her in I will rescue her and then I will *kill* you. I will *eat* you. Do you hear me?'

It wasn't clear if Aeron *did* hear her. He just stood and stared ahead. It was as though he had forgotten all about the girl tied up in his boat.

Then Kelda caught another voice on the wind. Or rather, voices. They were singing something Kelda knew well – something Uncle Abe had played often enough, on his fiddle. It was a song for victory. A silverman song.

Kelda clambered across to another rock, nearer to Aeron. 'Aeron! Did you hear me?' Then, as a wave lurched the little boat among the rocks: 'Watch the *boat*! Isla – I'll catch you, I promise, don't be scared . . .'

Isla's voice was thin, whipped away by the wind. So close, and now even the wind wanted to steal her.

Kelda peered in the direction of the singing. She could make out the bodies through the spray now, on the rock ahead. Bodies that shouldn't live at all; bodies that were not quite fish, and not quite human. Were they looking at Aeron, or out to sea, to the bound brimghast they sang their victory song for? She couldn't tell.

'Aeron. You're going to sink the salted boat.' Isla was crying, Kelda was sure, although so much was lost in the wind. Still Aeron just stared. He was searching among the singing faces; he had clearly understood what the folk were. Kelda had to make him listen.

'Fossy isn't with them, Aeron. She was seen belly up, remember? Some people live, yes. But Fossy's dead.'

A huge wave came and flung the boat wildly; for a heart-stopping moment Kelda glimpsed the rope-bound bundle of Isla, and it looked as though she would fall. She crouched, ready to dive. But the boat righted itself, and dreamlike, Aeron paddled them a little closer to the merfolk – further among the rocks.

'Aeron, *no*.'

She didn't even hear the crack of wood over the wind and the waves. She just saw the boat lurch like a wounded animal, then tip its back end in the water, and Isla with it.

In the same moment, Kelda was underwater, and lengthening out into a beast again, full of a howling fear and rage.

The wyrm that was Kelda pulled its wild mind back to Isla, Isla, Isla. It hunted through the blackness for a ripple that was wrong, but there was so much of it, with the sea so choppy and the pieces of the boat tumbling . . .

It dived towards them, feeling for something falling that didn't want to fall, and found her at last. It wrapped her in one great loop of muscular body, and heaved upwards. Clumsily, it dropped her to the nearest rock above the surface, unclenching.

From the rock, the merfolk looked down at her.

The wyrm wanted to tell them to keep Isla safe, but all that came was a rasping hiss. But perhaps they understood. One stroked Isla's hair as she retched and sobbed, while another began to unknot the ropes around her wrists; and still they sang, and sang, and sang.

Afterwards, Kelda always said it was the thought of Uncle Abe that sent her back into the sea – of the look on his face, when she had wanted to leave the others to die.

It took longer to find Aeron. He was no longer flailing, and the water was no longer protesting his arrival. But at last there was the gentle downwards tug of something falling. The wyrm looped under his unresisting weight, and surged upwards.

It dropped him with considerably less care, before condensing inwards and downwards and crouching, human, on the rock. Isla was shaking violently, and blue with cold. She stared up at her sister.

'Kelda?'

'Hello, little one,' she said.

'But you . . . you were . . .'

'Yes.' She wrapped herself around Isla. 'Guess you get a spirit for a pet after all.'

'Kelda, they . . . they wanted . . .' And she was sobbing into Kelda's chest, and Kelda knew that some part of her little sister was still drowning out at sea, and would be for a long time.

'I know,' she said, squeezing tight. 'I know. But you're safe. I'm here now.'

Around them, the merfolk were changing their song. It wasn't a song of celebration any more. It was a casket song: a song for the dead.

She had been too late.

She looked at Aeron Jupp's body. She had never seen a salted death. His skin looked bloated and rubbery. He was grotesque, a parody of a human being.

'Did you mean to? Did you do it on purpose?' she asked the merfolk.

But they only smiled sadly at her, and sang their song of mourning: a song for the boy who had followed his grief, out among the rocks, all the way into the sea.

32

The merfolk refused to help Kelda at first.

'Please. I can't get her back to land without taking her underwater again. We have to hurry, look, she's *blue*.'

Sad shaking of heads. Kelda could have knocked those heads together.

'I thought you helped the pure of heart.'

This annoyed one man enough to make him break his silence. 'In their struggles with the silvermen,' he said, 'not with every petty favour they ask uss.'

'Right. Fine.' She pointed to the ranked torches waiting on the shore. 'There they are. Will you carry her past them, at least? No further. *Please*.'

This was a dilemma for them. They conferred in low, hissing voices. Kelda had the distinct impression that they hadn't reached an agreement, but one long-haired man hissed something defiant, then said to Kelda: 'I will do thiss.'

'Great. Thanks.'

'But no further.'

'Understood.'

The man placed Isla over his broad shoulders, and began a

gentle breaststroke across the waves. Sometimes the choppy water crashed over Isla, but it was at least better than taking her silverside.

Kelda slipped under, and forced her huge mind to focus only on swimming round the promontory, inside the firth, and away from the silvermen.

The merman stuck precisely to his word. The moment they were far enough from the last silverman to be swallowed by the dark, he deposited Isla on the shore, where she promptly vomited hugely on the sand. Kelda emerged to find him backing away, nose wrinkled. She had the distinct impression he felt his moment had been ruined. He turned to Kelda.

'Thiss is as far as I may help you, Kelda Pade, wyrm of Loch Ness.'

'Yep. Thanks.'

He considered the shaking bundle of Isla.

'She iss not well,' he said thoughtfully. 'She may yet die.'

Kelda did not stop to reply. She had Isla in her arms, and she was hurrying to the lighthouse.

Isla was too heavy to run with, and Kelda's legs were weak with exhaustion. She stumbled almost more than she ran. When a voice called her name she very nearly fell, and was only caught by the arm belonging to the voice.

'Woah, careful now. You don't need concussion on top of everything else.'

'Maggie?'

Maggie didn't bother to confirm. 'That's Isla?' She put out a hand to the shivering bundle. 'Lord, she's in a bad way. Get her home, wet clothes off, wrap her in blankets, get warm drinks in her. Don't leave her alone, you'll need to keep her airways clear if she's still spewing seawater.' As she spoke, Maggie was fumbling at her waist. She produced a key for the lighthouse, and pressed it on top of Isla. 'Blanket for you too, young lady, why are you naked?'

'Where are the others?'

'Oh, we were caught on our rescue mission. Naturally. Terrible plan, but we had to try. I got away; I've been prowling around waiting for a chance to help the others.'

'Oh, *River*.'

'Go, you've got to get Isla warm. I daresay the others will live.'

'But—'

'The mood was turning your way when the tide was normal. Which I'll be wanting to hear all about later, by the way. And your brother was doing sterling work, and a lot of people were unhappy with this New Weard business to begin with. I'd be astonished if there's appetite to kill anyone – except perhaps her' – here she indicated Isla, with a jerk of her head.

Kelda's arms tightened. But her legs seemed paralysed. 'What about Douglas?'

'Who?'

'The wyrm . . .'

Maggie looked at her, nonplussed. 'Kelda, I think you're in shock. Look. You have to get Isla back, she looks at death's door. And besides, you've got to hide her – this isn't over yet. You understand?'

Kelda nodded. She understood. Isla still needed her. Isla always needed her.

'So, *go*,' said Maggie. And she gave her a little push on the back. Dazed, still stumbling, Kelda went.

At the lighthouse door she fumbled with the key for an age, and then it seemed to take forever to work out the lamps, and by the light of the lamp to build a fire in the open-stove-thing in the wall. She took blankets from her own unused bed, and the cotton dress for herself. She stripped Isla of the sopping clothes, and wrapped her in the blankets at the fireside. Isla was still blue, and her breaths were much too small – and then occasionally huge, as she heaved, and regurgitated more saltwater than seemed possible for such a small body.

For the second time in Isla's life, Kelda kept vigil by the little trembling body as the night wore on. But this time, no one else watched with her. The room stank of the waiting chowder.

Kelda was not sure how many hours had passed when Maggie returned.

'How is she?'

'Sleeping.'

Maggie looked down at her thoughtfully. 'More normal colour, at least.' She sat herself at the table. 'Thought I ought to update you. It's all right out there. They've sorted themselves out into one of your chitterings, and I earwigged. So far they've overturned the use of Old Lore, and been so good as to remind themselves they have no jurisdiction over landmen. But Peter and Judith have stayed, to speak on Isla's behalf. Her fate's the great business of the day.'

This was hard to take in. Kelda nodded slowly.

'Firth's doing brilliantly. I didn't know he was such an orator.'

Kelda raised her eyebrows. 'Neither did I.'

'Well, he's pulling out all the stops. Certainly knows his Lore.'

'What about my parents?'

Maggie shrugged. 'Under your modern Lore they won't be killed. So there's no immediate danger. Exile, maybe – all depends on the arguments about Isla. Which are very boring. River Lore is interminable.'

One of the many knots in Kelda's stomach untied, a little. Her parents were safe. There was still Isla's fate to be decided. But she was hidden in this strange landman house, for now; there was hope. 'What about Douglas? What are they saying?'

'The wyrm boy? He's all right. A little red-headed chap made a long speech on his behalf about new wonders revealed and marvellous advances to be had in medicine. And cried a great deal. Almost as much as he talked.'

'So they aren't hurting him?'

'No talk of it. There's not exactly a precedent for a case like that.'

Kelda breathed out. 'Good. Right. Good.'

'So.' Maggie sat up, alert, as though to say that the small talk about trivial things was over, and the real business had begun. 'You transformed! And you stopped the brimghast.'

'Yes.'

'Well. I suppose I shouldn't interrogate you about it now. But – well done.' And she smiled. By the firelight Kelda could see that she was flushed with the night's excitement, and it made her somehow more human.

Kelda hadn't really stopped to think about what she and Douglas had done. She didn't quite know how to respond. All she could think of was to say, 'I think you were right, by the way – about the spirit being provoked by all the muck in the rivers. It's hard to describe . . . at the river mouths there was this *anger* in the water. It was hard to swim past the Thames.'

'Ahh,' said Maggie – and it was partly a sound of satisfaction, but it seemed to be partly sadness, too. Kelda supposed Maggie would like to have been the one to know the ocean so intimately. For a few moments, they were both silent.

'You know,' said Maggie at last, 'if they hadn't tried to kill your sister and sent you running up here, I daresay the whole island would have been lost. And your brother can't forgive himself for ratting on her, but as it all turned out, it was the best thing he ever did.' At this, she actually laughed out loud: a single, barking *ha*. Her curls bobbed wildly. 'You see?' she said.

Kelda was not sure she did, and was a little distracted by Isla, who was stirring in her sleep. But Maggie was waiting expectantly, with an air of great triumph, so she said, 'Um?' to be polite.

'No guarantees,' said Maggie, with enormous satisfaction. She stabbed the table with her finger, twice: '*No. Guarantees.*'

Just then, Isla opened her eyes. Kelda forgot all about Maggie, and leaned in closer.

'Isla? I'm right here. How are you feeling?'

'Thirsty.'

'I'll get you some tea. Hot tea. Do you think you can drink?'

'Uh-huh.' Isla propped herself up on one elbow. 'Where are we? Can I have food? I'm hungry too.'

'*Yes*,' said Kelda; and suddenly all the relief of the night was on her at once, everything they had survived crashing down over her in one great wave of joy. 'Yes, you can. I'll make you the best breakfast you've ever had, Miss Isla Pade.'

'Oooh,' said Maggie. 'Me too please.'

So Kelda made tea and eggs, the only things she understood in Maggie's galley, and Maggie introduced her to hot-buttered toast. Then the three of them ate and drank. When they were full, Isla leaned against Kelda, and Kelda did her best to explain how she had spent the night. She tried to make it sound exciting, and wonderful, and like something from a River story. She tried, as best she could, not to let Isla dwell too long on what it would mean for them: that Kelda was not going home. Not to live there, anyway. She was a wyrm now. She would never truly go home.

All the time she was telling her story, the dark outside was lifting, and the shape of the world could be seen in shadow, and the sun began turning the sky and the sea to blue; and, from their lighthouse refuge, high above the waves, they watched the dawn come in.

33

Mam, Dad, Firth, Judith and Peter arrived at the lighthouse around noon, exhausted, with Willig and Douglas in tow. Douglas had a bandage around his side, but he was upright, and the right colour again – and someone had given him fly-silks, so he looked more silverman than ever.

Everyone knew roughly what had happened from Douglas, but they clamoured for Kelda's explanation too, loudly and excitedly; it took an effort to persuade them to tell their news first. But the news was good. After a long chittering, Mam and Dad had not been sentenced to exile. Firth had leaned heavily on Isla's half-silverman status, and a surprisingly intense knowledge of past trials and sentences, to argue for a relaxed interpretation.

'*And*,' said Mam proudly, recounting the morning, 'he argued his way out of Isla's sentence.'

'Your exploits last night didn't hurt,' said Willig to Kelda. 'Young Firth certainly made *excellent* legal arguments, but after Dougie had recovered enough to give his testimony of the night's events there was also a general feeling in your favour, to put it mildly.' He looked at his son as he said this, with an air of bemusement – which was fair enough.

'And our landmen friends here were a huge help,' he added, turning to the Parsons, who were hovering in the doorway. 'Explaining all about the landman pollution, how it might be causing a lot of the hard season we've had.'

Judith smiled at Willig, and Peter nodded. They didn't quite look at the reunited Pades – especially not Dad.

'So, Isla can just come back?' said Kelda. Somehow, she didn't feel surprised. She had survived the brimghast: the day was a brilliant blue. This was, of course, what came next.

'No,' said Dad. He was installed in a chair by the fire, very stiff and upright. It didn't look as though anyone had taken particular care over his injuries while he was a prisoner. Mam was fussing around him now, with a box of Willig's ointments and bandages. He addressed himself to Isla: 'They've backed down, but it's still exile – to leave here by noon tomorrow, and not to live on the waterways again.'

'*What?*' said Kelda. 'After everything?'

'Yes. It was the best that—'

'How *dare* they? We saved their salted lives. I—'

'Kelda,' said Isla. She said it so firmly that Kelda was stopped in her tracks. She sounded stronger than she had all morning, but there was something else, too; something new, that was hard to place. Kelda noticed that she had found her little wooden horse, and was holding it tightly.

'It doesn't matter,' she said. 'I don't want to stay.'

This momentarily floored Kelda. 'What?'

'You're not coming back with us, are you? And Uncle

Abe's gone . . . I don't want to live on our boat without you. And I don't want to live like all of the rest of our lot again, ever ever.' Her face was set. 'I hate them.'

'Of course you do. I do too. But—'

'I'm not like them. I don't *want* to be like them. Peter already said if it was ever safe, I could still live in the cottage and learn all the herbs and things. And have a horse' – here she held up the wooden toy, as though to clarify what a horse was. 'So I can do that now. Can't I?'

She said this last to Peter, who looked back at her with an expression so pained that even Isla faltered. 'You are so tremendously welcome,' he said, after a moment's pause. 'But I – it's not for me to . . .'

'We'd be grateful,' said Dad. All eyes went to his chair, where he sat stiffly; he was looking only at Peter. 'She needs a home on land. Lyn and I just want what's best for Isla. We love her.'

There was a long look between the two men. For the first time, it occurred to Kelda that they used to be friends. The look they shared now definitely wasn't friendly, but there was an understanding in it – though Kelda didn't know, exactly, what was understood.

'So I can go?' said Isla.

Mam took Dad's hand in hers. She nodded. 'Of course, love. If that's what you want.'

'You'd be so very welcome,' said Judith.

And what could Kelda say?

That afternoon, they slept.

The others planned to travel with Isla the next day, to see

her settled in her new home. Kelda would visit soon, but she knew she couldn't take her body from safe water for that long yet. Douglas promised her it would get easier, but right now, she needed the sea and the lochs.

Kelda slept on a bed between Mam and Dad, as she had when she was very small, before Firth and Isla had existed. Lying there, Kelda talked to them about staying behind at the lochs, and all three of them were strangely calm. They had guessed, Mam and Dad said, when they heard what had happened to her. She promised to visit often. They told her they loved her. She already knew.

The family would all stay at Camberley while a new boat was built. Their old home had survived the tide, but someone had set fire to it shortly after. Apparently Aeron had been furious. It was not anywhere in the Lore, the burning of boats; it was an improper way to grieve.

Early that evening, Mam and Dad and Isla went out together. Kelda wanted to spend every last moment with all of them, but an annoyingly sensible part of her knew that Isla was in desperate need of her parents. Douglas was with Willig. Kelda sat by the porthole, and looked at the sea, and itched. She didn't want to go in yet, when the others might come back any minute; she didn't trust her wyrm-mind to get her back here in time.

So she was almost glad when Maggie came in and announced that they were going out. 'Want to show you and your brother something,' she said. 'But you'll have to put up with my boat.'

This was a mysterious statement, until they saw the boat.

It was the very newest in landman boating – it had an outboard motor, and thrummed like a very annoyed ocean-going bee, and smelled awful. Firth looked deathly pale the whole time they were on board. Kelda didn't love it either, although at least the sea didn't terrify her any more. But Maggie just whistled to herself, and ploughed on through the waves.

When at last she steered the thing into land, she just pointed up the sloping shore, and said, 'Straight line. You'll know it when you see it. I'm going on to the next town for some errands, I'll be back here in an hour or so.'

They didn't talk much as they walked up the hill, shadows long in the dimming light. They saw it up ahead, long before they reached it: a great carved stone. It was weathered and faded, and they couldn't make out the carvings until they were close.

There were soldiers and headless sacrifices and horse-spirits, and guardian knots of all kinds, and other symbols Kelda couldn't make out. Kelda traced her fingers along the shapes, while Firth just stood and stared.

'Maggie told me about these,' he said. 'The landmen call them Pictish stones.' At last, he reached out to touch it. 'Isn't it beautiful?'

'It really is. This must be older than most of the Lore, even.'

'So we *were* here before. That bit's true.'

Kelda nodded. 'Lots of it's true. Just not all of it.' She looked at her little brother. 'Makes life complicated.'

'Keeps it interesting, I guess.' He squatted to study the knots better. 'I don't think these ones here are our knots. Do you know them?'

Kelda crouched beside him, looked where he pointed, and nodded.

'So this is *your* Lore,' he said. 'Sea Weard!'

'I guess so. I'll have to start studying Sea Lore. I'll tell you all about it.'

'D'you think Isla'll be the next Land Weard? We're going to need one – someone who can make them see reason.'

Kelda hadn't really thought about that. 'Probably. Makes sense.'

She sat down next to him, leaning against the stone, and shut her eyes as he continued to exclaim at the carvings, and poured out everything he had learned so far from Maggie, about knots of silver found buried near the Firth, and Sea Lore, and – at some length – about landmen and river health. Something about pumping aquifers seemed to particularly irk him. Kelda let it wash over her, only half-listening, but enjoying the old familiarity.

When he had finished, she made appropriate noises of interest, then said, 'So. Just you going back with Mam and Dad. Will you be all right?'

'I'll be fine.' He said it lightly, the weight of his mind focused on the carvings. While he studied them, Kelda watched their shadows in the grass: sometimes two separate things, sometimes merging together into one, as Firth shifted his balance. Then he sat, and they were one body, but with two heads – like something from an old history.

'Will *you* be all right?' he said. 'Without us – without Isla.'

'Yes, I think so,' said Kelda. And this seemed true, even though it seemed so achingly sad at the same time.

'I know you were set on staying together.'

'Well – I didn't know how it would be.'

'How d'you mean?'

'Just . . . well, I wasn't expecting be a wyrm for a start.'

Firth laughed. 'Sure. No one expects to be a wyrm.'

For a minute they watched the sea, a rich indigo now, striped with shifting lines of light and dark like rolls of velvet. Something wild inside Kelda ached with longing.

'I've been thinking,' Firth said. 'When we build the new boat, we should paint it cherry red. With white trimmings.'

'*Firth!*' Kelda forgot all about the sea and the wild aching, and was entirely Firth's big sister once more. 'Those were *private!*'

He held up his hands in mock-defence. 'I know, I know. I always used to look at the stuff in your chest. I dunno . . . I was little when I started, and then it just never seemed like a big deal to look just one more time. And I liked the boat sketches. I sort of imagined I'd have a hammock in the galley, like Abe.'

'Idiot. You should have just said, I'd have drawn on an extra bedroom.'

'I'd rather have the hammock. At the heart of everything, you know?'

'I can see that.'

An ant had crawled on to Firth's finger; he held it to a blade of grass with careful concentration, making sure it returned safely to its own world. 'I don't really feel like Abe's gone, do you?'

'Nope.' Kelda shook her head. 'Not at all.'

*

299

After dark, it was time for Uncle Abe's casket-night. Everyone briefly endured Maggie's boat again, to take them inland, and from there they walked down the silver ribbon of the River Ness. Then they set the empty casket on the current, which carried it away, flowing on and on, unstoppably out to its end.

Each in turn took a spoonful of the chowder, then gave a spoonful to the river, and said: 'Aberforth.'

With all the Pades and Parsons and the two Willigs, there were a lot of them there to say goodbye. By the time the last person had taken their turn, the casket was out of sight.

'PREFACE' IN:

THE WATERWAYS: ESSAYS ON A HIDDEN WORLD

....

The true head of a river is often a shifting, unplaceable thing. In much the same way, it is hard to say when my resolve to write these essays truly began.

I have written them in fervent hope of cordial relations with landmen, and improved treatment of the waterways, which I believe is increasingly crucial to the survival of my people. I hope that these secrets will be received in this spirit, by those to whom this volume is entrusted.

I have received much support while writing these essays, but also some anger. Many have asked how I can be sure that my disclosures will not provoke violence from landmen. To this I must answer that, although I have weighed my actions seriously, I cannot be *sure*. I write the pages of my life in hope, as we all must.

I am forever grateful that I was shown how to hope. I dedicate these essays to the memory of my uncle, a great friend to landmen, and the greatest friend of all to me: Aberforth Pade.

– Firth Pade

34

By the time they were home again, Kelda needed the loch. The lighthouse was overcrowded anyway, and disproportionately full of Maggie and Firth earnestly discussing the sickness of the River and its causes, which was the last thing Kelda wanted to think about right now. So she and Douglas said good night to the others, and went down across wet sand to the water's edge.

'Look, I have to tell you something,' said Douglas, as they neared the sea.

'What?'

'I lied. About the gingerbread house. There isn't one in the loch. It's just a loch.'

Kelda laughed. 'Well, I guess you'll have to build me one. You can put it on the island.'

They were at the edge of the sand now; the waves sent tendrils of foam over their feet, welcoming them. He stopped walking, and put both arms around her waist. 'You'd like that? I can try.'

'Yes. Gingerbread castle, please.'

'That's a lot of gingerbread.'

'With some of those little flag things, in icing.'

'Whatever you say, soldier.'

'Are we getting in the water or not? My skin hurts.'

'Not yet. I haven't kissed you yet.'

'Oh, is that an important part of wyrm survival skills now?'

He smiled at her. '*Very* important.'

35

Not long after dawn, Kelda went back to the lighthouse with Robin Hood in her arms. He had been more than happy to be scooped up from the shores of the loch, in his slightly-stupid way. The morning felt fresh and light, not yet weighed down by the waking world; at this time of day, topside felt almost like silverside.

No one else at the lighthouse was awake yet, but Isla of course was up and fidgeting, ready to go. The two sisters sat on the lighthouse steps and talked while the sun drifted west, until it was almost time.

'You'll come and visit?' said Isla.

'Lots.'

'And I can visit you?'

'I'm sure you can. You'll have to ask Judith, but I bet she'll say yes. You could come and stay with Maggie.' This wasn't exactly the same as always and always. Kelda was going to have to unpromise that particular promise.

Isla leaned against her. 'Is it nice in the loch?'

'Yes.' It was, now. Kelda's horror of it that first night seemed far away. 'The water's amazing there. Sort of silky. You'd like it.'

Considering this for a few moments, Isla reached a decision. She turned, and pressed Robin Hood into Kelda's arms.

'He should live here with you. He's happy up here. And that way he can say hello to you from me every morning.'

Robin Hood gakkered amicably enough at this, and looked up at Kelda with his bright little eyes.

'Well,' said Kelda, 'that'll be lovely.' And quite unexpectedly, she meant it. She could never have guessed the duck would seem so precious.

Isla stroked his head, then gently hugged Kelda – careful not to crush Robin Hood, resting her head above his on Kelda's chest. They could hear the others coming down the stairs now. It was time.

'I can hear your heart,' Isla whispered.

'That's good,' said Kelda. 'Still alive then.'

Acknowledgements

It is more or less impossible to find a map of all British rivers. It would be equally impossible to chart every act of kindness and support that flowed into this final book. Still, some of the major tributaries must be mentioned:

Thank you to my early readers: Jehan Azad, Uri Bram, Caitlin Campbell, Anna Kemp, Sam Plumb, Aube Rey Lescure, Dylan Townley and Alice Winn, for your wise comments and priceless encouragement.

Thank you to my fellow writers from all over the world who join me on zoom every day: the Writers With Faces. This book was written alongside you all, wherever you happened to be, and I am so grateful.

Thank you to my excellent editors, Chloe Sackur and Charlie Shepherd, for invaluable help shaping this final story; and Eloise Wilson for the meticulous copy-edit.

Thank you always to agent of wonder Bryony Woods, for finding a home for this book, and for wise-and-patient guidance in the face of Many Questions.

And thank you to Jack Noel for the design, Thy Bui for the beautiful cover, and Rebecca Freeman for the map of my dreams. You have made this book too beautiful for my silly mortal eyes.

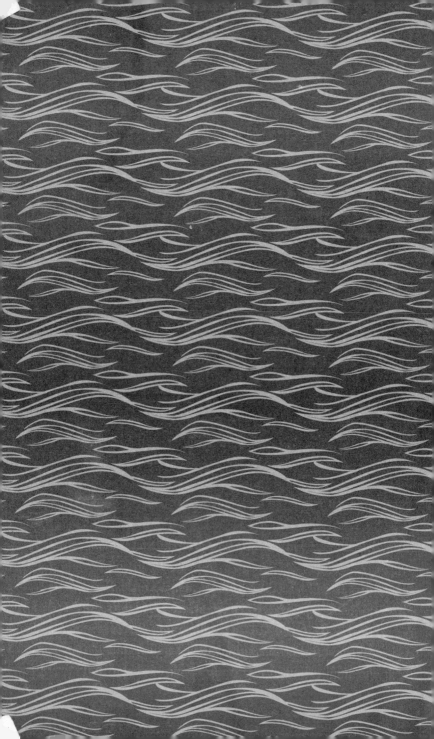